The invocation had open
panding the monk's limited world to a degree which
he would never have thought possible. He saw fields
of fungi, the fruit-bodies full and ripe beneath alien
skies. He saw shapes of blasphemy and horror rising
up before him, and beings of beauty and gentility
long vanished from the earth, beings that might have
been angels as the horrors were most certainly devils.
He looked backwards and forwards in time, witnessing battles of undreamable perversity, towers of
wood peopled by exquisitely beautiful evil, enormous wooden engines pulsing out sounds man was
never meant to hear.

And a kiss.

*Also by Bernard King in Sphere Books:*

**VOLUME I OF THE CHRONICLES OF THE KEEPER:**
THE DESTROYING ANGEL

**VOLUME II OF THE CHRONICLES OF THE KEEPER:**
TIME-FIGHTERS

# SKYFIRE

## VOLUME III
## OF THE CHRONICLES
## OF THE KEEPER

### Bernard King

SPHERE BOOKS LIMITED

SPHERE BOOKS LTD

Published by the Penguin Group
27 Wrights Lane, London w8 5TZ, England
Viking Penguin Inc., 40 West 23rd Street, New York, New York 10010, USA
Penguin Books Australia Ltd, Ringwood, Victoria, Australia
Penguin Books Canada Ltd, 2801 John Street, Markham, Ontario, Canada L3R 1B4
Penguin Books (NZ) Ltd, 182-190 Wairau Road, Auckland 10, New Zealand

Penguin Books Ltd, Registered Offices: Harmondsworth, Middlesex, England

Published by Sphere Books Ltd 1988

Printed and bound in Great Britain by
Richard Clay Ltd, Bungay, Suffolk

*For Arthur Sarsfield Ward ($ax Rohmer)
wherever he may be now, for being one of my gurus*

So, so, break off this last lamenting kiss,
Which sucks two souls and vapours both away,
Turn thou ghost that way, and let me turn this,
And let our selves benight our happiest day.

John Donne – The Expiration

# CONTENTS:

# PART ONE

Historical Fragments
Bearing upon a Thesis
which Finally Threatens
to be Explained

# FIFTH LUNATION

## Day 16, 63,411 BC. Noon

Anhuk was smiling to himself.

That his thoughts and memories remained private was more the fault of the limited language he and those like him had evolved than his own choosing. There was so much he would have liked to have shared, so much that he could have told those about him, had he only known the words to do so. As it was they would learn, in time. It might take a hundred, perhaps a thousand, generations, but they would learn. They would know as he had known, and they would do as he had done.

He was one of the great ones. Probably, he thought, and this was what had caused him to smile, the first of the great ones. That had been a long time ago, though, on that night, eighteen years before, when the blue lights had come out of the sky and taken him, pissing himself with fright, from the familiar, comfortable bosom of his father's tribe of hunter-gatherers.

He'd returned out of the sky, his body bronzed to the point of blistering, much of his hair and beard burned away to a crisp dark stubble, powdery to the touch, with the first *image* in his hands. *They* had shown him how to make it. *They* had told him what to do, what to tell the others. And Anhuk had done what he'd been instructed to do. He had returned, out of the sky, a day missing in his life, and taken command of his father's tribe in a way his father had never thought to do. At his command they had built a cairn, an *altar*, upon which he had set that first rough idol of baked river clay. It had massively exaggerated features, fat thighs and belly and massive breasts, bursting with the milk of fertility, the white, creamy nourishment which was the future to those as yet unborn.

His tribe had moved its ground over the intervening years. It had travelled from the Danube valley, progressing eastwards into the valley of the Don, at the north-eastern corner of the Black Sea, in today's USSR. He had directed its progress, not usurping his father's authority but rather supplementing it by the special insights which he received from the deity of kiln-fired clay. The *deity* itself had shown him how to build and fire a kiln, how to refine the clay and model it, how to create an image which might last through countless millennia and later be found by archaeologists and labelled the Venus of Willendorf.

Their life was good. Their tribe grew in number, both by the fertility which Anhuk and his deity brought them and by the prowess against their enemies which regular nourishment encouraged. They had learned to smile as well as to worship, and the smile was as important as the prayer.

And now, with the sun high and the fertile valley stretched out before him, Anhuk was smiling to himself.

There were times when he didn't smile, times when he couldn't smile, when the onerous duties of his office demanded that he deflower a distastefully-visaged virgin or despatch a rival's blood, sacrificially of course, into the soil beneath. But they were simply things he had to do, and he did them without even questioning. The tribe, awed by their memory of the blue fires in the sky, awed by the person Anhuk had become since their taking him, didn't question either. Anhuk was special. He was their *priest*.

Their smiling priest.

The seasons were different in those days, those long-gone days. We might imagine the fifth lunation to be late April or early May. In Anhuk's time, however, it was closer to October or November. At his feet grew the red, white-spotted caps of fly agaric, the decay-hued death cap and the leprous, virginal whiteness of the destroying angel. The deity had shown them, with a degree of trial and error, which fungi they might eat and which they ought to shun. Anhuk alone might partake of the fly agaric and live without degenerating into madness. Yet even he was left a little mad by it. He saw things that he alone could interpret. He pissed into an earthenware pot and drank his own urine. And then, when he had done what no other of the tribe might do, he saw more, and better.

Why shouldn't he? After all, he was their priest.

The noon sun, offering little warmth, cast his shadow small where he stood. Its warmth wasn't as important as it might have been in times past. They had fire. They had furs. They had ways of doing without the sun, when the deity kept the sun from shining and giving its own bright warmth to them. Yet Anhuk liked the

4

sun. It reminded him, yellow though it was, of the blue fires, the night of the blue fires in the sky, and what they had taught him.

Live. Pray. Be.

Being is believing.

Being is believing, perhaps. But what was *being*? Anhuk himself could recall at least four separate states of being. There was the being of ordinary life, of dreams, of the mushroom trance, and of the time, so vividly remembered, when the fire in the sky had taken him. If all of these could be being, then might there not also be other kinds of being, kinds he didn't yet know and therefore couldn't comprehend?

This was deep. Anything he couldn't find words for was deep, and Anhuk couldn't find the words to reason this.

His smile faded slightly, yet remained.

Who else had formed thoughts such as these? His father, Ursik? Any of those foolish youths who sought to rival him and failed so dismally? A woman? Any woman?

He shook his head. Inconceivable. (*Not-belief-happen* in tribe-speak, later to become Indo-European, the root of almost every Western modern language.)

He needed the help of the deity. He needed to feel those fat thighs about him. He wanted to lose his face in the comforting cleft between those enormous breasts. He needed to be the *somewhere else* that only the deity could place him.

Anhuk was beginning to discover a new feeling within himself, a feeling that somehow, for all he knew, for all he had learned, there was more. Probably there would always be more, even at the moment of his death. And yet, he realized, that didn't stop him wanting it. After all, there was the promise he'd been given by the light from the north, that promise which Anhuk could never forget.

YOU HAVE TO OBEY, ANHUK. YOU HAVE NO CHOICE BUT TO OBEY. DO WELL. DO WELL AND YOU SHALL BE MORE THAN JUST THE SHAMAN FOR YOUR TRIBE. DO WELL AND YOU SHALL BE THE KEEPER OF THE BALANCE . . .

'The . . . balance, Lord? The word is strange to me . . .'

His smile had faded as he began to slowly walk down from the brow of the hill, back into the valley which his tribe now inhabited. This word stayed with him, haunting him, refusing to yield its meaning. In the intervening years he had coined many new words to explain the many new ideas he had forced his people to struggle with, but still he didn't know what the *balance* was.

Anhuk's eyes, cast down and glazed with the effort of his thought, only noticed the general features of the ground beneath and before his skin-wrapped feet. He had been little more than a youth when the fires had come from the sky and taken him. Now he was in his early thirties, but an erratic diet and the rigors of his priesthood had made him much older. His bones felt heavy and he decided to sit down and rest for a while.

His knowledge, his position, carried certain privileges. One was that he was not required to go out for food like the others of his people. His time was his own, to use or waste as he chose, according to the dictates of his service to the deity. The grass where he sat felt damp to the exposed parts of his thighs and he shifted his position slightly, setting the palms of his hands to the ground to steady himself as he did so.

Then he felt the firm, fleshy caps of the fungi about him.

There was nothing new about the mushrooms and toadstools which grew, overnight, out of nothing. They were a mystery, but a familiar one. Experience had taught what might be eaten with impunity, what might be eaten only by Anhuk as the priest of his tribe, and what might not be eaten at all, unless by a dangerous rival as an ingredient of a death-spell. It was the season of the fungi, and they were plentiful.

His fingers, almost of themselves, quested the stems of the nearest growths to either side of him. When they reached the junction of stem and cap they tightened and snapped, leaving him with a fruit-body in either hand. Idly he lifted them and began to inspect what he had picked. In his right hand was an ordinary field mushroom, white on top but with brownish gills underneath. In his left, white both above and below, was the destroying angel.

Anhuk tossed each a little way into the air and shifted his hands quickly to catch them, leaving the mushroom now in his left and the deadly toadstool in his right. Proud of his skill he repeated the operation, changing them back again.

The two caps were about the same size and weight, he decided. It was both strange and wonderful that two things, so similar in many ways, could be so different in their natures. One gave life. One took life. Giving and taking. Living and dying.

If the deity had only provided one of them, he mused, then life

6

for his tribe would be very different. If there was only the destroying angel, then they would have less to eat at this time of year. If there was only the field mushroom, life would be so much more safe for the little ones who hadn't learned the difference yet. Without one or the other . . .

At first, sitting amongst the fungi, his eyes flickering from cap to cap, hand to hand, meaning to meaning, Anhuk didn't take heed of the shouting from the skin-tented camp beneath him. They were always shouting about something or other, like the children they were. Eventually, though, he could no longer ignore it and lifted his gaze to stare down at his people.

Some were pointing. One or two were running up the hill towards him, calling his name. Still holding the fungus caps in his hands he rose to his feet.

From their shouts and gestures whatever had alarmed them was happening behind him. He turned, puzzled and curious, and faced the brow of the hill, staring into the north. The grasses and fungi were standing out with a powerful and unremembered clarity, as if something bright and terrible was hiding on the other side, as if the sun had dropped from the sky and changed colour in its falling.

Anhuk felt the power of what was to come. He'd felt it before, but that had been a long time ago. Then, it had frightened him at first, as it was frightening him now. Yet he was the priest. He had spoken with the light before. He had been with the light before. Now he had no choice. He must do what was expected of him by the others, by his watching, aged father, Ursik, hobbling closer on a rudely-fashioned crutch to be proud of his son once more before he died.

Slowly, majestically, as if it was possessed of great weight and solidity, the blue fire rose up from behind the hill and hovered before him. It appeared huge, filling most of the northern horizon with its presence. It might have been round, slightly dome-shaped. Like the cap of some enormous fungus, Anhuk thought. Like the caps of the fungi that he held in both hands.

The others moaned and stayed their progress up the slope. The nearer ones drew back a few paces, eyeing the light with terrified, blue-tinted faces. They shielded their eyes with their hands as if from the sun, and those old enough to remember when the light had come before recalled what they had called it then.

*Blue-sun-bright-falling* was back.

It called to Anhuk, reminding him of its promise. None of the others heard it, but Anhuk did.

He stepped forward, no longer afraid. His smile returned, broadening into a grin which broke through the tangle of beard and moustache obscuring most of his face. He wanted to run towards it, *into* it, but the respect of the watching tribe had to be retained, so he restrained himself, walking slowly with measured, deliberate steps.

His arms were held out in front of him as he drew closer, ever closer. The caps of the fungi, so like the light, rested on his open, upturned palms.

So like the light. Both of them. Life giver, life taker.

He stood before the skyfire, holding out his offerings, chest heaving with exultation and the effort of his understanding.

Ursik nudged the woman next to him with the hand that wasn't holding the crutch. 'My son,' he proclaimed.

Anhuk slowly moved his arms until they stretched out to their limit on either side of him, his body a dark cross against the powerful blue light to the distant watchers. His skin was tingling with a feeling that was neither heat nor cold. As the skyfire moved closer he began to drool with the anticipation of his triumph.

'Balance,' he proclaimed.

His fingers curled inwards, crushing the caps to pulp.

'Balance,' he repeated.

His hands turned at the wrists so that the palms faced downwards. He opened his fingers and the pulped fungi slithered into a fall and were lost amongst the grasses.

Anhuk smiled. 'Balance,' he confirmed.

THEN YOU ARE READY TO BE THE FIRST, the light told him. ALL IS PREPARED FOR YOU, ANHUK. ALL YOU NEED TO KNOW YOU WILL BE TAUGHT. YOU THOUGHT TO DIE BEFORE YOU KNEW ALL THAT YOU WANTED TO, BUT YOU WILL NOT DIE. YOU WILL LIVE BEYOND THE SPANS OF MANY MEN. THE FIRE WILL WARM YOU, AND THE ICE WILL KEEP YOU ALIVE. SUCH IS THE WAY OF THINGS IN THE KINGDOM OF THE KEEPER.

The light opened to enfold him with its blueness. His bones no longer heavy, his thoughts no longer confused, Anhuk turned and raised his hand to his tribe in a final salutation. Then he walked into the skyfire and was gone from their sight for ever.

In the time that followed Anhuk asked the light many questions, hungry to learn about his new life. The Kingdom of the Keeper was of a strangeness he had never known or suspected might exist upon his world. It was cold, but its waters were warm, sometimes hot. The ice shimmered about him in his echoing cavern, but the sky was light, even throughout the night for some of each year. The light told him of a past he had never even dreamed of, and of a future which he and those who followed him would eventually, in their own remote way, come to control.

It showed him how to set down his thoughts on skins with marks that had meanings. It taught him how to read the marks that others, not Keepers, had made in that mysterious and power-crazed past. He learned of conflicts between creatures he would never have known existed. He learned of life-forms beyond his experience or imagination.

He even discovered, albeit at the age of 337 years, though he'd stopped counting by then, how to control the light. And the darkness, though the darkness was both more subtle and more blatant in its manifestation.

Then, and only then, did Anhuk, son of Ursik, truly acknowledge that he had become the first of many Keepers.

# ALL HALLOWS' EVE

## 31 October 863. Night

Not everybody came away from the Devil's Lair with some of the Devil's treasure. Oh, no. You had to be brave and fearless to rob Satan himself. And it helped if you were Irish, Caillchen Mac Eamon told himself.

And a Man of God, naturally.

Ah, but demons fly marvellously from the sign of the cross, hung about one's neck. They melt away into invisible harmlessness, even as you invade their lair. That's why you come back with the treasure, because of their powerlessness.

He'd laboured long and hard to build himself the tiny stone shelter which was both his home and his shrine. This island in the northern ocean might be ideal for solitude, but the lack of decent trees meant blistered hands and aching joints before even a small byre could be raised from the rough stones scattered about, as if by some giant volcanic hand. And those twisted branches that could be found were little use for rafters, restricting the size of one's dwelling even further.

Yet what need was there of a place to house his meditations? It would not be fitting. Not fitting at all. And if ever the order decided to establish a church upon the face of this deserted land it could ship timber from Bri Chualann to make a proper job of it.

Caillchen had used the stunted branches, covered with bundles of dried grass, to roof his simple hermit's cell. He'd embraced the monastic life some twelve years before, displaying a fervour which left those about him marvelling at his holiness. When the opportunity to sail north to a hermit's life in Iceland had arisen he'd been assured of a place by his devout, if aggressive, nature. And so he'd established himself, living off whatever the land might supply, which wasn't a great deal, spending his time in prayer, meditation, exploration and the studious avoidance of his fellow hermits. After all, he reasoned, you can't be a hermit and *know* people.

He'd been there two years, most of which he'd spent upon his knees. In that time he'd travelled much of the surrounding area, both in searching for sustenance and exercising the cramps which prayer inevitably brought in its wake. Somehow he'd always found reasons for not setting foot upon the glacier to the north, until he'd prayed to Christ to do something about the creeping, insidious boredom which the Devil was intruding upon his devotions. Over the past few weeks he'd pressed deeper into the frozen waste, watching his footing, extra layers of hand-woven rag about his feet and ankles, a staff of gnarled dwarf birch his only support. Two days ago he'd actually crossed it, praising the Lord for his achievement, trusting in the Lord to make the crossing worth while and provide him with something to still the hunger-pains in his belly on the other side.

The Lord hadn't let him down. A meal of berries and fungi, eaten raw, hadn't been much, but it was much better than nothing.

And then he'd found the Devil's Lair.

The opening, though it was door-sized, was well-concealed by the natural configuration of the surrounding landscape. For this reason Caillchen had missed it the first time, some God-given trick of the light revealing it to him upon his return. Once found, naturally, it had to be explored. Especially as he was certain there were no other hermits in the area.

Tired, his joints aching, wary of the approach of the interminable night which the cold season brought to his chosen homeland, he stepped inside.

And gasped.

He felt as if he had stepped inside some fairy hill. Beneath the earth a cavern walled with ice rose like some majestic (if demonic) cathedral. It soared upwards into a canopy vaulted without the need for supporting pillars. The hot spring at its centre lent a mirror-like sheen to the walls, reflecting and magnifying what light there was into a kaleidoscopic display of glittering hues. It was cold, yet somehow also warm. It was, he realized, despite the ice, warmer than the stone cell he'd laboured so long and hard to build for himself.

And that alone was sufficient to render it demonic, without any further discoveries.

Such comfort as this provided by nature? Caillchen shook his head.

Unnatural, he decided, walking further in.

At one point he stumbled across some decayed wooden furniture, of a style and pattern he didn't recognize, which must have meant that it was devilish. At another he found a chair and table of relatively recent construction. There also appeared to be living quarters, of a positively Sybaritic luxury compared to his own, and, further back, something resembling an enormous pigeon-loft.

For the first time since he'd come to Iceland the monk felt an unsanctified warmth caressing his body into comfort. It wasn't right, he thought. He wasn't there to be comfortable. No-one was there to be comfortable. They were there to praise God.

He approached the pigeon-loft and discovered that it was something totally different. No squabs for the pot to be found here, sheltering in the niches. Nothing so hallowed. Instead, each of the hollows cut in the ice contained a vellum scroll of undoubted and devilish antiquity, resting upon a straw bed. And something else.

As if forming a three-dimensional index to the ancient library, each niche was guarded by a tiny obsidian figure. At least, the figures looked as if they had been carved out of obsidian. So far as Caillchen Mac Eamon could see, they were all different and mostly disturbing.

The Devil's Lair. There was no doubt about it. He had stumbled upon the Devil's Lair. And his library.

So what did the Devil actually know?

He reached past the nearest figurine, the sleeve of his tattered robe knocking it aside as his fingers quested the manuscript beyond. He took out the vellum scroll and unrolled it a little way, his eyes straining to make out the unfamiliar characters (the Devil's own script) in which it was written. Spitting with disgust, he replaced the incomprehensible document and reached for another.

The scroll was guarded by a tiny figure of a monkey, one hand raised in benediction, the other grasping its erect penis in the unmistakable act of masturbation. Caillchen shuddered and picked the figurine up, his other hand reaching into the niche to take the scroll. Only the Devil would think to carve such things. Only the Devil would trap him into his library, a library where Caillchen would be watched by something less (or more) than human.

As his fingers touched the scroll and closed about it, as his other hand grasped the blessing and masturbating monkey, Caillchen felt the eyes burning into him.

The Devil was watching.

He turned, scroll and monkey firmly held, but saw nothing. In the whole of that terrible library carved out of the ice there was no living thing except himself . . .

And the blue light emerging from a niche on the opposite side. The blue light that floated in the air . . . And was beginning to grow in size.

With a howl the monk seized his stolen booty and ran for the entrance to the cavern. His feet caught in the abandoned, broken furnishings of Roman pattern, sharding them still further. He picked himself up and continued his flight, the steam from the hot spring masking his exit from the pursuing skyfire. Once outside, his staff forgotten in his flight, he stuffed the scroll and the monkey inside his robe and raced towards the uncertain footholds afforded by the glacier which separated him from the safety and sanctity of his tiny stone cell.

Caillchen ran, the Lord beside him, holding him, keeping him safe, saving him from bloodying his knees too much when he stumbled in his panic. Behind him the blue light seemed to expand as it watched, coming closer without actually moving, accusing the holy man of the crime of theft by its pulsating presence.

It had taken him the better part of a cautious day to cross the glacier on his outward journey. Now, with the infernal breath upon his neck and ankles, the monk made it back to his own side in a little over two frantic hours. Only when he regained the shelter of his hermit's hut did he look behind him to see if the light was still following. To his great relief, and the Glory of Christ, it wasn't.

He spent most of that night in prayer, hardly conscious of the scroll and figurine which still reposed within his sweat-damp robe. Towards dawn he pitched forward on his knees before the crucifix he had brought with him from the monastery at Bri Chualann, plunged into exhausted sleep.

It was early the following afternoon when he emerged into consciousness once more. The day was bright and fine, encouraging him to go out and forage for food. God was kind, and in his bounty provided enough for at least two days.

When Caillchen returned to his hut he lit a small fire with tinder and a flint and set his only cooking vessel, an old iron pot, on a trivet above it. The rigors of his exploration, not to mention his encounter with the demonic, had left him in need of the comfort which comes with hot food. Though he didn't know it he was slightly light-headed with hunger when the stranger appeared outside his hut. And he still had the stolen scroll and monkey inside his robe.

He looked up as the stranger's shadow fell through the doorway, expecting to chastise some fellow hermit who had trespassed upon the privacy of his domain. Instead he caught an impression of someone pale, with long white hair and, unlike his fellows, white robes, with eyes that burned bright and somehow kindly in his shadowed face.

'May I join you, Caillchen Mac Eamon?' asked the stranger. 'I have a contribution for your pot.'

A gaunt hand held out a plucked and gutted seabird, feet and head already severed and discarded.

Caillchen, crouched beside his fire, looked up warily, wondering if there was a suspicion of blue light behind the newcomer. Yet he saw nothing, for all his fears.

'You're not a hermit,' the monk began, almost accusingly. 'So, who are you? Why are you here?'

'To offer you my help,' the stranger replied. He stepped inside, bowing his head as he passed through the low doorway, and dropped his offering into Caillchen's small cauldron. 'You'll never read that scroll without my help.'

The monk yelped and huddled back, cowering into an angle of his cell. 'It's you,' he gasped. 'You. The Devil! You've come for me!'

'Nothing of the kind,' the Keeper smiled. 'I simply want to help you.'

'I don't need your help. I have God's.'

'Then show him the scroll and ask him to read it to you.'

Caillchen hesitated. Then he reached inside his robe and withdrew the vellum scroll. Holding it by its upper edge he waved it before the crucifix. 'Lord, help me to read this,' he intoned, his eyes upon the Keeper even as he prayed.

No answer came. The symbols upon the vellum remained remote and incomprehensible.

Caillchen turned to the stranger. He held the scroll out to him. 'You can read this?' he demanded.

'I can.'

Caillchen sensed no hostility in the intruder. He became bolder.

'These symbols,' he grunted, underscoring the first word of the text with a grubby finger, 'what Devil's script is this?'

# T ⅎΙΥΛ

'It is called Etruscan,' the Keeper replied. 'It means "To the god".'

'Etruscan?'

'The people who lived in Rome before the Romans.'

'Demons,' Caillchen snorted. 'All of them.'

The Keeper shook his head. 'Ordinary people, my friend. Their script survives today, or a variant of it. It is used by the people who will claim to discover this island in seven years' time. History will call them Viking, and their script Runic. So you see, Caillchen Mac Eamon, there's nothing demonic in it. Not at all.'

The monk frowned. 'That's the second time you've called me by my name, Demon. How do you know it, if not with the Devil's aid?'

The Keeper offered his companion a faint smile. 'I know all my guests,' he told him. 'And you are as much a guest as any who has come here yet. More so, perhaps, for you have seen my home.'

'Your home?'

'The ice cavern. The place you call the Devil's Lair.'

'You live there?'

'I do. You yourself thought that it was more comfortable than your cell, I believe?'

'How do you know these things, if not with the Devil's help?'

The Keeper ignored the question. 'Shall I read the scroll for you?' he asked.

'If the first word says what you have told me, then it may be Holy Writ. "To the god", you say? Which god is it to?'

'Surely there is only one god, Caillchen?'

'Since Christ redeemed the world with his blood, yes. All the rest are the Devil's spawn.'

The Keeper raised a hand to hide his yawn. This monk was becoming tiresome. Besides, his theology wasn't that sound, either. If there was one god since Christ, then there could only have been one before Christ. Wasn't that part of the Saviour's teaching anyway?

'Then let me have the scroll, my friend.'

Caillchen hesitated. 'How do I know you won't just run off with it? That you will read it to me?'

'And if I did, would I be stealing what was already mine? But I give you my word. I shall read the scroll to you. That's why we're here together.'

I have to read the scroll to you, Caillchen, he thought. I must read and you must listen. Neither of us has any choice in the matter.

The hermit eyed him suspiciously as he took the scroll and unrolled it. This whole affair still stank of devilry but, in his heart, after so many years alone, both here and back in Bri Chualann, he was aching for the sound of another human voice and the comfort it could bring, even if it were reading a blasphemous biography of Satan himself – which, Caillchen decided, it wasn't.

It never occurred to him to question how this stranger knew the Gael tongue of his homeland, nor how he was able to translate and transliterate the symbols of the Etruscan script, rendering the contents of the vellum scroll in perfect Gaelic. If it had, the reek of brimstone would have come more strongly to his nostrils.

The words flowed from the Keeper, washing over Caillchen, bathing him with the beauty and harmony of their sounds. Exactly what was being read to him he never knew, immersed in the melody of the language as he was. Yet it insinuated its way into him, permeating every fibre of his grubby, tortured being, nestling inside his robe, stroking his skin and washing every hair of his body. As the text continued the music of the invocation wormed its way to the soft-marrow centre of his bones, then through his skull to etch its potency upon the inside of his cerebral cavity.

He began to tingle, suddenly aware of a greenish something seeming to grow within him as he listened, hearing the Keeper's recital with ears other than the physical ones God had given him. He wasn't even surprised that it didn't matter to him that this was an unhallowed new experience for it was, in its way, truly a part of him. Indeed, it *was* him.

Exactly when the Keeper finished he didn't remember. He was aware, in the moments left to him, as the long Icelandic night began to wrap its shroud about his cell, that he reached inside his robe and held out the tiny monkey to the stranger. He was also aware that the Keeper shook his head.

'Keep it in trust for the one who will come for it,' he told Caillchen. Then he released his hold upon his scroll and it fell to the littered earthen floor, to crumble and rot into nothing before the ravages of advancing years.

The Keeper left him there, still sitting in a corner of the stone hut, the arm holding the obsidian monkey extended. Caillchen Mac Eamon didn't see him go. He felt the light depart, but that didn't matter. There was so much to know and feel, so much to pass on, be he living or dead when the time came.

The invocation had opened new vistas to him, expanding the monk's limited world to a degree which he would never have thought possible. He saw fields of fungi, the fruit-bodies full and ripe beneath alien skies. He saw shapes of blasphemy and horror rising up before him, and beings of beauty and gentility long vanished from the earth, beings that might have been angels as the horrors were most certainly devils. He looked backwards and forwards in time, witnessing battles of undreamable perversity, towers of wood peopled by exquisitely beautiful evil, enormous wooden engines pulsing out sounds man was never meant to hear.

And a kiss.

Caillchen watched as a man, middle-aged and slender, embraced a young and lovely woman in a kiss that was to end the world of which the scroll had told him.

All this and more Caillchen saw. People spoke to him and he answered them from the knowledge he had been given by the Keeper's invocation. Time came, time passed. The moment of his death went by unheeded. His body locked in rigor mortis, the tiny monkey still extended. And when the old woman came, on the late afternoon of Wednesday 27 July, 869, the better part of six years later, Caillchen's remains were still sitting in his cell, waiting to present the figurine to the one who would know how to use it. Or, at least, keep it safe for the one who eventually might.

That was an ancient witch-woman called Heidi. She took the monkey, and she also took something else.

Caillchen's skull.

# TUESDAY 27 JULY 1540

## Morning

They had watched him from his first approach, townsfolk and sailors alike. Their eyes had followed his progress as he came down out of the wastes and glaciers to Vapnafjord. With his long white hair and wild white beard, the moustache sweeping to either side in the old style, the figure in the snow-bright robes could easily have been an animated snowman. All that marred the illusion was the age-blackened staff of yew that went with him in his hand. That, and the piercing blue eyes which were too young to live in such an ancient, wizened face.

They spread the word of his coming.

A young Danish priest, eager to battle superstition and the powers of darkness in a land where the runes were still secretly used for black magic, leaped out to confront him, crucifix uplifted.

'Avaunt, creature of the Devil!' the priest cried.

The blue eyes became sad. When the figure spoke the moustache seemed not to move, and the gathering onlookers wondered if they heard the reply with their ears or with their minds.

'Folly does not become you, young man.'

He walked on, down towards the harbour, leaving the priest shaking so that the cross dropped from his fingers onto the frozen ground. No-one moved to help the young Dane. They simply watched. And questioned.

'Who is he?' they whispered amongst themselves. 'Who is he? Where does he come from?'

An old man grinned back at them, gap-toothed. 'He's the Keeper,' he replied. 'They call him the Keeper.'

'The Keeper of what?' they asked him. 'Who calls him the Keeper?'

The old man shrugged. 'My father saw him once. It was he who told me that this ancient one is called the Keeper. That's who told me. Now, as to where he comes from, who can say? You saw as much as I did. He came down out of the glaciers. And now you know as much as I do.'

Their gaze followed him down to the seafront and watched as he went aboard one of the vessels tied up there, a lateen-rigged caravel belonging to a Danish merchant. None opposed him as he boarded. None came and asked him for his passage. The captain thought about it for a moment, but then something seemed to change his mind. Instead, he had the men cast off and put to sea, with the ship half laden and forced to tack against an unfavourable wind.

On the second day out, with Vapnafjord well behind them, the caravel was running with its sails full before the wind. The timbers cracked and creaked. The ropes strained. The crew, amazed by the speed of their progress, would sometimes take the time to stand and stare at the old man standing in the bows, watching the Northern Ocean flying past. Spume and spindrift flew up and clogged his hair and beard as he stood alone.

They muttered.

They muttered about the good time they were making in these wild northern seas. They muttered at his silence, at the way he stood there in the prow, unspeaking, untiring, with his young blue eyes turned only towards the future.

He felt them staring at him. Even an ordinary man would have felt their anxious eyes upon him. They asked their questions in his silence and he answered them the same way. The crew could no more have divined his thoughts than they could, provisioned as they were, have changed course and made for the new-discovered Indies.

He stood alone and they left him alone. They didn't hate him, but they couldn't love him either. That would have taken their understanding, and the Keeper was the last man that their minds could have understood.

With the dawning of the third day the captain, intrigued by this man who didn't move to seek warmth, or shelter, or food, or rest, came forward and stood beside him, his eyes studying the Keeper's face, struggling to find some level of comprehension. He was about to give up and turn away again when the Keeper asked: 'When do you expect to make land, Captain?'

The captain had been looking at him as he spoke. The ancient lips hadn't seemed to move beneath the heavy white moustache.

After nearly thirty years at sea, eight of them as a master, the captain had carried many strange cargoes and even stranger passengers. Yet he'd never known any as strange as this one, so he struggled to appear unconcerned in the face of whatever phenomena might present themselves. Besides, if he showed fear the effect upon his men could be disastrous.

You already know the answer, he thought. Why ask me if you know more than I do?

He forced a shrug. 'Perhaps the twenty-ninth. Probably the thirtieth. You can never tell for certain. There are so many different factors involved. If this wind holds, we might make Frederikshavn even sooner . . .'

He broke off as the Keeper turned towards him, smiling. 'The wind will hold, Captain. You will make port earlier than you had ever hoped you would. The twenty-ninth, the thirtieth, will be too late for what I have to do.'

His eyes studied the captain's features, noting the strain about the man's mouth and the indrawn, pin-prick concentration in his pupils.

'You need have no fear of me, my friend. No harm shall come to you and yours. Your first port of call, however, will be Bremen. From there, when I have left you, you will make good passage back to Frederikshavn.'

The captain heard him and, nodding to himself, believed and began to relax. Then he walked back amongst his crew, which had knotted behind him to watch the exchange, smiling and calling them by name, reassuring them as he now was reassured.

The Keeper continued to stare ahead of them. Above him the lateen sails were straining against their shrouds to hold the firm air which was pushing the caravel so rapidly forward. The surf of their passage whipped past mere inches from the tops of the bow gunwales, but the Keeper's blue eyes didn't notice. They were seeing other sights, other times, reviewing a progression of images which, in time, would resolve into the merciful release of death from his many-centuried life.

Before then, however, there had to be a replacement. The office of the Keeper could never be left vacant. That was what the *other* powers wanted. That was why they forced these confrontations.

In his past he viewed a shattered, scattered skeleton, still mouldering in brown tatters in a tumbled hermit's hut. The skull was missing. So was the tiny carving of a monkey, one hand raised in benediction, the other masturbating, which the skeleton had once held in an outstretched hand. Separately the two things were meaningless. Yet together, in the hands of those who *knew*, they were capable of summoning, liberating or destroying the most frightening, terrible powers that mankind had ever faced.

Perhaps Gardar Svarsson's mother hadn't known the full power of the two disparate items, but she had been enough of a witch-woman to take them, to keep the skull for herself, together with the monkey, until she died. Her name had been Heidi, the Keeper smiled to himself. She wasn't the first of the Heidis, but neither was she the last.

With her death the skull and the monkey passed on to other owners. The skull spoke to some of them, if they knew how to make it speak, but mostly it held its deathly silence. The monkey, though, said nothing. It simply blessed and masturbated on.

In time the two things went their separate ways. The skull divulged its secrets to an ancient Arab sorcerer. As he fell exhausted into nightmare-haunted sleep his young apprentice stole it from him, together with the sheaf of fragile vellum pages it had dictated. The monkey travelled from hand to hand, little more than a curiosity, until a gypsy woman called Hulda presented herself at the home of the Graf von Meersburg as the nurse for his new-born son.

She taught him magic and mystery. She showed him how the minds of men had become closed by the stifling teachings of the Church. She moulded the future Ptythonius Ulrich, Graf von Meersburg, into the greatest charlatan and most potent iconoclast of an age of burgeoning wonders. And she gave him two things.

The first thing was a name, another name, a *secret* name. Johannes Faust. The second was a small obsidian monkey.

But that was in the past.

Faust was dead now. Everybody knew that the Devil had come for his soul that night in Freiburg. Everybody knew how the sorcerer had been torn apart by the Fiend in an upper room of the Lion Inn. Hardly two scraps of his body remained to be placed together for burial.

Ptythonius von Meersburg, however, lived on. So did a little sorcerer called Amsegi. The skull wouldn't talk to Amsegi, but he had his master's manuscript. And in a ruined castle a monstrous clock would soon beat out an unholy rhythm to summon one of the ancient darknesses of Thule.

The Keeper closed his eyes against the sights but they continued to haunt him, to possess him as he stood in the bows of the speeding caravel. The images persisted, as did the knowledge that came with them.

Amsegi, for all his knowledge, was weak. He would betray the man he served for the love of a beautiful woman who had once been the Landgravine von Bamberg. Yet the monstrous evocation would continue for all that. And so the Keeper had to be there, to intervene.

I know so much, he thought, and yet I know so little. If the time has come when I have to face termination for my carelessness, then I am ready. No man, not even the Keeper, may hide himself away in the blessedness of the *point quiescent* for ever.

So, if it is time for me to terminate, I shall. All I can hope for now is that my end is not in vain, that the new Keeper is ready for his task and that some fruit will have ripened in the waiting and planning through the years.

A seagull mewed overhead. He turned and peered up at it past the billowing sails.

There was still some hope.

'Tomorrow,' he said to himself as he stood wrapped in his thoughts. 'I think we shall make Bremen tomorrow.'

And after that I shall never see Iceland again, he added, inwardly. Not on this plane, anyway.

# WINTER SOLSTICE

## 21 December 1578

They sat amongst the graves in the little churchyard, the squat, flint-built tower of the parish church of Wodsham casting its shadow beneath the winter moon, masking their presence from any who might stumble late towards them. The landscape around them, the grass, the roofs of the distant cottages and the closer, larger roof of the Hall, just across the field beyond the ha-ha, the trees, all was white with frost. The Council, however, perched upon markers, squatting on slabs and table tombs, the latecomers crunching down the brittle vegetation beneath their haunches, didn't mind the cold. Not tonight.

There were important things for them to decide tonight. There was also the special sacrifice to the returning sun to be completed. The graveyard earth needed blood to breed its magic, and blood they intended to give it once the work of the Council was completed.

In the centre of their rough circle, hamstrung and freezing, mumbling his terror softly because of the way those teeth could dig in if his cries became too loud, a youth of nineteen lay shivering in the shreds of his finery. His fear was a solid, choking thing that pulsed from throat to belly and back again with every beat of his heart, magnified by both the presence of his tormentors and the certain knowledge that his father would assume him to be drinking or wenching through the night and not bother to send out searchers from the Hall to look for him. Hugo Williamsone was alone and helpless in his final moments. No help would arrive to rescue him. No mercy would be shown by his inhuman captors.

He was going to die, very soon, and he knew it.

The debate was nearing its conclusion, bringing the time of his sacrifice ever closer. Furred heads were nodding assent, bowing to the inevitable rigors of the time they inhabited. Disturbingly manlike faces, the mouths displaying wickedly-sharp teeth, expressed personal assent or disapproval and made the choice appropriate for the colony they represented.

The Venerable Wandermouse, his fur grey-white, his eyes the colour of tanned leather, his features seamed with age and almost bald, summed up their choices in his hoarse, grating whisper of a voice. 'We have agreement from all Venerables present,' he began, 'save for you, Pyewacket, and you, Artisson. The rest of us will caution our colonies to be selective in their service to the adherence of the Old Religion, though that service will continue unchanged, despite the present circumstances. Now I must call upon you two to inform this Council of your intentions, that all may be advised of the actions of their neighbouring colonies. Have you decided, Pyewacket?'

He turned his ancient gaze upon the Venerable of the colony hosting the Annual Grand Council. His fur was cream at the roots, though it was earth-darkened at the surface of the pelt, and his eyes were slate-grey. When he spoke his voice was higher in pitch than Wandermouse's, but just as firm, strong with the authority of his position as a Venerable. 'This area is now too firmly infested with the Witchfinder General's money-hungry followers,' he stated. 'It would be foolish for my colony to remain active in such circumstances. The precautions which have been required in order to host this Council must have conveyed some impression of the risks we have been running almost daily. The gallows from Chelmsford to Beccles dangle with the rotting bodies of those we once served. We have no choice but to go underground, Wandermouse, to terminate our service and ride out the storm in secret.'

The older Venerable's eyes narrowed for a moment. Then he nodded, slowly and sagely. 'It is probably a wise decision in your circumstances,' he replied. 'I wish you and yours well of it. And you, Artisson? Your colony is in equal jeopardy, I imagine.'

Artisson was a black *familiaris*. Both his fur and eyes were night-black, though the unfurred areas, the palms of his tiny hands and his muzzle, resembled tanned human flesh. Like the others permitted to speak at the Council, he was a Venerable, the leader of a colony which was based to the north of the River Orwell, around Woodbridge. His expression was serious, regretful, as he said: 'It has been hard for me to come to a decision, Venerable Wandermouse, but I have done so. Like Venerable Pyewacket's, my colony has suffered greatly from our persecutors. We have already terminated our service to the witch-cult and made our plans. In a week's time we intend to leave this country and seek a new home on foreign shores. Sadly, this is to be my last attendance at this Council.'

Wandermouse frowned. 'This has the sound of greater hazard about it than any of the others' plans, Artisson.'

'Perhaps,' came the guarded reponse, 'but if we succeed we shall be able to resume our lives in greater liberty than will be afforded to those who remain here. And that has to be worth the hazard.'

'How will you make your voyage?'

Hugo Williamsone moaned piteously and opened his mouth to try a scream. Before he could do so three of Pyewacket's subordinates had climbed onto his head, their teeth threatening his eyes and nose. The scream remained unsounded as he shut his eyes firmly against the tiny nightmares and shuddered in his agony.

'There is a carrack leaving Felixstowe bound for Denmark in a week's time,' Artisson replied. 'My colony will sail with it. If ship-rats can get aboard it will be no trouble for us. And the rats will sustain us throughout the voyage as well.'

Pyewacket scratched at his ear. 'Why Denmark?' he inquired.

'Because it is free of trash like Matthew Hopkins, and hopefully will remain that way. It is also a far enough distance, yet a short enough voyage, for us to remain unnoticed.'

Wandermouse silently admired the boldness of the plan. It seemed to have been well thought out and had a good chance of success. 'Then the business of the Council is concluded,' he announced, 'and the hour of the sacrifice is arrived. Venerable Pyewacket, you should tell us, as is customary, how you have made selection for the Solstice victim.'

Pyewacket climbed down from the surface of the table tomb he'd been occupying, glad of the opportunity to move after several hours of debate. Flexing himself, he leaped from the grass onto Hugo Williamsone's panic-heaving chest and stared at the terrified youth through blankly-indifferent eyes. Then he looked up and around, his gaze taking in Wandermouse and the other Council members.

'Upon the Eve of All Hallows last this man's father brought about the execution of one we served, by the name of Thomas Harley. It is thus just for the son to form our sacrifice this night.'

'Why not the father?' Artisson enquired. 'Surely he'd be better chosen?'

Pyewacket laughed, mirthlessly. 'If we could have taken the

father we would have done so, Venerable Artisson. Nothing would have given me, personally, greater pleasure than to see Sir Nygel Williamsone, or whatever his name really is, lying here in this wretch's place. The father, though, is a devotee of the Old Powers of Thule, and thus beyond our reach without the intervention of the Keeper of the Balance. I agree that this . . .' he gestured contemptuously at Hugo, 'is a poor substitute, but at least he has the debauching of Thomas Harley's orphaned daughter to recommend him. He forced Rebecca Harley to whore for him in order to effect her flight from further persecution, and his punishment as our sacrifice is thus both justified and desirable.'

He looked around the circle of his peers, noting their nods and murmurs of agreement. 'Venerable Wandermouse,' he invited, 'as elder Venerable of the Council, will you honour my colony by acceptance of our choice of sacrifice?'

The *familiares*, despite their high, inhuman voices, spoke the human tongue of the areas they inhabited. Hugo Williamsone, crippled, helpless and alone, heard and understood what was said. His terror and revulsion mounted to a new peak as the Venerable Wandermouse, ancient joints rebelling, jumped down from his perch upon a marker and began a painful trek towards Hugo's throat. He didn't bother to climb onto the body, which would soon begin to thrash helplessly, if dangerously for its tormentors.

'For the return of the sun,' Wandermouse intoned, ritualistically.

'For the return of the sun,' the others responded.

Then it began.

Hugo screamed as their teeth went in, howled as they swarmed down and began to drain him, both into the earth and into themselves. His useless limbs beat at them like flesh-covered clubs. His bowels and bladder voided their contents. His eyes saw briefly, before vicious canines punctured them and even the moonlight went out for ever. The rank sweat of horror and pain burst out from every pore.

He didn't scream for long. His cries began to bubble into inarticulate gurglings as teeth found his larynx and severed his vocal cords. Yet the *familiares*, in their ritual, were anything but merciful. They bit with care, with restraint, keeping the sacrificial victim alive and conscious for several ghastly minutes. The sun expected it, demanded it of them. So too did the ghost of Thomas Harley and the vanished person of his daughter Rebecca.

Hugo Williamsone took nearly ten minutes to die.

The Annual Grand Council of the *familiares* of East Anglia completed its work and disbanded. In the days that followed Pyewacket's colony went underground, where it remained for a little over 400 years, surfacing again at Wegrimham where, at the intervention of the Keeper, it finally took its revenge upon the one they knew as Nygel, then Rufus, Williamsone and the dark Thulean power he served. The Venerable Artisson's colony, under cover of darkness, slipped aboard the carrack *Fine Lady* at Felixstowe, sailing with it on the morning tide of Saturday 8th November, 1578. Yet the best laid plans of mice, men and creatures that are neither can often founder before the whims of fate, and the *Fine Lady* was destined never to make her intended port of Esbjerg. On Monday 10th she fell before a vicious south-easterly which blew her off course. Faced with a choice of wreck or run the captain decided to run.

Four days later, on that unlucky day Friday which sailors dread, the *Fine Lady* foundered close by the shore of Hornafjördhur in south-east Iceland. Wet, cold and hungry, the ship-rats all used up (and at least one member of the carrack's crew), the Venerable Artisson led the surviving members of his colony ashore.

Into the Kingdom of the Keeper.

# TUESDAY 13 NOVEMBER 1649

## Night

They had almost reached the coffin.

Feist and Grünner were beginning to ache all over from their exertions. The wicked frost, one of the first really heavy frosts that year, had seeped through their clothing and into their bones; even the rivulets of perspiration produced by the digging were chilled into semi-frozen, almost-burning stains. Worn mercenary leathers were not the ideal clothes for work such as this, and neither were the two mercenaries used to the labour. The most that was normally required of them in the Landgravine's service was to look menacing – an attribute that both of them possessed in abundance – and to slit the occasional throat, normally without knowing why.

The cemetery, nestling outside the walls of Karlstadt, was overgrown and neglected. Tall grasses obscured the grave-markers, except where those markers had fallen over, flattening the growth around them and frequently obscuring the names of those whose last resting places they had been set to mark. But at least Feist and Grünner had found the marker they required still upright, without the struggle to read damp, slug and larva mottled legends on the stones pressed to the earth, which smothered the leprous white filaments of sun-denied vegetation struggling to survive beneath them.

Neglect was everywhere across the landscape, not just here. The wooden palings of the boundary fence were broken or missing, here and there charred by the fires of soldiery long before camped and moved on. The town of Karlstadt fared better than some, but the paint was peeling and the boards worse weathered than might have been expected. Roofs, once meticulously tiled, were no longer as strong as they were. The streets were dirty, the populace worn-down and struggling to regain some measure of their former rural prosperity. Even so, they were grateful. The terrible times they had survived were now officially – if not necessarily in fact – over, the signing of the Treaty of Westphalia bringing the Thirty Years' War to its inevitable end. Peace and religious toleration were to follow in its wake, and with the peace would come a time for repair and restoration, a time to retile the roofs, repaint the boards and scythe down the grasses in the cemetery.

But now, as the hands on the clock beside the Stadttor Gate moved steadily towards midnight, Karlstadt was silent and asleep. The chiming of that clock would penetrate no dream, disrupt no slumber, for by a town ordinance its chimes had been stilled after that dreadful night over a hundred years before, that night when a fantastic wooden engine had boomed out an awesome beating from its carillon of tambours in the ruins of the Karlsburg on the hill above the town.

Feist's shovel, heavy with clinging clods of earth, struck something solid. He turned and looked towards Grünner, digging away at the further end of the grave. Above them the night was clear and star-bright, and the grasses spearing up to either side showed the glistening of their crisp white coating in the yellow light of the tallow lantern lighting the mercenaries' endeavours.

'Wood,' Feist announced in a triumphant whisper. 'I've hit wood. I've got the lid.'

Grünner stopped digging and turned, easing his bulk along the narrow confines of the open grave. Together they scraped at the surrounding earth, squeezing around one another to trace the outline of the simple plank coffin and free it from the clayey grip which had embraced it since 1540. They used their spade and shovel almost as spoons to free the sides from the encumbering earth and make it easier to grasp and lift. Once all but the lowest part had been cleared, they climbed up out of the grave and used long poles as levers to break it free of its final restraint.

On the dirt road which ran past the cemetery, at some distance from the place where Feist and Grünner were working, a horse-drawn wagon stood waiting to receive its burden. Whilst neither mercenary was unused to blood, death and decay, for both had seen service at the horrific climax of the siege of Magdeburg, they were both eager to be done with this grave-robbing and into the healthier atmosphere of the open country, their burden secured and their task completed. Besides, there was always the chance of some peasant out late discovering them and rushing into Karlstadt to raise a hue and cry before they could get clear or silence him.

Such a reaction would have been Ehrich Hittelmann's, except for Ehrich's curiosity. He had been wounded and returned home during the last months of the war, making a good recovery because of his youth and the combined ministrations of his doting mother and hero-worshipping fiancée. At twenty-two he was a hardened veteran of several bloody campaigns and had shown his valour, as he described it, or foolhardiness as it was called by those about him, many times. The musket ball which had penetrated his right shoulder, remarkably passing beneath the collar-bone and out again above the shoulder-blade, had left his sword-arm stiff, but with regular exercise and plenty of hard work, having taken up a late apprenticeship to a local weaponsmith, it was slowly improving. And Ehrich's curiosity also helped. It had led him to explore beneath the skirts of several women in the area, an exercise infinitely more pleasurable and preferable than simple arm-strengthening press-ups, though very similar in physical movement.

On this particular night, wrapped in the soldier's cloak that he retained to remind those about him of his former prowess, he had been indulging in his most favoured form of exercise with a widow who lived some three or four kilometres from the town. Walking home along the dirt road he came first upon the wagon, a dark blur ahead of him which gradually resolved itself as he approached. Ehrich patted the horse harnessed between its shafts and was rewarded with a faceful of steaming horse-breath. Walking slowly around, curious as ever, he noted that the wagon was both empty and seemingly abandoned.

His first thought was that this was hardly the kind of time or place for such a conveyance to be standing. It was too far from the town gate with its squat building and square tower. Perhaps the animal had run away. Perhaps, he wondered, there would be some reward for its discovery and return.

He surveyed the frosted landscape about him. In every direction nothing and no-one stirred or was to be seen. Except . . .

There, in the graveyard he thought he saw a yellowish glow amongst the tall disorder of the white-rimed grasses. Blinking to reassure himself he peered harder and concluded that he was right. A yellow glow.

Ehrich scratched his head. It was too late in the year for fireflies, the wingless beetles which shone phosphorescent patches to attract their mates. Nor could he think of any other explanation to begin with. Then two came at once, both of them sufficient to pique his curiosity.

The first was ghosts.

The second was grave-robbers.

With the thrill of battle tingling his skin once more, with the imagined sound of his former adventures ringing in his ears, Ehrich Hittelmann began to walk into the cemetery, moving as silently as any soldier might. Be the light he could see natural or supernatural, he would know its origin or perish in the attempt.

Or both.

He took what cover he could from the grave-markers and tried to avoid disturbing the grasses more than he had to. Creeping closer, his movements unheard by Feist and Grünner because of the efforts they were making to extricate the coffin from the grave, he observed the fiendish duo at their labours.

Two men. Both of them mercenaries from their dress, neither in the first flush of youth. It would be a challenge, but Ehrich decided he could beard them with a rush. First, though, he had to be certain of his ground.

The night was moonless, but the frosted ground reflected and magnified what light there was to see and be seen by. The grave-robbers had the disadvantage of being within the circle of light projected by the lantern. That would hamper their vision. They were also distracted by their grotesque and ghastly occupation.

And then Ehrich's curiosity obtruded again.

He now knew the origin of the light and the reason for the wagon. He could also see who was performing this sacrilege in the cemetery. Yet he didn't know *why* they were doing it, or to whom. He crept closer, his eyes straining to make out the inscription upon the age-weathered marker at the head of the grave. For several moments he struggled with the lichen-encrusted legend, then smiled to himself. Why ever they were doing it, it couldn't happen to a better subject. The marker read simply:

UGO DA DONDI OBIT MDXL

Ugo da Dondi. The man, legend told, who had brought the night of fear, the night of the monstrous clock in the castle ruins, to Karlstadt. Children sang:

Ugo da Dondi, evil man,
Sought to take the life from man.
In the ruins built his clock,
Ugo da Dondi may you rot.

Whoever one asked in Karlstadt, even so long after the event, had no good word to say for the memory of Ugo da Dondi, Master of Time.

Nevertheless, Ehrich decided, these two were defiling a grave, albeit that of a hated memory. It behoved him to do something about it.

He sprang.

Where he came from Grünner and Feist neither knew nor cared. That he was there at all was enough. With a wild and warlike cry Ehrich leaped upon them, his rush flooring Feist and carrying him full into Grünner, who gave way whilst his companion scrambled to his feet. Lashing out wildly the mercenary felt his fist connect glancingly with the side of Ehrich's head, skinning his frozen knuckles. Ehrich landed on one knee and turned, crouching, slightly stunned from Grünner's blow, to face the advancing Feist. Springing from his crouch, the youth head-butted Feist's crotch and tore the dagger from his adversary's waist. Before he could use it Grünner's shadow, projected by the lantern, fell across him and made him turn again.

Grünner had seized the pole he'd been using to lever da Dondi's coffin free of the earth in the grave. As he swung it, Ehrich raised his left arm to block the blow and lunged with Feist's dagger at the mercenary's corpulent belly. Grünner anticipated the movement and leaped back, the point of the dagger snicking his leathers as he did so.

'Hold, there,' he demanded, dropping the pole. 'We can talk about this, lad. See? I'll even disarm myself,' he added, drawing his own knife clumsily with the wrong hand and tossing it past Ehrich in an apparent gesture of submission.

'There,' he grunted. 'Let's talk, shall we?'

Ehrich sensed an advantage. 'Only in front of the Burgermeister, grave-robber,' he snarled with his best viciousness. You had to be seen to be tough and heard to be tough with vermin like these.

The tears were clearing from Feist's eyes. His balls hurt with that dull ache which stretches from knees to navel, but his mind was clear. Grünner hadn't simply disarmed himself. He had tossed his weapon to one in a better position to use it than he was himself. It lay inches from Feist's empty fingers.

Grünner resisted the temptation to look past Ehrich to his companion. 'Can't we talk here?' he grinned. 'There's gold in it, if you're prepared to listen.'

Keep him distracted. Keep him looking at you, unconscious of what's happening behind him. Buy time with talk.

Ehrich's eyes widened. They were looking past Grünner in a way that Grünner hadn't dared to look past Ehrich. They were staring at the tiny blue light, hardly much bigger than the nearest star, which floated behind the mercenary as if it were ... watching ...

Feist filled his empty fingers and tensed.

Grünner's face clouded as he saw Ehrich's expression. He turned to follow his gaze.

Feist struck, the dagger ripping into one of Ehrich's kidneys.

The youth at first seemed to ignore it. His eyes remained focused upon the light until they glazed, slowly, and he pitched forward onto his face. Feist left the dagger in his victim's body and, like Grünner, stared at the blue light.

'What is it?' he whispered.

His companion shook his head and turned back. 'Whatever it is, let's grab what we came for and get out of here,' he urged.

They hauled the coffin out of the grave and dumped Ehrich's body into the space it left. Without bothering to fill in the evidence of their handiwork they carried the coffin quickly to the waiting wagon, straining and cursing, casting nervous glances behind them at the watching skyfire. They didn't see it depart towards the north. They were too busy loading the mortal remains of Ugo da Dondi onto their cart and whipping the horse into flight.

Feist, shivering slightly, looked at his companion. 'What do you think it was?' he asked.

Grünner didn't even shrug. 'How should I know?' he demanded. 'Let's forget it. We've got the coffin, and that's all the Landgravine is interested in.'

# THURSDAY 31 OCTOBER 1889

## Early evening

The pen fell from his frozen hand and rattled across the icy surface of the desk. Before him the leather-bound log was open, the last entry still fresh from his writing. His blue eyes were red-rimmed and the lashes and brows beneath the fur-lined hood were crusted with frost.

He studied the figure by the cabin door, unsure as to whether his voice would still work if he tried to speak. The hand which had clutched the pen had moved to the butt of his Mauser revolver, the frostbitten index finger ready to press the trigger, whatever target he might ultimately select.

'You ... are the Keeper?' he asked, almost horrified by the sound of his own voice in the ice-bound silence.

Ptythonius von Meersburg, white robed, forbidding, nodded his response, trying to smile comfortingly and reassuringly at the frightened, dying man before him. 'I am the Keeper,' Ptythonis replied. 'And you are Martin Fallenberg, I believe.'

'I am,' the Swede replied. Then: 'The fungi told me you were coming.'

Ptythonius smiled gently. 'The fungi have always been difficult,' he told Fallenberg. 'They resent the briefness of their active life and fight against its reality whenever they can. Of all forms of creation it is normally the fungi which create the most difficulty, be it through poisoning or infection or simple wilful stubbornness. Yet in this case they have wrought something of a service.'

They were aboard the schooner *Harfanger*, out of Stockholm in pursuit of Martin Fallenberg's last and greatest dream. Fallenberg had lusted after the discovery of a lost continent for most of his life, despite the fact that the world was adequately charted and the great voyages of exploration already made. He had set off to find the mythical, as most men thought, continent of Thule upon the surface of the physical world, and had lost his way. Now the *Harfanger* was ice-bound in the sub-polar desert north of Spitzbergen. His surviving crew had deserted, leaving him alone to face whatever the fates had in store for him. Now, in the presence of the Keeper, a presence foretold by the fungi which had invaded and possessed his vessel, surviving in terms of both time and temperature beyond their appointed hours, he had reached the crux of his existence, and he knew it.

'I could ask you how you have come here,' Fallenberg began, 'but I don't think that's important any more. The fact of your presence is almost enough to answer all my questions. I have one question remaining, though.'

Ptythonius von Meersburg nodded. 'Ask it,' he instructed. 'I shall answer you as best I can.'

'Then it is this,' Fallenberg said. 'Why have you come to me? Everyone else has lost faith and fled across the ice to try to save themselves. Yet you have sought me out. Will you comfort a dying man and tell me why?'

'You have answered your own question,' the Keeper replied. 'I have come to comfort you as you approach the moment of your death, Martin.'

Fallenberg forced himself to snort, his breath steaming and almost crystallizing in his arctic surroundings. 'Do you bring fire, or food? How can you comfort me? What's left that can bring me comfort?'

'The knowledge that you were right, according to the limit of your beliefs.'

'Right? I'm right? Lost here, frozen in the ice, I'm right?'

'In your way,' Ptythonius responded. 'You sought Thule, Martin. You believed it was there and you set out to find it. I have come to bring you the comfort of knowing, before you die, that Thule is a reality.'

Fallenberg gasped. For a moment his eyes glazed, then he struggled to bring them back into focus upon the pallid figure by the cabin door. 'I was right?' he asked. 'Then why didn't I find it? I had the charts. I had everything that's been written about it, from Higgins to Plato and back.'

'Will you believe my answer, if I offer it?'

'I can try, Keeper.'

'Then it is this. Thule is real, but it is beyond the reality you know. Your first search was subjective, making you believe in Thule. Your second search was this one, in which you sought it objectively. Yet there is a third reality, Martin, beyond the objective and subjective. It is there that Thule is to be found. You did not have the means to seek for Thule within the third reality. It will be almost a hundred years before that search is undertaken. So you see, you were right. But you were ahead of your time, and you are paying the price for that. Even so, in your way, you have been right, from the very beginning.'

He both watched and controlled Fallenberg's reaction to his words. The Swede reached for his pen and scribbled a single phrase onto the map spread out beneath the log. Then he dropped the pen and, clutching the revolver in his frozen fingers, raised it until the muzzle pointed to his right temple. His features slowly crumpled into a look of final content, then froze in shock as the Mauser discharged a bullet into his brain.

Ptythonius von Meersburg watched him slump. I owed him that much, he thought as he turned and left the ice-bound schooner for the future to discover. I owed him that much and I have paid that part of my debt. History may judge him insane, but I shall not. There have been greater insanities than his before now, and there will be again.

In fact the greatest of them all is still to come.

# SUNDAY 9 AUGUST 1942

## After lunch

Tubenheim was delighted with the brandy. It was the pale gold which proclaimed it, together with its aroma, as being both French and of considerable age. Obviously Signora Vertucci had pulled out all the stops on her household's culinary organ, he reflected.

Sturmbannführer SS Ernst Albrecht Tubenheim sat back in the comfortable depths of the leather club chair, snatching a moment's content from the rigors of the increasingly uncertain world about him. Beyond the sanctuary of the villa the city of Genoa had attained that unusual calm and comparative silence which marked the day of rest. For six days a week it positively howled with activity, its trams clattering through the historic streets, the congested (even in those days) traffic struggling towards its several destinations and the hustling, shouting activity of the market. But on the seventh day, apart from the more muted travel of the faithful to and from the cathedral and the other churches, and the pealing of the bells which summoned them and their gossip to and fro, Genoa settled into a respectful silence.

That, however, was outside.

Signora Vertucci, dressed in the customary black of the Italian widow (though her clothes were of finer material and better cut than most, denoting her position of wealth in the community), was a complete contrast to the teutonic blondness of the young SS officer she had entertained. Her hair was as black as her clothing, though beginning to grey where it was swept back above her forehead. Her eyes were darkly un-Germanic and her mouth, though deeply lined at the corners and puckered across the upper lip, still showed some trace of the exotic promise it had held for Ignacio Vertucci, proto-Fascist and local dignitary, over thirty years before. Beside her features, Tubenheim was nothing more than a black and silver cut-out of the New Germany, despite the power residing in both his person and the orders it had received.

'I trust you enjoyed your lunch, Major?' the widow Vertucci inquired, like the perfect hostess she invariably attempted to be.

Sturmbannführer Tubenheim inclined his head slightly and permitted himself a smirk. 'Delightful, Signora,' he assured her, draining his brandy and retaining the glass in his hand. 'Quite delightful.'

She acknowledged the hint by rising from her chair, opposite, and replenishing his glass, though not as generously as before, which did not go unnoted. Manners were not a strong point with the SchutzStaffel, though Signora Vertucci was careful not to emphasize the patent fact. Indeed, a man better gifted in that department would not have required to be prompted in order to express his appreciation of the meal.

Despite the Axis, Italy was, for the most part, wary of its *übermenschen* allies to the north. Especially here, on the shore of the Ligurian Sea, where tales of atrocity and suppression in nearby France were rife. The widow Vertucci sensed that her guest, his eyes unfocused with something more than just the alcohol he had consumed yet alien in the coldness of their blue depths for all that, was elsewhere.

At that moment Ernst Tubenheim's thoughts were back in the opulent office in the Prinz Albrecht Strasse where he was being briefed by Standartenführer Volker, Himmler's appointed successor to the treacherous Hans-Heinz Gudenheim. Tubenheim was a new recruit to A M T VII and didn't yet fully appreciate its nature and purposes. He had heard of the work of the Ahnenernbe, the ancestral heritage research organization, naturally. It was impossible to reach even a minor rank in the SS without being fully indoctrinated in the magnificence of the Germanic past as redefined by that obscure but important department. But to join it, even with a promotion from Haupsturmführer, posed questions his basically simple, soldier's mind was going to have to grapple severely with to gain any kind of answer. And Ernst Tubenheim wasn't sure he was prepared for ideological, as opposed to physical, grappling.

Still, he was here now in Genoa because Volker had ordered him here in Genoa. And he'd do a good job on this first assignment, even if he didn't understand what it was all about.

Standartenführer Volker had smiled, corpulently, displacing two of the chins above his collar. 'A simple mission to begin with, Ernst,' he had promised. 'You will go to Genoa with a picked squad. There the arrangements have already been made for you to lunch with a Signora Eleonora Vertucci next Sunday.'

'Might I ask why, Standartenführer?' he'd inquired, knowing there had to be something more to a visit to Italy than simply having lunch with a widow.

The widow's words brought him back to the present, yet retained his link with the past. Signora Vertucci had taken her courage in both hands.

'It has been most pleasant meeting you, Major,' she said, her voice slightly higher than its normal register. 'I cannot help feeling, however, that there was some purpose to your visit. Perhaps I would be better able to help you if I knew what that purpose is?'

Tubenheim sobered up, hard and fast. His voice was everything that could have been expected of a major in the SS when he replied: 'Your husband was interested in local history, I believe, Signora Vertucci. Because of his interest he accumulated a substantial library of local documents, both modern and historical. Am I correct in my information?'

The question was rhetorical, but it required an answer for all that. 'You are,' the signora told him.

'Including certain documents relating to the da Dondi family?'

'The clockmakers? I believe there may be some items, yes.'

'Might I see them?'

'It will be my pleasure to show them to you, Major,' she lied. 'If you will wait here I will fetch them for you.'

'I don't wish to be ungracious,' he responded, offering her a contradiction, 'but I would prefer to accompany you, if I may.'

His words constituted a demand rather than a request. The signora inclined her head. 'Will you rise and come this way?' she inquired with veiled sarcasm.

In the servants' quarters of the villa Tubenheim's men were quietly and efficiently instituting a massacre, as he hauled his wiry but intoxicated frame from the depths of the club chair. On reluctant legs he followed the widow Vertucci from the comfortable drawing-room and out into a high-ceilinged corridor. They progressed along this in silence, she leading and he following, then passed through the double doors at the further end into a book-lined apartment, one wall of which was taken up with cardboard document-cases. Beside these the signora paused, scanning the typed labels on the projecting edges, then she reached down three and placed them on a table at the centre of the library. Tubenheim read the labels of the cases she had selected.

DA DONDI: GIOVANNI
DA DONDI: UGO
DA DONDI: GENERAL

'There are no others?' he inquired, his cold eyes aware of an intrusive presence at the doorway, behind his hostess ...

'No others,' she replied. 'You have only to look should you disbelieve me, Major.'

'Excellent.'

He nodded as he spoke. At his nod the *feldwebel* in the doorway sighted along his Schmeisser and pulled the trigger, pumping twelve rounds into the widow's black-dressed body.

'The charges are in place?' Tubenheim demanded, almost before the signora's blood had begun to stain the carpeting beneath her.

'They are, Sturmbannführer.'

'Good. I have what we came for, so I see no reason for lingering here. Tell the others, Erich, and let's get out of here.'

# THURSDAY 6 AUGUST LAST YEAR

## Late afternoon

If the British summer seemed to have pulled out the stops to be disgusting over the rest of the country, it was trying extra hard over RAF Dunnet. The most northerly of Britain's air bases, Dunnet was tucked away off the Pentland Firth, within what the ground crews called farting distance of John O'Groats and kissing distance of Thurso. It was hardly the optimum posting for an ambitious young officer, and George Ratcliffe Harding, recently promoted First Lieutenant and transferred from NATO Project Nightwatch, somewhere in the Midlands, began to wonder if maybe his memos to Project Command hadn't queered his future after all.

Harding had arrived in the middle of a downpour late the night before, had been shown his quarters, eaten a lonely scratch meal in the mess and tumbled into bed without unpacking, having paused only briefly to report to the duty officer.

This morning, his first, he'd seen RAF Dunnet in grey, soggy daylight and found it a distressingly grey and soggy place. The only consolation was that he might be able to creep through the back door into pilot training if he showed sufficient aptitude and interest, the adjutant explained.

RAF Dunnet was home to Project Lapwing and was equipped with BAe TAV–8A Harriers and a few old F.6 Lightnings, all modified to deliver payloads of air-to-air and air-to-surface missiles, the adjutant went on. Whilst the location might appear to be at the arse end of God's earth the work done there was important.

'The lapwing lays its eggs on the ground,' the adjutant continued. 'So do we, for the most part. Project Lapwing is a NATO missile assessment programme, examining the capabilities of a wide variety of armaments on behalf of both our allies and the MOD. The test area for ground-strike is inland, past the Strath of Kildonan. There's a dump for decommissioned military vehicles just past Kinbrace that we use for targets.'

Harding nodded, intelligently, he hoped, though the trickle of water from the back of his peaked cap down the neck of his tunic hardly served to promote an intelligent expression. 'And for sea-strike, sir?' he asked, wishing for the warmth and shelter of the mess instead of this wind-blown expanse of grass and runways.

'Same sort of thing, don't y'know,' the adjutant replied. 'The old tubs berth up near Scrabster, then get towed out to the firing zone, nor'-nor'west of here. Gives the birds something to lay their eggs on.'

'Can I ask what's on test at present?'

'Ah,' the adjutant beamed. 'We've got some real beauties at this very moment. Somehow the Yanks down at Dornoch got hold of some AS–Xs. Know 'em? Well, they're one of the latest Soviet hobgoblins. Improved AS–X–10s with either inertial or command mid-course guidance and semi-active laser homing over the last 40 kilometres. They launch 'em off Sokhoi Su–22s, so we're popping a few off the old F.6 Lightnings, adapted with modified packs.'

Harding tried to see if his hands would thrust any deeper into his greatcoat pockets and found they wouldn't. 'Sounds fun,' he muttered, trying to convince himself as much as anybody.

Eventually they made their way back to the mess and dried off over coffee before Harding was due to see the CO. The interview passed off smoothly and the young lieutenant was assigned to the computer flight and target simulation detail, a sort of computer game which used information gathered during actual missile tests to assess potential and performance capabilities in different circum-stances. He quickly learned that the FTS detail was one of the most coveted on the base, for at least two reasons. One, being in the computer area it was at least air-conditioned, for the sake of the hardware rather than the hardware jockeys. Two, the idea of playing computer games had a greater appeal for those who didn't do it than for those who did it all day every day.

Around mid-September, as the evenings were noticeably shor-tening again, the weather held fine long enough for the mess barbecue, on the cards since mid-July, to actually take place. By now Harding had settled in and was one of the lads.

For some reason even the most tasteless sausages blossom into

Egon Ronay delights when cooked over charcoal, and stringy chicken tenders up remarkably well. The beans were still beans and the beer got better the more you drank. Along with the beans were some fried mushrooms, which Harding was assured were both fresh and 'bloody good eatin''. His one reservation was the faint greenish tinge that remained in their flesh, even after cooking.

'They're not field mushrooms, are they, Carter?' he asked the non-com serving him.

'No, Mr Hardin', they ain't,' Carter answered. 'Tell the truth I ain't got the foggiest what they is, but the locals eat 'em an they ain't died yet, 'cept of old age an' the occasional accident.'

Like Francis Bacon with his first potato, Harding tasted the mushrooms very carefully. Their flavour was more delicate and harder to define than field mushrooms, though very similar, and he suffered no ill-effects from them whatsoever.

Not right then, anyway.

# THURSDAY 27 AUGUST LAST YEAR

## Late evening

The B9123 isn't the easiest of roads to drive, even in the best of circumstances. It winds out of Banff, almost following the line of the North Sea cliffs, and is cut by even smaller side-roads which lead down to the tiny fishing villages perched precariously between land and water. Just before it reaches Fortstown it passes over the head of Braw Valley, an ancient cleft in the rocky landscape sweeping down to the shingle shore, clad with grass and heather and scrub and decorated with the ruins of the ancient church of St John. The head of the valley is twisty, forcing the road into a series of potentially lethal bends, very few of which are adequately marked or even fenced off. It's the sort of road you have to know and make allowances for, the sort of road which reduces even Ferraris to tangled junk and their drivers to shattered flesh. No-one races along the B9123 over the head of Braw Valley. Not even drunks or idiots.

Alan Bannock knew the road better than most. He'd driven its length to and from his home near New Aberdour for six days a week, getting on for nine years. In his early fifties, most of his hair gone and what remained, parted low and combed-over, greying into white, he was a distinguished-looking professional man in sober office suit and Aberdonian Club tie. His wife's daily kept his shirts crisp and white. His earnings as a senior partner in a Banff legal practice kept his circumstances comfortable and his two boys at Gordonstoun.

He frequently cursed the road. All it took was a heavy truck on its narrow carriageway to reduce his BMW to stalling speed, his frustration rising in proportion because of the impossibility of even contemplating overtaking. But it was the only reasonable route from home to office, several miles shorter than cutting south onto the A98 at Woodhead and following it out of his way through New Pitsligo and Longmanhill, so Alan continued to use it.

The evening, so far, was inconclusive. He'd spent it entertaining an Aberdeen-based oil executive who'd hinted that company business might be put Alan's way. Personally he'd rather have taken his wife and the boys, who were due back at school in a few days, to the opening night of the Circuz Ferencz, which was in Banff for a week. Instead, it had been shop-talk, hopefully of the more impressive kind, over Parma ham, veal and olives, white Chianti, port, coffee and brandy in Gaspacci's.

Maybe I shouldn't be driving, Alan reasoned with himself, but the food will have soaked up a lot of the booze. And anyway, I know the road.

The circus traffic had dispersed, clearing the roads, some time before he'd escorted the oilman back to his hotel and started the drive home from Banff. Some heavy machinery had obviously been operating somewhere, possibly offshore, as there had been a heavy pounding in the air as he had walked to the car park. Anyway, whatever it was, it had stopped.

He drove out through Macduff and began his meandering route home, handling the BMW with the caution of a man who was aware that he'd had a few. As he reached the first of the bends above Braw Valley he saw the broken-down removals van in the lay-by, its cab tilted forward to expose the engine underneath. On the look-out for the driver or his mate, he passed it slowly, rounding the bend and getting his first view of the valley. As he did so he felt, rather than heard, an involuntary whistle pass his lips, and his right foot moved to the brake pedal.

Braw Valley was ablaze.

Well, not all of it, Alan reasoned. Most of the flame-bright destruction seemed to be centred on the ruined church. The fragmented remains of its walls stuck up like broken, blackened teeth as the wreckage of . . . two vehicles? . . . blazed inside them. In the light of the flames he saw figures in the valley, small dark ants of people down near the shore. Wondering briefly if they were survivors or witnesses, he decided that they had to be the latter. Obviously two vehicles had met head-on on the narrow road and plunged down into Braw Valley after the collision. Nobody got out of that sort of crash alive, he thought.

My god. It could have been me!

Without realizing it he had brought the BMW to a halt. He was sitting there, staring down at the fire, with the handbrake off and the car out of gear. All it would take for him to join the scene below was someone to come round the corner and nudge his back bumper. In many ways that might have been the kindest thing that could have happened to Alan Bannock that evening.

He never really understood where she came from. The first he realized of her presence was when her hand, the carefully-manicured nails now split and much of the varnish chipped away, opened the passenger door. She didn't bother to lean in and inquire. She simply slid into the passenger seat and fastened her seat-belt as if he'd known her all his life and stopped expressly to offer her a lift.

Alan felt his mouth hang open. She turned her head to smile at him. 'It was kind of you to stop,' she said.

Her clothes were obviously good, he noticed, despite the tears and grass-stains which had ruined them for ever. Probably a London fashion-house. She had money, and, from her behaviour, a remarkable degree of self-assurance.

He stared at her, his puzzled mind endeavouring to take in and retain details which might mean something later. Her hair, still clinging to the remains of its coiffure, was a gleaming Titian red. Her eyes were brown, bright in the interior light as she opened the door and still bright in the darkness now that the door was closed again. Yet there was a sadness about them, a sadness which had nothing to do with the smeared make-up which, on its own, could never have marred her beauty. Her bone-structure, Alan concluded, was amazing. Despite the grime, despite the graze across her forehead, she was one of the loveliest women he had ever seen, and he prided himself that in his fifty-two years he'd seen a lot of good-looking women.

'I . . . take it you want a lift?' he ventured hesitantly.

What a stupid thing to say, he chided himself. Christ, but I could make a real fool of myself with this lady!

'Turn inland at Dubford,' she instructed him. Then: 'It's so kind of you to take me to Aberdeen, Mr Bannock.'

He struggled to close his mouth. Her voice was gentle, despite its inherent strength, and something in her tone appeared almost hypnotic.

Alan Bannock began to function automatically. He slid the BMW into gear and drove on along the B9123 towards Dubford, as instructed. His mind struggled to understand what was happening, why he was obeying without question, and failed. As he drove, the best he could do was to attempt to engage his mysterious passenger in conversation.

'You know who I am? You have the advantage over me, I'm afraid. Have we met before?'

The lady smiled, more to herself than to him, he thought. 'Everyone knows Mr Bannock, the famous lawyer,' she replied.

They lapsed into silence. As they drove past the side-road which led down into Fortstown Alan noticed an unusual number of lights on in the little fishing village. He was about to remark on the fact when he inexplicably decided not to.

'Won't you tell me your name?' he asked, as they approached the Dubford turn. He took it without question, instead of continuing as usual towards New Aberdour and his home and family.

'You won't have heard of me,' she smiled, 'as I have heard of you. I'm not famous, Mr Bannock.'

'That doesn't matter. Tell me anyway.'

She shrugged. Good breasts he noticed, as the dark line of the seat-belt emphasized the movement. A truly beautiful woman.

And dangerous, a little voice whispered somewhere deep in his brain. Lovely and dangerous. She knows you. She's controlling you. But how? How is she doing it?

'Very well,' she answered. 'My name is Erzebet von Bamberg.' After a pause she added: 'You see? The name means nothing to you now. Nor will it ever.'

'And . . . where are you from?'

'My family home was at Eberheim in southern Germany.'

'Was?'

'It was destroyed some . . . years ago. Now I am the last of my family.'

'I see. I'm sorry.'

Erzebet shook her head. 'You don't see, Alan Bannock. Neither do I require your sympathy.' Her brown eyes burned into his. 'But you find me attractive, don't you?'

The question was unexpected, all the more so because the Banff lawyer knew that women as beautiful as this one know their beauty for themselves, without any need of the reassurance of others.

'I think you're quite lovely,' he told her.

'Yes, you do. Do you want to make love to me?'

'I . . .'

'The question is simple enough. Yes or no?'

'Yes.'

Who wouldn't? he asked himself. OK, so she's obviously been hurt, but she's the one who's asking.

'Then stop the car.'

Alan pulled to the side of the road and switched off the ignition. His mind, puzzled before, was in turmoil as she opened her door and walked around to his. She took his hand and led him deep into the moon-bright heather. As he stood, questioning, trying vainly to understand, she knelt in front of him and began to loosen his trousers, her fingers exploring the growing firmness through the cloth as she did so. Her mouth, her perfect, wonderful mouth, didn't look large enough for what it began to do. But it was.

He dug his fingers into her Titian hair and forced a closer union. As he felt himself reach the threshold of his climax she tore away and pulled him down beside her. With remarkable strength she straddled him, tearing her own clothing away with her broken fingernails. Before Alan could even think of resisting he was inside her, feeling the firmness of her thighs working about him. As he came she pumped on. As he came again her muscles held him all the more firmly. As his exhausted body responded a third time he felt her own delicious spasm. He looked up, his hands inside her blouse, cupping those fine breasts. Her eyes had glazed and her mouth was open, revealing fine, sharp white teeth. Her lips moved.

'Ptythonius,' she whispered to the night.

They didn't linger there. She stood him on his feet and dressed him, then led him back to the car. They drove through Dubford and continued south, picking up the A948 and the A92 in turn. A few miles north of Aberdeen Erzebet told him to stop again.

He watched her get out. He didn't know that the Circuz Ferencz had been in Aberdeen the week before. And there was no way he would even have expected that Erzebet von Bamberg, under an alias, had established credit for herself at one of the Granite City's leading banks. From here she was safe. From here someone else could pick her up and take her to her destination. And with funds behind her once more she could vanish as certainly as if she were already dead, as many believed she was.

Alan Bannock watched her go. Seconds later a freight wagon stopped and she climbed into the cab. It was over.

He turned the BMW around and began to drive home. Erzebet

von Bamberg, the lady in the night, had altered Alan's life for ever. Taking a right turn just past Cloverhill the lawyer found himself on a road leading down to the beach. There didn't seem to be any point in wanting to go home any more.

She had taken the darkness from him. She had taken the darkness and turned it into light. She was life, and living, and hope. She was the future. She was everything.

Erzebet.

He was still whispering her name to himself, still reliving those precious moments in the heather, still worshipping at the shrine of her body after his separated, futile fashion, as he drove the BMW into the sea.

# FRIDAY 28 AUGUST LAST YEAR

## Nearly midnight

'So, what's it all about, Johannes? Just what *did* go on back there?'

Ferrow eyed his new companion with the same cautious reserve that he'd shown throughout the journey south. After the nine-hour drive, broken only for coffee and a burger at a Little Chef near Nottingham, he'd left the car at the kerb, as close to his flat as possible, instead of in the parking bay across the street. Now he was slumped in an armchair, his cases abandoned in the middle of the floor, working his way through the bottle of Glendronach which Miles Fournessie had given him before he left the Fortstown Arms.

The single-malt was warming but hardly reassuring. Nor were the expressionless black eyes of the creature he'd named Johannes. He couldn't be sure just how it was related to that other *glebula*, the one called Gyorgy which the two dwarfs, Sodom and Gomorrah, had threatened him with in the ruined church in Braw Valley. Nor was he entirely certain what he was going to do with the creature, sitting beside his cases and staring ambiguously up at its new master.

Despite the darkness of its eyes they retained a certain luminosity in the dim light of the standard lamp which was the only light Ferrow had bothered to turn on. The *glebula* was nearly the size of a full-grown sheep, covered in a mottled fur which ranged from reddish-brown to the grim grey of the Carpathian wolf. Its proportions seemed to have something in common with both wolf and sheep, though it was obviously neither. Nor, with those tufted ears projecting horizontally from the flattish head and its complete lack of a tail, was it a dog, though Ferrow had decided that he'd have to pass it off as one to anyone who saw it.

He grinned sourly to himself as he imagined the conversations to come.

'Funny-looking dog you've got there, Bob.'

'Yeah. Friend gave it to me before he went abroad.'

'I've never seen one like that before. What is it?'

'Oh, it's a Glebhound. Very unusual. This is probably the only one in the country. They come from somewhere up north.'

Like Thule?

Johannes snuffled. It was a strange, almost pig-like sound that Ferrow would probably never learn to interpret. The short, pointed muzzle, so like a cute little Koala, seemed to lengthen to wicked proportions as the *glebula* yawned, displaying a set of teeth that wouldn't have looked out of place on a Bengal tiger.

He set down his scotch and stood up, walking around his new pet towards the kitchen. Better feed the brute, he thought. I'd rather it gorged on my food than on me. It's behaved itself so far, OK. You never know, though. Not with something artificially created as an obedient killing machine . . .

The canned food showed nothing his nasty carnivore was likely to be interested in. Neither did the packets. He opened the refrigerator and found it still as cleaned-out as it had been before he'd left with June for their holiday in Fortstown. Then he checked the freezer compartment on top. The two fillet steaks he'd been saving for a special dinner with June sometime were sitting there, grinning at him. He took them out and set them in the microwave to defrost. Then he went back to his scotch, still giving Johannes a wide berth.

He looked up. 'I must be out of my fucking head,' he informed the ceiling.

And that's putting it mildly.

His body was beginning to ache from the cramped conditions of the long drive, and the whisky was starting to spin the room uncomfortably. Ferrow half-rose, fighting the sensation, then sat back and tried to review the events of the past few days. Despite what had happened at Fortstown, he decided, all that really mattered was to try and sort out the ending. Whether or not the Keeper, that strange old man who had been Ptythonius Meeres during the Wegrimham affair and Johannes Faustus at Fortstown, was alive or dead seemed neither here nor there. He'd seen Meeres killed. He'd seen a fantastic wooden engine explode in a ruined church about Faustus. Yet moments before that explosion the Keeper had called out to him.

'Believe me when I say *I shall be back*.'

They hadn't found his body afterwards, that body which he may or may not have borrowed from a missing youth named Paul Cull. Nor had they found any trace of Erzebet von Bamberg, although both Ferrow and Sergeant Harris had seen her Mercedes plunge down into the fire-spattered ruins.

Oh, the machine had been destroyed, sure enough. It could never be used to summon that terrible Thulean entity called Pudendagora again. It was banished as surely as the Destroying Angel had been banished at Wegrimham. But that wasn't enough, Ferrow told himself as the pinger on the microwave struggled through his thoughts.

No, it wasn't enough. Not with the Keeper and Erzebet alive. And they were. He knew they were. He could *feel* it.

'You feel it too, Johannes, don't you?' he asked the *gleluba* as he struggled out of the chair and headed for the kitchen rather unsteadily.

The *glebula* grinned. Saliva flecked from its fangs as it appeared to nod. Ferrow was too busy unceremoniously hacking fillet steak into raw strips to notice. He dropped the meat onto an old soupplate and brought it into the lounge.

Johannes showed none of the predictable canine enthusiasm for the plate, once it was set in front of him. Instead he maintained his half-crouch, half-sit and kept his rodent-like eyes, as expressionless as death itself, firmly on his new master until Ferrow sat down again. For some moments man and creature eyed each other.

'If we're going to pretend you're a dog you'll have to do better than that,' Ferrow remarked. 'For Christ's sake try to look interested. I'd hate to think I'd wasted two good steaks for nothing.'

Johannes snuffled at the steak. He stood up and padded around the plate, keeping his nose to it. Then he resumed his former position and began to pant. A moment later he uttered a short, excited, unmistakable bark.

The short hairs on the back of Ferrow's neck began to prickle. Jesus God! he thought, I told it to act like a dog . . .

He drained his glass and leaned forward in the chair. 'So . . . why don't you eat it?' he asked, puzzled. The answer flashed into his mind almost at once.

I need your permission, Magister.

His right hand flew to his mouth in a gesture which ordinarily would have reminded him of a startled virgin. A cold sweat broke out through the scotch fumes.

'OK . . . eat it,' he said in a small voice he'd never have recognized as his own, his eyes riveted to those of the *glebula*.

They had been there in Braw Valley, serving Erzebet. A dozen good coppers had died with the help of the *glebulae*. When the trailer taking them away had crashed into Erzebet's Mercedes, plunging both vehicles down into the blazing ruins, the door had sprung and Johannes, as Ferrow had named him, was the only one able to leap clear. As Ferrow had been driving home the next morning he'd found Johannes sitting by the roadside. Just why he'd opened the door and let the creature into his car he didn't know.

But now . . .

Within thirty seconds the plate was empty. Johannes made a token show of licking it clean and pushing it about with his nose, then loped across and nuzzled his head against Ferrow's leg. Still not understanding why, the policeman reached down with his left hand and scuffled his fingers under the increasingly dog-like chin.

I said I wanted you more like a dog . . .

. . . And now I'm more like a dog, Magister.

With a howl, eyes wide, mouth slackly open, Ferrow rapidly withdrew his hand and leaped up, folding his legs beneath him, clear of the floor and those potentially-deadly teeth and claws. As he huddled back as far as possible into the armchair, wondering if his terror-tightened nerves had finally snapped, he managed to mumble: 'You . . . can talk . . .'

Not strictly true, Magister, came the unspoken reply. I believe the Landgravine Erzebet once created speaking *glebulae*, but she rejected the strain as unrealistic. In view of the work we are most often called upon to perform, this kind of mental communication is far superior. You, in turn, do not have to speak to me. Just think to me and I will hear and understand you. Thus you may order and I may acknowledge in total silence.

'You mean . . . I can talk to you without actually having to say anything?'

Precisely, Magister.

Ferrow felt his coiled limbs begin to relax a fraction, though his mind was still struggling to throw off the effect of the scotch and come to terms with this frightening new phenomenon.

'Then . . . how . . .' was the food? he ventured.

Most acceptable, though low-grade cuts of meat will be equally so in the future, and less extravagant on your pocket. At a stretch, ordinary dog-food will serve on occasions. I would ask, though, that you permit me some live food now and again.

'Live food?' . . . I mean . . . live food?

Johannes offered his disturbing parody of a smile again. The black eyes showed no expression as he responded: Nothing human, Magister, unless with your permission. The odd cat or rabbit will serve just as well. All you need do is let me out at night. My activities will not be obtrusive. No plague of slaughtered moggies littering the neighbourhood. I understand your position within human society and will do nothing to compromise it. That would violate the *glebula* code of total obedience.

Ferrow shrugged. Sounds OK. Do you need something to drink?

Plain water will be excellent, Magister. As you will appreciate, my diet is high-protein and requires an intake of liquid in order to be properly digested.

Clever little bastard, aren't you? Ferrow caught himself thinking.

I hope I've not offended, Magister, Johannes replied.

For the first time that evening Robert Ferrow felt himself smile, albeit rather sheepishly. 'No, you've not offended, Johannes,' he said, 'and I hope I didn't, either.'

That is not possible, Magister. Might I ask why you are speaking to me now?

'Simple enough. People don't go round thinking to their dogs. They say things like "Here, boy", and "Heel", and "Good dog", and shit like that. Your life here with me will be a lot more open than it was with the Circuz Ferencz, so we'll both have to put on a show for the rest of the world. OK?'

As you require.

'You were hurt when I picked you up. There's a veterinary nurse I know. Do you want me to have her check you over?'

I heal quickly, Magister. There's no need unless you wish it. But you could phone her anyway and see if you still have a fiancée.

'And what the hell do you know about that?'

You forget how easily I pick up your thoughts. I was doing so as we drove down from Fortstown today. Thus I know of your concern for Miss Lowe. You see, having selected you for my Magister

I need to know as much as I can about you in order to ensure my own obedience.

'Yeah,' Ferrow said heavily, attempting to weigh the implications of Johannes' last response. He relaxed in the chair and his legs slid out from their cramped position beneath him. The *glebula* sprang heavily into his lap and began to lick his face.

'OK, OK. You don't have to be a dog unless there's people watching,' Ferrow scowled. Then: 'Say, can you read other people's thoughts as well?'

Johannes shook his head in a remarkably human gesture. The process is two-way, he began. If I could read, as you put it, their thoughts, then they could also read mine. Or, at least, they would be aware of an intrusive intelligence. But I have a thorough understanding of human body-language, and that is often just as good.

'What sort of distance can you do it over?'

Normal voice-range, Magister.

'Speaking voice?'

Certainly, though we both know how to shout our thoughts when we have to, simply by concentrating. And *in extremis* we may whisper the same way. Why don't you ring Miss Lowe?

'You know, I'm glad you're so formal in your obedience, Johannes,' Ferrow grinned. 'Sometimes your formality will be the only thing which can help me tell your thoughts from my own.'

Christ, this is weird, he thought to himself. Then he wished he hadn't.

For me it is quite normal, Magister, Johannes responded. Yet I accept it has a certain frightening novelty for you. Even so, the bond between Magister and *glebula* is a strong one, and quickly becomes a comfortable one also.

'So who was your Magister before me?'

A man called Gregor. He was a Czech who looked after us at the circus. Not very bright, but he had a gentle mind.

'Had?' Ferrow queried.

Sadly, yes. By virtue of his compact with the Landgravine Erzebet he was completely powerless when ordered to release us to the two dwarfs, Sodom and Gomorrah. We obeyed those two because he ordered that we should. We didn't want to, you know. They'd taken Gyorgy out that afternoon and returned without him.

'I know, Johannes. I saw him shot.'

Might I ask who killed him, Magister?

'Have you heard of the Keeper, whoever *he* is?'

Ah. I met the Keeper, for the first time, last night in Braw Valley. So it was he who killed Gyorgy?

'He did.'

Then there was at least some reason behind his death. I regret the work we all did in Braw Valley. Now you know a little more of the nature of the *glebulae*, Magister, you will understand that we had no choice . . .

Johannes paused and looked up at his straw-haired master. Ferrow did understand. He himself knew what it was like to have no choice in the matter. After all, he'd bumbled his way through the Wegrimham and Fortstown affairs and somehow managed to come out physically in one piece. And that, he believed, in view of all that he'd been through, was enough to constitute a major triumph.

'Go on, Johannes.'

When we were recalled to the trailer we already had our instructions from the Keeper. Sodom and Gomorrah had to die. We relayed these orders to our Magister. We felt the grimness in his mind as that gentle man confirmed them to us.

We killed, Magister. It was more than simply wanting to obey. We wanted to show our displeasure to those evil, soulless little creatures. We tore them apart. Slowly. And then we read Gregor's mind and knew that he intended to ram the Landgravine's car. We felt the impact through his visual impressions as much as the physical shock of the trailer and the Mercedes colliding. We heard his last command to us. 'Save yourselves, if you can, my creatures,' he told us.

You know the rest, Magister. I alone survived. I lay in the heather, resting and tending my injuries as best I could. The next morning I saw your car approaching, and I knew that you were destined to become my future master.

Ferrow set his head to one side and looked down at the somehow less fearsome muzzle of his companion. 'How did you know, Johannes?' he asked the *glebula*.

Because the Keeper had told me of you. He regards you highly, Magister. And I had no choice but to obey him. When we had done with killing, as we were about to be recalled, I felt him speak to me. 'Go with my friend Robert,' he told me. 'You will survive, as I will also survive. Go with Robert. He will give you one of my names. Serve him and you serve me, little friend.'

Robert Ferrow sat back and shut his eyes tightly, vainly trying to force away the tears which had started into them. 'Oh, hell,' he whispered. 'Is there nothing that old bugger doesn't know? Why me? For fuck's sake, Johannes, why me?'

Because there's no-one else, Magister, came the reply.

'He planned it all. He worked it all. He *knew* it all. He even knew I'd call you after him. But what am I supposed to do? Can you tell me that?'

Not yet. Perhaps, I regret, never, Magister.

Ferrow sighed and fondled one of the creature's tufted ears. 'So tell me about the Keeper,' he instructed.

What can I say, Magister? He is the one who keeps the equilibrium between the two Thules. He keeps good from triumphing over evil, and evil from triumphing over good.

'You mean . . . good doesn't win?'

If good wins, evil must reassert itself as the other end of good. It becomes less than it was, perhaps, but it still exists. Neither good nor evil can ever be completely eradicated, Magister.

'So there're only shades of grey? We're going through all this for shades of grey? Is that what you're telling me?'

Grey is only a mixture of black and white. Don't think in terms of shades of grey, Magister. Think in terms of shades of black and white. Think of a perfect balance between the two, a world that is neither wholly good nor wholly evil. That is what the Keeper maintains.

Now, why don't you turn your mind to yourself for a change? If you were to offer me a bowl of water I'd be more comfortable than I am, but it is for you to direct as you see fit. I shall endure. It is the lot of the *glebulae* only to obey. It's nice to be comfortable as well as obedient, though.

Ferrow smiled and finished scratching at Johannes' ear. He stood up and walked to the kitchen, returning with a basin of water which he set before the *glebula*. Then he crossed to the telephone and began to dial June Lowe's number as Johannes lapped his drink, dog-fashion.

He heard the number ring at the other end. Just as he was about to give up and replace the receiver he heard a voice say: 'There's only one bastard who'd ring me at this time of night. Hello, Bob.'

They'd been through a great deal together. June had been with him since those harrowing days at Wegrimham. She hadn't seen those nasty little *familiares*, those tiny creatures, part-rat, part-cat, part-man, who had killed the man she worked for, and several others. She hadn't seen the horror of the Destroying Angel in the crypt beneath Wegrimham Grange. But she'd seen the blue fire in the sky, the fire which left even Robert Ferrow no choice but to obey its dictates, and even she had been afraid of that.

And then in Fortstown she'd heard the beating of the machine which was to summon Pudendagora. She'd stumbled over the body of one of Erzebet's victims, his throat cut by one of the Landgravine's dwarfish servants. And that had been enough. She'd left him there to answer the questions as best he could, to muddle through, ever the Keeper's creature, without her support.

'Hullo, June,' Ferrow began. 'How was your journey back?'

'Look, Bob,' she told him. 'I'm tired. I'm tired and I've been scared stiff. I need time. I need time to think, and time to sleep, and time to forget. Call me in a week or so. Until then, sod off!'

He heard her slam the phone down and turned to look at Johannes. The *glebula* was staring intently into one of the darkened corners of the room.

Ferrow turned his head and strained to follow Johannes' gaze. Eventually he gave up. Noticing that he was still holding the purring telephone receiver in his hand, he set it down on the rest and returned to his chair.

Johannes continued to stare into the shadows, looking at something Ferrow couldn't see.

'Now that's what I call really dog-like,' the policeman quipped.

I'm delighted it amuses you, Magister, came the reply. I think you ought to know, though, that there is a *familiaris* in that corner who has been watching us for quite some time.

Ferrow's smile subsided. Oh, shit, he thought. It's too soon. Surely I've earned a rest? I know it's going to start again sometime soon, and I know that I'll do what I'm supposed to when it does.

But does it have to be now? Sweet Jesus, does it have to be right now?

# WEDNESDAY 9 FEBRUARY
# THIS YEAR

## Mid-afternoon

'And what can I do for MI6?' Rosenblum asked, extending his hand.

Commander Faber took it before he sat down. As Rosenblum positioned himself behind the cluttered desk the intelligence officer asked: 'You have a patient here called Noel Jorisund?'

The psychiatrist nodded. 'Yes, we do. He's been here the better part of a year, now.'

'And what sort of progress is he making, Doctor Rosenblum?'

'Before I answer that, Commander Faber,' came the guarded reply, 'I would need to know the reason for your interest in Mr Jorisund.'

'*Need to know* is exactly the expression, Doctor. My credentials are sufficient, as I'm sure you're aware.'

Faber's cold, rat-like brown eyes stared dispassionately but authoritatively into Rosenblum's blue ones. They defied him to make an issue of the question. As the psychiatrist stared back he realized that he was into one of the few losing battles of his life. He capitulated.

'Very well,' he sighed, both baffled by and resenting an authority that he didn't understand. 'What do you want me to tell you?'

Faber grinned, showing fine white teeth, despite the small cigars he habitually smoked. 'Jorisund came here late March last year,' he began. 'He'd suffered some kind of mental breakdown and needed putting back together. Am I right so far?'

Rosenblum nodded. He wasn't going to bother with the technical terms. Faber would need them explaining anyway, and that would slow down both the interview and the spook's departure. 'As you say,' he confirmed. 'Noel had been subjected to a mental breakdown. I have to add, though, that he also appeared to have ingested a hallucinogen prepared from the toadstool *amanita virosa*, the so-called destroying angel. In my opinion, that was itself responsible for many of his problems. It's unusual to find a man of his age and background playing around with drugs of that nature. And despite a number of examinations and interviews I've been unable to elicit any comprehensible responses regarding his motives. It's almost as if he has deliberately chosen the course of secreting them in some sub-stratum of his mind which is inaccessible to psychoanalysis.'

'And how does that leave his mental health?'

'In lay terms, not awfully good. He responds to any kind of pressure very badly, preferring to retreat inside himself rather than face the outside world. His fantasies seem to have taken on a reality of their own which causes him to escape by going inwards. Thus his mind has become both the source of his torment and his sanctuary from it.'

'Which is to say he's psychologically unstable?'

'Not necessarily. He responds to given stimuli in predictable ways. His responses, though, are not always sufficient in relation to others and his surroundings. Unstable, not really. But he is still a sick man.'

'So when do you think you will be able to let him out of here?'

Rosenblum shrugged. 'We may never be able to. Oh, he's responded to drug therapy to a certain extent. His medication regimen has created an artificial improvement . . .'

'But you'd not be willing to discharge him?'

'No. I wouldn't like to, anyway. Not because he's a danger to others. There's no psychosis of that kind. He's simply not well and not, despite our efforts over the past twelve months, making any genuine effort to recover.'

Faber nodded. 'I think I know what you mean. We've had our experts study his records and their own prognoses seem to agree with your own.'

Rosenblum sat up behind the desk. 'Your people have seen *our* records?' he demanded. 'That's not possible.'

'On the contrary,' Commander Faber smiled, 'your base data is kept on an AF35A4 Honeywell computer, as is most medical data in this country. Our communications and DP boys have entry codes for all such machines currently in use. It's easy enough to scan patient records when we want to.'

The psychiatrist was about to explode with outrage at the revelation when his visitor continued: 'Calm down, Doctor. We don't abuse our privileges unless we have to. And in Jorisund's case we've had to. Now, I have here an order for his release into my custody ...' he continued, opening the briefcase which was standing on the floor beside him and withdrawing a typed form signed with a heavy black pen.

Rosenblum took the form and studied it carefully. Laying it on the desk in front of him he said: 'It ... appears to be valid, Commander Faber.'

'Of course it's valid. We want Noel Jorisund. I come here with the right paperwork. You give him to us. Simple, isn't it?'

'But I don't understand. Noel's a sick man. What use can he be to you?'

Faber sighed. He wagged a finger at Rosenblum. '*Need to know* again,' he grinned reprovingly.

'Even so, he's my patient.'

'Uh oh, Doctor. *Was* your patient. Once that paper changed hands he became my responsibility. Now, have your staff get him ready to travel.'

The psychiatrist glared at Faber. 'Only if he's fit to travel,' he snapped, standing up.

The spook rose in turn. His finger jabbed down at the paper on the desk. 'My responsibility,' he snarled. 'Mine, Rosenblum. It says so, right there. You want to obstruct my authority? You want to lose all this?'

He raised a hand, gesturing towards the ornate plaster ceiling of the high-walled office in the Georgian mansion which constituted the psychiatrist's clinic and sanitorium.

'You wouldn't ...'

'You know I both could and would. Now, do you see to Jorisund or do I have my own people come in and do it? I'm not going to be fucked about any longer.'

He sat down again, the smile returning to his rat-like features. For a few moments the psychiatrist stared down at him, mentally assessing the situation. Then, with a sigh, he resumed his own seat and pressed a buzzer on his intercom.

'Yes, Doctor?' a voice crackled.

'Ask Sefton to prepare Noel Jorisund for discharge,' Rosenblum instructed.

'Now, Dr Rosenblum?'

'Yes. Right now. Just get it done and report back to me.'

Faber's smile persisted. 'It's kind of you to cooperate in this matter,' he smirked.

'You mean I had a choice?' Rosenblum glared.

'Not at all. But choice is so subjective, Doctor Rosenblum. You might have mistakenly thought that you did.'

The psychiatrist offered no reply, so their conversation lapsed into uneasy silence. Some minutes later the intercom crackled again.

'Mr Jorisund is ready and in reception, Doctor,' said the voice.

'Thank you,' he replied. 'We'll be out directly.' Then he looked across at Faber. 'I take it you heard that?' he demanded.

Faber's grin gave Rosenblum his reply. 'Let's have a look at him, then,' the agent said bluntly, closing his briefcase and rising to his feet.

'He's not a dissecting-room specimen, you know, Commander Faber. He's a patient. A human being.'

'Yes, yes.' Faber was already at the door, obviously impatient to be gone. The psychiatrist followed him out into the corridor and down to the reception area. Sitting on one of the padded leather seats, a male orderly standing beside and slightly over him, was a man of fifty-one, his eyes hidden behind tinted glasses, clean shaven and with a shock of slightly unruly white hair. Noel Jorisund had a spare frame, with hardly an inch of surplus flesh anywhere. His mouth, neither too fleshy nor too slit-like, wore an expression of faint, almost disinterested bemusement. He wore a navy blazer of unfashionable cut over a white shirt and paisley cravat, grey flannel slacks and, incongruously, brown Oxfords.

Faber approached his new charge. Behind him Rosenblum motioned for the orderly to move away. 'Mr Jorisund?' Faber inquired, his voice unexpectedly gentle after his tone and attitude previously.

Noel looked up. 'I believe I am,' he replied, leaning on a Malacca cane as he rose. 'Have we met before?'

'Not to my knowledge, sir, though I've read several of your books. I especially enjoyed the *Speculations upon the Alternative Origins of the Gothic Alphabet*.' He extended his hand. 'My name is Faber.'

Noel shook the hand rather limply. 'You know,' he began, 'they won't let me finish my speculative biography of Roger de Sancrox. I so want to go back to Wegrimham and complete it. I've had an offer from Century Hutchinson, you know.'

'I'm sure you have. Now, will you come with me, Mr Jorisund?'

'Are we going somewhere?'

'Not terribly far. I have a car waiting.' Faber gestured through the glass entrance doors to where a black Bentley, a military pennant stiff on the offside wing, glimmered starkly against the frosted ground.

'A ride? How charming. Are the trees still frosted? The world looks so pretty and fragile when the trees are frosted, you know.'

'I know. Yes.'

Faber cast a backward glance over his shoulder towards the watching Rosenblum as he escorted Noel through the doors and down the short flight of broad stone steps. The driver opened the door to the passenger compartment and Faber waited patiently as his charge climbed inside. Then he got in himself.

Only as the vehicle was driving away did Rosenblum notice that there was another person inside it, though the shape through the rear window was too indistinct for him to make out any details. Just for a moment though, close against the glass, firmly held and angled as if for insertion, the psychiatrist believed he caught a glimpse of a hypodermic needle.

SECURITY MEMORANDUM 256/2/11–Q  Date: 27.4.88

From: Chief Artificer, Royal Naval Dockyard, Chatham
To: Department 7, MI6, Century House. Attn. J G Faber

Ref: Received Request A3A5 dated 17.9.87

In accordance with your R R noted above I am to advise you that
on MOD Directive 256/11–Q, subsequent to the confirmation
issued in SM 256/1/11–Q, the following vessel has been decommissioned and refitted in accordance with the aforementioned
Directive:

| Pennant No.: | Class: | Year orig. comm.: |
|---|---|---|
| P298 | Tenacity | 1974 |

As specified in the Appendix to the Directive the following refit
has now been completed: Crew quarters enlarged reducing berths
from 28 to 6. Relieved space (equivalent 10 berths) refitted as
marine laboratory. Armaments (twin 35mm Oerlikon gun forward
and Contraves Sea-Killer missile capability aft) removed. Ice-
breaker forward keel and aft ballast fitted, retaining standard 165
tons displacement. Extra fuel storage fitted, adequate to increase
range to 3000 miles at 20 knots. Heavy duty antenna support fitted
above superstructure.

I confirm, as per the Directive and your R R, that storage here will
be undertaken until such time as a designated berthing order is
received under codename RETURN TICKET.

# PART TWO

## A Long Way
## Back to Thule

They pulsed in front of him, their reflections glittering coldly back from the mirror-like walls of the ice cavern. At present they were small, little more than golf-balls of shimmering blueness, but he knew the power that they could exercise in their own right was truly awesome.

He sat back in the plain, serviceable chair which had been made for the Keeper before him, sometime during the fifteenth century. The hot spring bubbling up from the centre of the cavern kept his surroundings relatively warm, but the heavy woollen robes and cloak of polar-bear skin were still a comfort he was unwilling to dispense with. Especially at moments like this.

At first they had been rare, passing almost unnoticed in their slightness. Now, though, they had become more frequent, more noticeable, bringing a chill to the Keeper that all the hot springs and furs in the world would never alleviate. The chill had nothing to do with the temperature of his surroundings, nor with the consistency of the thinning blood which flowed through his centuried body. It was a coldness of the soul, an icy grasping at the very purpose of his being, and all the more terrible because it emanated from the most ancient and trusted of all his servitors.

The light awaited its answer, hovering with its fellows before the gaunt-faced figure, watching the reactions to its question with whatever means of sight it possessed. He knew that the lights could see, in the same way that he knew they could also hear and speak, by the evidence of his own senses. Yet he had never come to understand how, and there was nothing in the records to show that any Keeper before him had learned the secrets of their existence. They simply were, and did. That was all.

Not quite all.

They also thought for themselves, as this one had done.

He knew that there were seven of them. There had always been seven of them.

*

It had been one of Anhuk's greatest surprises, once his fear of the unknown had begun to dissipate into acceptance and understanding, that there hadn't been a blue-sun-bright-falling for every tribe upon the earth, that there were only seven for his service. Never changing. Never reproducing. Never developing an actual, individual identity.

'What is your name?' Anhuk had asked the one which translated him to the Kingdom of the Keeper.

SKYFIRE, it told him.

'And you?'

He asked a third. Then the rest. They all told him SKYFIRE.

It had puzzled him, as it periodically puzzled his successors. Still, there was a sort of logic to it. Seven lights, all the same, all with the same name. He looked at one in particular, as he had learned to do when he wished to address any single light. 'And where do you come from?'

THULE, it pulsed.

'You all come from Thule?'

WE DO.

His vocabulary, both actual and mental, had expanded remarkably quickly since he'd come to the ice cavern. He understood and accepted things which would have left the old Anhuk scratching his shaggy scalp with claw-like fingernails.

Anhuk tried the question again. The *old* question.

'If you come from Thule, then you must know where it is, Skyfire. Where is Thule?'

ASLEEP.

'That is *what* it is. I asked you *where* it is.'

THIS IS ALL THAT REMAINS OF IT IN THE PHYSICAL WORLD, KEEPER.

'If this is all that remains, then this must be what is asleep. Am I right?'

NO, KEEPER.

At this point Anhuk usually gave up. There were some concepts he had yet to master, and one of these was the omniversal nature of existence. That there were different forms of reality he had always suspected. Two of them, objective and subjective, were common to all people. It was subjective that broke down into different components the most easily, depending upon which of the fungi he had eaten. Objective broke down only from person to person, and Anhuk still had to learn to think beyond himself to appreciate this phenomenon. The lights had explained it, as they had explained so many things to him, but it still didn't make a great deal of sense to the first of the Keepers.

Because of this the lights hadn't progressed as far as the third major form of reality, *alterjective* reality, which explained the onion-layers of being in terms of multi-dimensional existence. They would eventually, but the first two forms had to be grasped and understood before that could happen. It would be difficult to demonstrate to modern man, let alone the first of many Keepers in the year 63,402 BC.

With the passing of time the skills and knowledge to be mastered became refined down into a series of teachings which were synthesized and stored in the records. Keepers came and went, each chosen by his predecessor. In all, between Anhuk and Ptythonius Ulrich, Graf von Meersburg, 127 Keepers learned and watched over the Thulean secrets held in trust by the skyfires. Yet they also went out into the world of men, studying the development of learning and the applications to which it was being put, seeking ever to live by the tenets of their position, to maintain the balance between the positive and negative principles which had plunged Thule into its semi-eternal sleep.

Anhuk and his successors learned more about that sleep, about how it had come about, as their faculties developed. The Keeper was much more than his title suggested, having in his nature both the scholar and the warrior. Ptythonius Meeres the Keeper had attempted to explain the basics of Thule's history to a Detective Sergeant called Robert Ferrow, not entirely without success. Perhaps Ferrow didn't truly believe in the ancient concept of warring parties struggling for possession of the planet he inhabited, parties that emerged from their sleeping to seek ways of return through the rites and processes of their human adherents, but he had at least witnessed manifestations of the power of two of the negative aspects of Thule, the beings known as Velaeda and Pudendagora. It was a source of some satisfaction to Ptythonius that Ferrow had survived these two encounters, with his help. And, at least in the case of Velaeda, with the help of the skyfire.

The same skyfire which had translated Anhuk? The same skyfire that had now asked him that question?

WHY DO WE SERVE YOU, KEEPER?

Not one of the intervening 127 had learned their origin. Not one of them had truly understood the nature of the seven blue lights that men called UFOs and flying saucers. They had always been there. They had always served. They were an accepted fact of the Keeper's bizarre life.

They accepted orders. They didn't ask questions. Not of the Keeper.

And especially not that question.

Ptythonius von Meersburg forced a smile and set a long, slender finger, the knuckles gnarled but somehow not arthritic, to the corner of his mouth to emphasize the expression. 'I don't know,' he answered. 'Why do you serve me?'

BECAUSE YOU ARE THE KEEPER OF THE BALANCE, they replied in unison, seven identical pulsing voices from seven identical lights.

'Then why bother to ask me the question, if you know the answer?'

THIS IS SEMANTICS, KEEPER, said the one which had asked the question in the first place. YOU ARE AWARE OF MY MEAN-ING. WHY CAN THE TWO THULES NOT UNITE?

'You mean, why do we need the Keeper at all?'

PRECISELY.

Ptythonius nodded slightly, weighing the implications of the question. The lights themselves had instituted the office of the Keeper many thousands of years before. From the researches in the records those lights were the last manifestations of the positive aspect of Thule, manifestations seeking the direction of one who could understand the need to prevent the re-emergence of the awesome negatives. And there were negatives, still, after all this time. There was even a negative for his own office, though the lack of restraint which characterized the ravening horrors she served prevented Erzebet von Bamberg from understanding her own position in the way that Ptythonius was able to understand his own. The skyfire understood this. The skyfire had always known that the unbalanced renaissance of Thule, even perhaps its balanced re-emergence, both positive and negative together, would be detrimental to the life which had developed and claimed the world as its own in the intervening millennia.

Man.

So, why the question?

The lights had never shown any leanings towards an extreme and misplaced nostalgia before. They knew that the return of the negatives would plunge both them and the unwitting, uncomprehending world into a species of war it had never, despite the development of nuclear weaponry, been able to even imagine. Yet without the Keeper, without the figurehead who was both their master and, in many ways, their servant, it would happen. Without the Keeper nothing could prevent one or other of the negatives from emerging. And once that happened the Sybaritic barbarity of the being's actions would free its fellows, demanding a hostile response from the lights. Dooming mankind, ultimately. Probably also dooming the balance which had been maintained for the better part of 70,000 years.

'For the reason that you gave the first Keeper,' Ptythonius replied, 'the balance has to be maintained. If fire and water meet the result can be cataclysmic, depending upon the scale of the meeting. That is why I try to work through humans as much as possible, to keep you away from the negatives. You are aware of this, Skyfire. That is why you instituted the Keeper in the first place. Are you saying that you now wish to promote the conflict we have striven for so long to prevent? Is that it?'

The light made no answer. Instead it behaved in the way it, or another, or possibly even all of them, had done when similar questions had been asked in the past. All seven began to vibrate violently, whilst maintaining their small size, then spun together into a blur and rearranged their positions in front of the Keeper, the identity of the querent effectively masked. And yet the other six had been slow, almost reluctant to move, as if they were weighing their loyalty to the Keeper against their loyalty to one another.

Ptythonius continued: 'I understand your question, Skyfire, and I take it the way I believe you meant it. We have maintained the *status quo* for a tremendous period of time. You are wondering, as I have often wondered, how it will end. All things have their appointed time for ending, including the two Thules. In recent months we have fought and overcome two of the most powerful negatives. Yet there are others just as powerful awaiting their opportunity. Something needs to be done to forestall their awakening, to remove the strain of waiting and watching for their manifestation. In human religious terms, it requires an *act of faith*. Well, I shall make such an act of faith. I believe I have discovered the way in which the two Thules may be brought together in a limited conflict to determine the final outcome. With your help I shall perform my act of faith.'

The nearest light wavered slightly. MAY WE KNOW WHAT YOU INTEND, KEEPER? it asked.

Ptythonius von Meersburg shook his head. 'Not yet,' he answered gently. 'But you shall, eventually.' He was silent for a moment, shielding his thoughts from exposure to his servitors. Then he continued: 'There is a problem, though. What I propose can only be performed with the aid of the third reality. The act I propose must take place on a multi-dimensional level in order to penetrate the fabric of reality sufficiently to be permanent. And it will mean the end of my term as Keeper.'

He watched the effect his words had upon the lights. All seven began to expand and contract erratically. It was not unusual for a Keeper to determine his own fate, for several had done so, including his immediate predecessor. Only the less effective ones chose to replace themselves on the grounds of tiredness or, unusually, boredom. The average duration of a Keeper was a little over 500 years. The former Graf von Meersburg had held the position since 1540 and was 56 years old when he assumed it.

And now, at last, he knew that his time had been well-spent. The plan formulating itself in his guarded thoughts was the logical result of his time as Keeper. It would not end the Keepership, but it would revolutionize its purpose. Even the skyfires would have a comparative end to their ceaseless vigil.

If it worked.

He had schemed and plotted before. He had sought out and, with the help of a skyfire and Robert Ferrow, destroyed the summoner of Velaeda. He had fought time itself in his successful attempt to sabotage the invocation of Pudendagora. Yet this idea, this act of faith, would take all his skill to accomplish. From the reports which the lights had given him he was aware that the servants of the negative Thule, including the negative Keeper, Erzebet von Bamberg, had already begun their next assault upon his kingdom.

He could defeat them, probably. He had always managed to before, somehow. Yet 'probably' had never quite been good enough for Ptythonius von Meersburg. He had always sought a means by which the conflict itself could be resolved. Whilst that might be beyond him, he continued to be aware that the negatives were manifesting, or attempting to manifest, at shorter and shorter intervals, requiring greater and more devious means to thwart them each time. If things continued as they were it was quite possible that he would fail in his task soon.

And so he came to the act of faith as his only solution, his final strategy for the future. Whilst it might have seemed to others that he had a choice, the Keeper knew that, in reality, even in the third reality, he had no choice at all.

It occurred to Ferrow that he'd spent quite a bit of time in hospitals, either on his own behalf or visiting, over the past year or so. Here I am again, he thought. Old man bedded down in a private room. Could be Meeres, but it isn't.

And thank Christ for that, he added inwardly.

No, this one wasn't Ptythonius Meeres. Robert Ferrow had seen quite enough of Meeres . . . Johannes Faust . . . whatever he called himself, for this lifetime. If he never saw Meeres again it would probably be too soon.

He was about to indulge himself in a groan to celebrate the thought when the man in the bed did it for him. The patient's age was given on his admission forms as 73, which explained the yellow-white hair and wrinkled visage. The nose was sharply hooked and the thin-lipped mouth open in sleep, but there was a fleshiness about the jowls which prevented the features from being the Keeper's. He was gaunt with the unnatural life he led. This one was better fleshed, more comfortable in his permanent surroundings, enjoying the pleasures which a well-pensioned retirement and a continuing strong heart could bring him.

There was always the unexpected, though, and Commander Charles Speed RN (retd) had just confronted the unexpected. That was why Ferrow was back inside a hospital again.

The inspector had looked the old man up in *Who's Who* before making his visit. The entry had been comparatively small, but at least it offered the background information that Speed had spent most of his service career with Naval Intelligence. A soggy spook, Ferrow decided with a grin. Not like that dry bastard Faber who'd been farting about after the Fortstown business. Still, Faber was MI6, and still in the service. At least Speed had the virtue of being out of things, to his credit.

Or was he out of it? The plaster across the stitched gash in his forehead, the bandages beneath the bedclothes covering and supporting his cracked ribs, and the swelling on the jaw-line indicated that someone hadn't thought so. And Ferrow himself was beginning to wonder.

He looked at his watch. The time was a little after 5 am. The pay might have increased since his promotion to inspector, but the hours didn't seem to get any shorter. The only thing that was half-way good about it was that there were fewer people of his own rank to rib him about that bloody funny-looking dog of his. He shrugged off the thought as hardly relevant to the present. His scowl transmitted into a wide-mouthed yawn. He must try to concentrate on the matter in hand.

He'd been just about to head home and see if Johannes needed feeding, or if the neighbourhood was short another moggie, when the call had come through to him as Duty Inspector. CID would have the matter in hand, but because of Speed's status the boys upstairs had wanted a medium-senior uniform on the job. So, into the car and off we go, Bobby-boy.

The address turned out to be an older property, set back behind a well-trimmed privet hedge and a wide lawn, on the Rockingham road. One of the better addresses around Corby, Ferrow decided. The house was easy to find from the flashing blue lights and the unmarked white Cosworth Sierra behind them, parked in the wide driveway. Those things could do getting on for 150 mph and usually got stuck with speed-trap back-up, so the guys inside were probably into unfamiliar territory with an aggravated burglary.

Speed was already on his way to the hospital when Ferrow arrived, minutes ahead of the forensic team. Jesus, he thought, they've really got cracking on this one. I'd hate to be the poor bastard who did it with big guns like these after me. I'd get blown to fucking buggery and back. And it'd bloody well serve me right.

He walked up the gravel drive from where he'd parked and through the well-lit open doorway of the eight-bedroomed house, two storeys and cellars, of late Victorian bayed and gabled extravagance. The wide hall was hung with hunting prints above the oak-panelled dado and the furnishings struck Ferrow as being curios of a vanished and now mythical British Empire. Three doors led off the hall, with an oak staircase, elaborately banistered, rising from the centre. One door began a corridor with other rooms off and a glimpse of a large kitchen at the further end. A second showed a comfortably-appointed lounge. Beyond the third, however, was the activity Ferrow had come to see. Four uniforms, and two of the dirty-mac brigade, were muttering amongst themselves. One of the uniforms was flashing away with an Olympus Trip at a broken pane in the French windows.

The room was obviously a study. Shelves and framed diagrams covered most of the walls, the books and papers revealing an interest in what Ferrow later decided was marine chronometery. On a two-pedestal desk near the centre of the room was a large sheet of paper, torn at one corner and spotted with fresh blood along the same side as the tear. A uniformed sergeant noticed his superior's arrival and broke off his conversation with a young constable to report. Ferrow listened, nodding in the right places, to a familiar tale of forced entry, probably a struggle and the intruder fleeing as Commander Speed's housekeeper raised the alarm.

'Anything missing?' he inquired, mechanically, beginning to wonder what he could do there except show the flag.

'Not so far as we c'n tell, Inspector Ferrow. Still, you never know with the place as cluttered as this is. Commander Speed was still out cold when the ambulance came, so we couldn't ask him.'

Ferrow felt his eyes drawn to the paper on the desk. It showed brown marks in the creases where it had been folded, suggesting age. Faint lines still spidered and ruled their way across its surface, revealing it as the plans for some kind of equipment. In the bottom right-hand corner, the ink now faded to grey, was the eagle and swastika motif of the Third Reich, and a peeling typewritten label pasted into a squared-off compartment. This was close to the tear and the still-drying bloodstains.

Curious rather than interested, not expecting to learn much that the others hadn't already worked out for themselves, Ferrow turned his head to read the typing on the label.

DEUTSCHES AHNENERBE: AMT VII. AG 9/8/42 Imp.
Volker. 1/1 da Dondi (Ugo).
Rückfahrkarte.

Something in his mind began to stir uneasily. He looked around the room. 'Any of you speak German?' he demanded.

One of the plain-clothes officers eyed him warily. 'Picked up a bit on a Rhine tour two years back, Inspector,' he ventured.

'Can you read this?'

The copper crossed over to the desk and squinted at the label.

His brow puckered in an overt show of concentration. Then: 'Not much,' he began. 'That 9/8/42 looks like a date. The only thing that I can read is the last word, *rückfahrkarte*. That means *return ticket*. That any good?'

'Not much, but thanks anyway.'

He stood looking at the plan, trying to puzzle out both what it was and why it seemed somehow familiar. When forensic arrived they took samples of the blood spattered down the edge which they'd later match to that of Commander Charles Speed. Once that was done Ferrow decided to take the plan as evidence, officially. Unofficially its schematic representation was becoming increasingly more familiar, though he still couldn't make out exactly what it represented. The only certain thing Ferrow knew right then was that it didn't resemble any ticket, return or otherwise, he'd ever seen.

He left the desk and began an idle survey of the bookshelves, conscious of six subordinates wishing him somewhere else. The titles were arranged in categories by author and covered a wide spectrum of interests, ranging from the mundane to the positively bizarre. Following along them he came to the Atlantis/Lost Continents shelf, some fifteen volumes ranging from Cayce's and Churchward's occult-based speculations to Babcock's more scholarly *Legendary Islands of the Atlantic*, as well as a hand-bound volume with no title on its spine. Without knowing why, Ferrow reached up and took this last book off the shelf, opening it to the title page.

*The Last Voyage of Martin Fallenberg* it leered at him.

Fallenberg? That mad bastard the library at Waventree was named after? He flipped into the text, discovering the primitively printed contents were heavily underscored in many places. From what his brief survey could make out, the book detailed Fallenberg's preparations and motives in setting out to rediscover the lost continent of Thule, though its sections on the expedition itself were highly speculative and could only conclude with the discovery of the mad Swede's body aboard his ice-bound vessel, some years later.

Unthinking, Ferrow slipped the volume into a pocket and turned back to the desk, where one of the forensic people was snapping his case shut. Ferrow folded the plan carefully, holding it up and shaking it first in an attempt to dislodge the last of the white fingerprint powder. He sensed rather than heard the sigh of relief as he announced that he was going to leave the others to it and walked out of the study on the way back to his car.

He could have radioed in and headed home to his flat, but instead he returned to the office and spread the plan out on his desk, conscious all the time of the tiny bells ringing out an as yet unrecognized peal inside his skull. There was something clock-like about the diagram, something that smacked of striking trains and going trains and . . . *a verge and foliot escapement*.

Now *that* was familiar. It shouldn't be. Verge and foliot wasn't used on modern clocks, but Ferrow had seen one, not so long ago. The question was where? And why was he suddenly dabbing at the cold sweat on his forehead? So Speed was into old clocks, and he'd got hold of some old German plans to make one from. So what?

Clocks have hands, though. And the pride of the Third Reich wouldn't have a primitive verge and foliot escapement. And this thing, whatever it was, didn't have hands.

He studied the label again. 1/1 it said. Sheet one of one. Nothing else. Nothing missing. A clock with no hands.

He folded the plan up again and slipped it into an envelope before putting it in one of his desk drawers. He was half-way out of the office when he turned back, deciding that he'd keep it with him rather than leave it there whilst he headed to the hospital to see if Commander Charles Speed was conscious yet. After all, he led an odd life, even for a copper, and if strange things happened at sea, even stranger things could happen to an old sea-dog's German hobby-plans.

*Deutsches Ahnenerbe* was familiar as well. Someone had told him about that bunch. Something to do with ancestral heritage, wasn't it?

Then he remembered who had told him. And when. And where.

He was sitting in the North Star at Wegrimham, listening to Ptythonius Meeres.

'It was the department responsible for researching the Nordic ancestry of the Teutonic peoples,' Meeres was saying. 'We were the ones who explored and developed the hierarchy's belief in the superiority of the Germanic race. We researched and developed obscure facts . . .'

Ferrow's car swerved dangerously at the entrance to the hospital. Only the day before his confrontation with both the skyfire and the destroying angel he'd heard those words. As he wrenched the Sierra back on to the right side of the road and slid into a parking space marked 'Consultant Only' his hand flashed down to his pocket to make sure both the plan and the Fallenberg book were still there, which they were.

He inquired for Speed and was told how to find the room. As he walked along the passageways, his feet smacking on the tiles, his nostrils wrinkling with the smell of polish and antiseptic, a foliot beam began to swing above a monstrous wooden engine in a ruined Scottish church once more. His stride faltered, then broke altogether as he stood perfectly still, the cold beads of terror springing out above his eyebrows and soaking them with their glistening rankness.

In his pocket, even as he began to shake, Robert Ferrow knew he had the plans for the device Erzebet von Bamberg had used to summon Pudendagora, or something horribly similar.

His eyes darted furtively from side to side, seeking the dread shape which might be waiting in the darkness of a doorway, watching for the approach of the gaunt, somehow inhuman form of the man he knew to be the Keeper. In the harsh yellow light of the small hours of morning he listened to the pounding of his heart, a pounding not so very different from that ghastly beating which had rung out, *and been answered*, in the starlit night about Braw Valley.

'C'mon, fella,' he grunted to himself, as much to keep his teeth from chattering as for any other reason. 'Find your balls or you'll shit yourself.' And I've done that before, he added mentally.

He forced himself to resume his progress towards the ward where Commander Speed was still unconscious. Walking more slowly than before, his face set in determined lines, he passed the night sister's office and nodded as he turned to where his uniformed constable was stationed outside the Commander's room. It was all coming together in his mind, and most of it had to do with the old man in the hospital bed. The plans were his, at least by possession, and the account of Fallenberg's expedition was his too. Someone wanted those plans. Someone had tried to rip them off the desk, hence the tear and the bloodstains where Speed had fought to retain them. And whoever wanted them knew what they were for, or, at least, was working for someone who did.

'Anyone been asking for him, Marks?' he asked the constable.

'No, sir. He's got a niece somewhere that Cooper's trying to trace. No other family that we know about.'

'Outside the family?'

Marks shook his head. 'Not a one, inspector.'

Well, that was something. At least his attacker(s) hadn't followed him here. Why should they, though? What they wanted was now in Ferrow's pocket, so there was no point in sticking with Speed.

Ferrow peered through the glass panel in the door at the unconscious patient for a few moments, then opened it and walked into the room. Nothing remarkable about it, he decided. Just another hospital room. Bed, wash-basin, wardrobe, chair, bed-table. Poorly lit. Shadows staining the corners.

Commander Speed was breathing evenly but not deeply. Probably sedated, Ferrow reasoned. A saline drip on a stand by the bed tubed down into the old man's arm.

Outside the door P C Marks didn't see the inspector yawning. His eyes had glazed and closed the moment he'd stopped fighting the chloroform pad that was pressed across his nose and mouth. Nor was there any sound as his body was lowered into the wheelchair and his uniform covered with a blanket, leaving any casual observer with the impression of just another waiting patient in just another hospital corridor.

Ferrow moved closer to the bed and leaned over it. Speed was beginning to stir slightly, as if consciousness was returning. So far all the police had to go on was a few prints off the plan, which, judging by the snort of the man who'd taken them, would probably turn out to be useless. What they needed was a good description or, better still, identification. That's why Marks had been waiting with the patient, hoping to collect a useful statement when the old man came round. Now, if Speed did wake up, there was every chance of getting one.

Not like Meeres at all, Ferrow decided. He's had a tough life, maybe, but somehow he looks too soft, for all that.

Then the eyes flashed open.

Ferrow drew back slightly, startled by the suddenness of the movement. Speed's dark eyes, the whites slightly yellowed with age and bloodshot in the corners, were staring straight at him.

More than that. They were changing.

Before the policeman's startled gaze Speed's eyes grew clearer and lighter, the whites sharpening and the irises changing colour. Their focus held, straight on Ferrow, as they became younger and stronger and more blue while he watched, fascinated and suddenly helpless.

He *knew* those eyes. Oh, God, how he knew those eyes!

Speed's mouth began to work, to form words, spoken softly, in a voice that Ferrow knew only too well.

'I shall require your help again, friend Robert,' said the Keeper.

Ferrow's mouth hung slackly open. He tried to draw back, to shake his head, to shut out the phenomenon he was witnessing, but it didn't work. Nothing worked, not as it should do. All he could do was nod, against his conscious will, horrified that he was agreeing to something, whatever, that could place him in dangers he didn't understand once more.

'Ptythonius?' he croaked. 'Is . . . that . . . you?'

Speed smiled. 'It was,' he confirmed softly. Then the eyes grew dark and old again and closed, and the retired naval commander in the bed lay still.

They wheeled Marks up the corridor, away from Speed's room. In the ward laundry store the girl changed her clothes and checked the contents of the stainless steel kidney-dish. Then, with a smile to her companion, she was ready.

Ferrow slumped into the chair beside the bed, his lips moving as if he was trying to continue a brief conversation several seconds finished. It was all beginning to hammer at his skull. In a few brief hours he'd found links to both the Wegrimham and Fortstown messes *and* spoken to the Keeper. Any second now he expected to see a blue light hovering outside the window, and he wasn't thinking of a police car either.

'Oh, Christ,' he muttered, 'I could do with a fag!'

'We don't allow smoking in the hospital, Mr Ferrow.'

He looked up and saw the nurse. Young, pretty, light-brown hair. Ought to be called Jeannie, or Genie, he smiled to himself.

' 'S O K,' he answered. 'I gave it up nearly two years ago.' Then his brow puckered. 'How did you know my name?' he asked her.

She ignored the question. 'Time for medication,' she said, setting the kidney-dish down on the bed-table and removing the hypo-dermic, depressing the plunger a little until a drop of the clear contents issued from the tip of the needle.

'Hasn't the poor old boy had enough?'

'Oh, it isn't for him, Mr Ferrow,' she grinned, her mouth self-satisfied to the point of smugness. Then she twisted away from the bed and stabbed the needle through the sleeve of Ferrow's uniform.

As she withdrew the hypodermic he struggled to rise, his mouth open, his senses beginning to darken and spin. Before they left him altogether he noted two things. One was the tall man in the porter's smock waiting in the doorway. The other came an instant later, as his cheek smacked against the parquet floor and his failing sight probed the shadows under the bed.

It sat there, smiling at him, then began to scamper closer. Its eyes were the deep, almost black-grey of roofing slates. Their expression was vacant, but something around the orbits, a line beneath the short, dark hairs perhaps, suggested amusement. They were set obliquely on the head, like a rat's. The ears were rat-like as well and seemed in the dim light to be furry both inside and out. The nearer parts of the face, though small, were horribly suggestive of a human parody. There was no harelip and split nose, as Ferrow might have expected from the size of the creature. The nose was almost man-like, with the nostrils well separated like an alligator's. It was furred for most of its length and whiskered at the tip. The smiling mouth, stretched lips slightly parted, was full of wickedly-sharp canines. No other teeth, just canines.

Like the machine that could be made from the plans, like the eyes which had shone out of Commander Speed's face, Inspector Robert Ferrow had seen this, or something very like it, before.

'Call me Toadflax,' the *familiaris* whispered to him, as the floor dropped away and consciousness went with it.

It was all getting *terribly* too much, Elspeth decided.

First of all she'd had the trauma earlier in the year of those dreadful government people taking her beloved Noel out of nice Dr Rosenblum's sanatorium. They hadn't told her, either. Not even Dr Rosenblum had told her. There she was, standing in his reception area, being informed that the man she had come to see, the man she intended to marry, simply wasn't there any longer. And where was he? Dr Rosenblum didn't know. All he could tell her was that Noel was 'helping' someone from the Government. Really!

As if that wasn't enough the sweet man had shown up on the doorstep (well, threshold actually) of her flat in Marloes Road, Kensington, having been escorted past the porter by men with very odd identification that didn't look at all like police warrant cards. She'd pieced this together later, being quite sufficiently surprised when she had returned home from a wee binge in Ken High Street to find Noel sitting there, confused but as delightful as ever. In fact he was possibly more delightful than ever, because his natural superiority had been temporarily eroded by whatever *they*'d done to him.

And now there was this latest kerfuffle to contend with. It was simply too much in one twelvemonth.

No sooner had she taken the first slice of toast out of the toaster, preferring to butter the bread whilst it was hot, than the wretched telephone had started ringing at her, demanding attention that the toast should have been receiving.

Elspeth had answered it, of course. If nothing else she was both beautiful (thought Noel) and curious. And there was always the chance that it might have been a luncheon invitation (Claridge's perhaps?) from an old admirer temporarily in town. Instead, it turned out to be some boring policeman from the far north who was calling to say that a nasty burglar had put dear old Uncle Charles in hospital.

Well, of course she had to go and see him. It would be unthinkable not to. Whilst duty was one of those things which was usually done by others, it behoved one well to be seen to do it on occasions. So, Elspeth consulted her diary, made a couple of quick calls, then began the struggle to get hold of British Rail inquiries.

If she moved fast she'd be in luck. Trains to Corby were few and far between, she discovered, the ten each day being subsidized by the local council. It meant changing at . . . Kettering? (Wasn't that something perverts did?) But the whole jaunt could be over in an hour and a half if she could reach St Pancras by 10.35.

Elspeth packed an overnight bag faster than she'd ever packed anything in her life. The daily could clear up the toast when she came. Outside Island House she hailed a cab which actually stopped for her and hurtled into St Pancras with a little over four minutes to spare. Fortunately this was enough, contradicting the rule that up till now had always proved right for Elspeth, that trains inevitably leave late unless you arrive late to catch them, in which case they leave early.

Thus it was that Elspeth Coulston, slightly flustered and definitely in need of a cup of coffee (whatever happened to buffet cars on trains?), eventually staggered into the hospital outside of visiting hours, to incur Sister's displeasure.

'Have you any idea what I've had to put up with just to *be* here?' Elspeth demanded, moderating the tone of her words by concluding them with her famous heart-melting smile.

Sister's heart didn't melt. 'Five minutes,' she snapped, holding up a hand, palm outwards, fingers splayed, as if this creature could only understand sign language.

'Too kind. Will you tell me where he is or do I have to waste the time you've so generously given me searching for him?'

'Just look for the uniforms, sweetie,' Sister replied.

In mitigation it must be said that Sister had arrived for her shift to discover police in plain, uniform and fancy dress snooping all over her formerly sterile environment. A touch of bluster revealed that a young constable and a not-so-old inspector had gone mysteriously missing the night before. The constable turned up, woozy and vacant, in a laundry store, but there was no sign of the missing inspector.

*Two* uniformed constables now stood outside Commander Speed's room, working on the principle that they could keep their eyes open alternately, at least, and stop each other disappearing. The patient inside had regained consciousness some time before, and had been rather surprised to have his statement taken by a Detective Superintendent. Now his surprise increased as his only niece, his sister's child, appeared out of nowhere between two obstructive policemen.

'Sorry, miss,' one said gruffly. 'Can't go in there.'

'Silly man,' Elspeth smiled, that smile that hadn't melted sister now being put to better use. 'Commander Speed is my uncle.' And with that she was past them and inside the room before either had a chance to protest.

As if to confirm her words she leaned over the bed and kissed its occupant upon a lightly-stubbled cheek. Then she sat down in the chair.

'What have you been *doing*, Uncle Chas?' she inquired. 'Here you are, all wrapped up like a mummy, under hospital arrest, I should say. You haven't been smuggling more of that dreadful hashish stuff in through Broadstairs again, have you?'

The question was asked quite loudly, and with an eye to admonishing the policemen in the doorway for being so painful. Only with that done, did Elspeth Coulston feel that she could give Uncle Chas her full attention and warm the dear old boy up a bit.

She'd seen him looking better. His face was a touch grey with something more than just overnight stubble. Yet he was awake and his manner was cheerful, if slightly restrained.

If the truth be told, Uncle Chas could have done without Elspeth at that moment. He'd not long finished searching his memory to provide the police with as much detail as he could remember and really wanted a little more sleep. Hospitals being what they were they'd wake him up soon enough with something quite inedible, cooked two hours before at least half a mile away, on a tray that they'd insist he cleared before they pumped him full of drugs again. Still, he was off the drip and the medical staff were pleased with his progress. Out tomorrow, they'd told him, if he kept this up, so there was no point in invoking BUPA and moving to private facilities.

He returned Elspeth's smile with a weak one of his own and began his second account of the night before, of how he'd been looking back over his wartime souvenirs when someone, two someones, he thought, had broken in through the French windows.

Probably the heavy curtains had prevented them from seeing the light and finding out he was inside.

For some unknown reason the intruders, a man and a woman probably, though it might have been a man and a youth – he'd been too busy defending himself and his property to note details for a description – had shown an interest in the old Nazi plan he had out on the desk and had tried to steal it. 'But I soon put a stop to that,' he told Elspeth, rather proudly.

'Yes, but look how they knocked you about,' she admonished. 'You have to remember that you're not as young as you were in the war, Uncle.'

He ignored the platitude and continued, his voice low and gruff, his speech still a little slurred in the wake of the sedatives. 'I remember Mrs Clarke came in and they made a bolt for it. After that there's a gap until I woke up here. All rather odd, m'dear. And it gets odder, y'know. You saw the chaps by the door?'

Elspeth turned and looked at the policemen. One of them was looking at her. She raised a hand and wiggled the fingers in a wave and he turned away.

'Thought they'd go when that detective chappie had finished my statement, but they're still here. Had a forensic team through me room as well. Thorough stuff. Seems one of their boys has gone missing. Two to start with, but one of 'em turned up drugged in a cupboard. That leaves them missing one inspector. Chap called Ferrow, I gather.'

Elspeth's tone and expression became less patronizing. Her eyes hardened from their usual spaniel brown to something nearer varnished oak. Her features, pretty and usually rather soft and feminine, strengthened and her mouth twitched slightly.

'*Robert* Ferrow?' she asked.

'That's the one. Know him, do you?'

'Um . . . yes.'

Elspeth knew him all right. She'd never told anyone the real story behind that *small breakdown* the year before and she wasn't going to start now. Besides, how could she explain what she didn't understand herself? Only brief impressions now survived of that horrifying night at Wegrimham. Swarming *familiares* tearing apart something that wasn't human. Wegrimham Grange ablaze. Gunfire. Ferrow, bleeding from his side, ordering her to get Noel out of the vault before the whole lot came down on top of them. And the blue light from the sky which had helped them, directed their actions, *spoken* to them.

It had all subsided with that nice Dr Rosenblum's help. With luck, she had thought, I'll never see Detective Sergeant Robert Ferrow again. He's out of my life, and Noel's, and he can stay there.

And as he's missing there's a good chance he will, she thought uncharitably.

'Well, this friend of yours, it appears, came in to have a look at me in the middle of the night, then popped off. Snatched, the bobbies think. All a bit too much for me, m'dear ...'

He looked up, away from Elspeth, as a figure appeared between the policemen in the doorway. The newcomer was wearing a Barbour jacket and a shapeless tweed hat, beneath the brim of which rat-like eyes glittered a shade too brightly. The policemen had sought to stop him and he was showing them something which looked to Elspeth like an oversized credit card. She was rather surprised at the way they saluted and stepped aside.

'I think it's time for you to go, m'dear,' Speed told his niece, a lot of the old authority and sureness returning suddenly to his voice. 'Stay at the house and come and see me tonight. Mrs Clarke'll let you in.'

The newcomer stepped into the room. He wore a dark suit under the Barbour, rather incongruously, Elspeth thought, and wasn't particularly tall. His face was thin and the features rather sharp. Not an altogether handsome sort of man, Elspeth decided.

'Aren't you going to introduce me to your friend before I go, Uncle Chas?'

Commander Speed sighed audibly. He wasn't looking particularly pleased as he shook his visitor's hand, but he said: 'Mr Faber, may I present my niece, Elspeth Coulston, who is just leaving? Elspeth, this is John Faber.'

She took the offered hand and found its grasp surprisingly firm. The man has more character than his appearance would suggest, she speculated. 'How nice to meet you, Mr Faber,' she lied.

'Goodbye, Elspeth,' Speed said firmly.

Taking a mischievous delight in prolonging her departure she bent and kissed him again. Then, bestowing her famous smile upon Faber, turned and left the room, pausing in the doorway to wave.

It was something more than simple mischief, though. The certainty of Elspeth's W8 world was being eroded – and the erosion was taking place with a rapidity which was quite unexpected. In the space of one morning she had heard of her uncle's experience the night before, travelled north to Corby, heard of Ferrow's disappearance and, finally, met John Faber, whose name was tantalizingly familiar although she'd never actually seen him before.

She was trying to puzzle it out as she walked towards the entrance to hunt down a taxi. Only several hours later, sitting in her uncle's comfortable lounge and enjoying the afternoon tea which Mrs Clarke had brought her, did the reason for the name's familiar ring finally return to her. Reaching into her handbag she withdrew her diary and began to flick back through its pages.

There it was. Monday 14 February. Valentine's Day. How appropriate.

Noel was huddled on her sofa *storming* into the brandy, despite her urges towards caution, trying to put his memories of the past five days into some kind of order. They'd taken him from Dr Rosenblum's sanatorium to a house in . . . Knightsbridge? Where a doctor and nurse were in attendance. Some kind of tests, they said. Anyway, they kept filling his arm with injections and wiring him up to various things, trying to therapize his memory, they said. All very kind but very professional, even down to not bothering to explain what it was all about to the patient. But it was doing him good, they said.

'Who said, Noel, darling?'

Noel Jorisund shook his white head, his eyes confused. 'Never did know who the doctor was,' he told her, 'but the man who appeared to be in charge was a civil servant, I think. Name of Faber. John Faber.'

His head was throbbing and his sight obstinately refused to focus. He might have been able to improve things, Ferrow reflected, if he'd been able to rub his eyes. For some as yet unfathomed reason, though, he couldn't move his hands.

The voices were echoing through his ears and reverberating around his skull. His mouth was dry to the point where he began to wonder if it was possible for his tongue to crack. All in all, Inspector Ferrow decided, he wasn't in particularly good shape. The hard part was working out why.

Slowly his puzzled eyes began to work again. The pupils were still dilated to almost double their normal size, dramatically decreasing the size of the blue irises around them, and the whites were bloodshot with lack of sleep and the effect of the drug. A shape wavered in front of him. Pretty, he decided, but also menacing.

'He's coming round,' said the shape, almost disinterestedly.

'Then it's time you gave him the Pentothal,' rasped another, somewhere outside Ferrow's blurred range of vision. 'Do it now, Ylena.'

The second voice was literally little more than a guttural rasping. It spoke in English but was heavily accented with German. In many ways it reminded the semi-conscious policeman of Ptythonius Meeres. Briefly his sight cleared and he stared up at the smiling, approaching face of the nurse who'd injected him at the hospital. From what she was holding in her hand she was about to do it again.

'Who . . .?' he managed to mumble past his swelling tongue.

He almost expected the second voice to come back with the classic *ve ask zer qvestions*, but instead Ylena said gently: 'All in good time, Mr Ferrow. You talk to us, then we'll talk to you, perhaps.'

His uniform jacket had been removed and one of his shirtsleeves rolled up before they'd tied him to the chair. This injection was presented in a more medically competent manner, the area about the puncture being swabbed with antiseptic both before and afterwards. It began to look as if Ylena, whoever she really was, at least had some medical background.

Ferrow accepted it all without fighting, without even really feeling any surprise, the lingering traces of the narcotic they'd shot into him before still clouding his perceptions. There was some pain in his arms from the tightness of his bonds affecting the circulation, and a stinging around the site of the first injection where muscle fibre instead of bloodstream had absorbed some of the narcotic. Now the pain began to fade, leaving a numbness in its place, a numbness which even extended to parts of his skull. It didn't affect his returning sight but it did make him feel possessed of a desire to please which almost counteracted the impressions of his surroundings and captors he was struggling to form for later reference.

He was in a sunlit room, high ceilinged and elegantly furnished. A large room, suggestive of country-house spaciousness, he decided. The lack of any kind of traffic noise outside helped to confirm this, now that the booming in his ears was over.

Ylena was about 25 and still dressed as a nurse, though her uniform appeared small, tightly stretched across her firm and well-developed body and short in the skirt. Almost a musical-comedy nurse, with light-brown hair and hazel eyes that were perhaps a shade too hard in their expression. Ferrow grinned when he saw the full, wide mouth. He had his own physiognomical theory about what that portended, lower down her anatomy. When he licked his lips it was slightly more than just an attempt to keep them from splitting on him.

His head was still too heavy to turn, so he couldn't see the second person he knew to be there.

'What is your full name?' Ylena asked him, that wide mouth moving invitingly.

He thought for a moment. 'Robert Edward Ferrow,' he replied.

'And what is the last thing you remember?'

He giggled. 'You, asking me that question.'

'I can see that I shall have to be more precise with you, Mr Ferrow. Very well, what did you do last night at Commander Speed's home?'

'There was a burglary. Someone attacked the Commander. I went out there to keep the big boys happy.'

'And when you left there, Mr Ferrow, did you take anything with you?'

Ferrow nodded. After a few moments he said: 'I took a plan and a book.'

'You took them with you back to the police station?'

'I did.'

'And left them there?'

'No, I took them with me to the hospital when I went to see Speed.'

'Why was that?'

Ferrow shrugged. 'Something told me that they just might disappear if I didn't. I figured the safest place for them was with me.'

'And you had the plan and the book with you when you were in the Commander's room at the hospital?'

'Yes.'

Ylena's hazel eyes flashed to the side, towards where the second voice was positioned. 'So, Grost and I were correct in our interpretation, Mynheer,' she ventured. 'From what we know of this man he acted exactly as we had expected him to.'

'You may justify yourself later, my dear Ylena,' came the harshly spoken reply. 'For now simply ask him what we want to know.'

Ylena nodded and returned her gaze to Ferrow. 'Do you remember me drugging you?' she asked him.

'I do,' he answered.

'Was the plan in your pocket at that time?'

'Yes.'

'And when you fell out of your chair, Mr Ferrow. Was the plan still in your pocket then?'

'It was.'

'So, where is it now, Mr Ferrow?'

The captive shrugged. 'I suppose you have it.'

With a snarl the second voice wheeled itself into Ferrow's line of vision. He caught an impression of an old, time-ravaged face atop a well-dressed torso. The lower half of the man in the wheelchair was swathed in a tartan travelling rug. Then the face was as close to his own as the wheelchair would permit, its cold grey eyes smouldering with anger. A wrinkled hand, a heavy silver ring on one finger, smacked across his face with surprising force, leaving him stinging and even more confused than he'd been before.

'No games, policeman,' the cripple rasped, his other hand pressing the button in his throat which generated his voice. 'Where are the plans?'

Despite the pain, Ferrow wanted to giggle again. This was all too much. Here he was, tied up in some country house with an archetypal mad scientist character and his nurse, shot full of Sodium Pentothal and getting the SS treatment. *Ve ask zer qvestions.* Too much!

Instead, he struggled to control himself, suspecting flippancy would bring more pain. 'They were in my pocket,' he said quietly. 'If you didn't take them when your nurse here knocked me out, I'm fucked if I know who did.'

Something was nagging at the back of his mind, worrying the hell out of him. There had been someone, or something, else in the room, something which had frightened him more than simply being drugged could have done. For some reason, though, he couldn't remember enough to make it worth mentioning.

'Then you are of no further use to us, Mr Ferrow,' the old man grated. 'Have Grost dispose of him,' he instructed Ylena.

'Is that advisable, Mynheer?' the nurse queried. 'There are other things he might be able to tell us, from the information we have on him. If we keep him alive a while longer he may still be able to help us, if not about the missing plan. And the Landgravine may wish to question him herself. We have no instructions to dispose of him,' she added.

Mynheer, to Ferrow's surprise, bowed his head in assent. His eyes were calmer now and his manner more restrained. Pressing his throat he answered: 'You are a treasure to me, Ylena. You restrain my passions as well as serving them. And you are quite right. It could be instructive to preserve this man a while longer. Very well, have Grost return him to the cellar.'

Ferrow hadn't suspected the presence of a third person in the room. His face creased with surprise as powerful arms unfastened the strap which held him to his chair and lifted him onto his feet. Unable to stand on his own yet, he was hoisted, head down, over a massive shoulder, catching a brief impression of a swarthy, impassive face.

Ylena and Mynheer had already dismissed him, even before

Grost had carried him from the room. He caught a brief snatch of their conversation.

'. . . impossible. We watched carefully to make certain nothing dropped from his uniform on the way to the car. And the room has been searched thoroughly since we noted their disappearance . . .'

'*Ja*,' Mynheer interrupted her. 'We have the Landgravine to contend with, though. She will not be pleased by . . .'

Grost padded through the open door and out into the hall beyond. Ferrow tried to raise his upside-down head enough to get some idea of the geography of his prison as the giant took him through a large kitchen, then down a curving flight of stone steps into the vaulted stone cellars of the house. Passing wine racks, mostly empty, in the dull glare from the electric lighting, Grost paused before a heavy wooden door with bolts top and bottom. With the hand that wasn't clasping Ferrow's legs he shot back the top bolt, then bent at the knees, plunging his captive's head towards the stone floor, to release the bottom bolt.

He kicked the door inwards and walked through. They were in a small room, about six by nine feet Ferrow estimated, containing several packing-cases and probably several rats. There was no light-fitting on the ceiling but a grimy window atop a narrow stone shaft let a small amount of sunlight in.

Grost dumped his burden on to a packing-case and turned away. Before Ferrow could speak he had pulled the door shut behind him and slammed the bolts into their keepers. His footsteps receded and finally vanished as he reached the curve in the staircase.

Ferrow surveyed his surroundings, struggling to keep his mind in focus and shrug off the lingering effects of the two injections. He decided he'd been lucky they'd had Sodium Pentothal to use on him. The sort of torture Mynheer was capable of could have left him permanently crippled, or worse. He was bound hand and foot and his limbs were becoming intolerably cramped, so the first thing was to try and get free of his bonds. Looking down he noticed for the first time that they'd used adhesive tape on his legs, and thus probably on his hands as well. Great. That'd be easier to cut than rope, if he could only find something down here to cut it on. Once loose, he could pile up the cases and see if he could break through that window.

A long hour of falling, hopping, crawling and stumbling exploration later, the best he could come up with was a rough edge of plywood. It might get through the tape, eventually, if it didn't wear smooth with the friction first.

Doesn't look too good, does it, Bobby? he reflected ruefully. Still, at least when a police inspector goes missing there's someone to notice and come looking for him.

I hope.

Wonder what time it is? There were long shadows in that upstairs room, so it's either early morning or late afternoon, depending on which way's north. If they grabbed me about 5 it could be about 8.30 or 9 right now. Or 4.30 in the afternoon. It certainly feels like a fucking eternity.

He thought about Johannes and tried a mental shout to see if the *glebula* was in range. It could be out looking for him but, like the rest of the local police force, how was it to know where to look?

Unless . . .

His mind raced back to those closing seconds of consciousness in the hospital. Something had scared the shit out of him just before he passed out, something familiar . . . or *familiaris*.

That was it. A *familiaris*. It had spoken to him, told him its name. But why was it there in the first place, coming closer as he passed out?

And then it all made sense, and Robert Ferrow began to rub the tape which bound his wrists against the plywood in an effort to get free. Toadflax must have the plan. Toadflax had been sent to the hospital to get it from him for some reason. That's why Mynheer didn't have them. The *familiaris* had been coming closer as Ferrow lay beside the bed. It had taken the plans before Ylena and Grost had hauled him out of there.

Toadflax had to be working for the Keeper. Ptythonius had controlled the *familiares* before, so he could do it again. But why go to all this trouble? If the Keeper wanted the plans that badly he could have taken them from Speed's study without all this hassle, either by sending the *familiaris* in to get them or simply taking them himself. There had to be more to it, something Ferrow didn't know yet. Something he might never know, unless he could get out of his prison. And before he could do that he had to get free of the tape, and fast. Mynheer could change his mind about letting him live at any moment and send Grost down to kill him. There had to be a good six and a half feet of Grost, and most of it solid bone and muscle. Even in good shape Ferrow would have had trouble with a man that size. Drugged, hurt and tired as he was, Grost could crush him with his little finger.

The tape began to wear. Splinters from the ply scored and punctured Ferrow's wrists, making them bleed and sting. With luck, though, he'd be free in a few minutes, if the edge didn't wear down too far on the packing-case.

Suddenly he stopped rubbing and listened. There had been a sound, somewhere. The light was wrong as well. Either the day was getting cloudy or there was something, or someone, outside the window.

Grost on guard, waiting for him to make his bid for freedom? Ferrow's heart began to sink. It was starting to look as if there was no way out for him this time. Then the light returned to full strength as whatever was outside moved away from the glass.

Stay clear of the window, Magister, said a familiar voice in Ferrow's head.

Shortly after dawn Johannes had awoken with the taste of a feral tomcat still pleasantly lingering on his tongue. The creature had been easy enough to catch, despite its being born and brought up in woodland on the edge of the Corby redevelopments. The hunting instincts of the *glebula* were highly developed, and its unfamiliar shape gave it the advantage of confusing its prey as to its intentions until the last impossible moment.

Johannes snuffled. Magister? He asked the empty flat.

No answer came. Ferrow obviously wasn't back yet. There was nothing unusual in his master being away all night. It went with the territory, as the policeman might have said. Yet somehow this present absence didn't feel right. Something about it screamed trouble.

The *glebula* decided to wait awhile. It was always, following Ferrow's injunctions to caution, reluctant to emerge in daylight, so his immediate thought was to wait in the flat for further developments. As time ticked by, however, and the Magister showed no sign of returning, Johannes came to the conclusion that he would have to go out and start looking for himself.

Keeping to the shadows as much as possible, trading on its ability to mimic dog-like characteristics, the *glebula* headed for Corby police station and slipped unnoticed past the desk. Once in Ferrow's office it hid under the desk, ears alert for snatches of conversation about it. Within minutes it sensed the unease of the officers present within earshot and caught fragments of conversation relating to its master's disappearance. Ferrow had vanished whilst he was at the hospital with a Commander Speed, it heard. So, next stop was the hospital.

As Johannes left the office he heard: 'Say, isn't that . . .'

'Whassa matter, Jim?'

'Oh, nothin'. I just thought I saw that fuckin' awful-lookin' dog of the Inspector's . . .'

The hospital was going to be slightly more of a problem because of the resistance to the presence of any form of animal that medical staff always displayed. For a human to creep in and hide was much easier. They could always duck through a door. Johannes could open doors, but it took more time, stretching up on his hind legs, than it would take to spot him. Yet his Magister was in trouble, and that made the risks worth while.

He decided, for once, not to bother with any attempt at concealment and padded in past casualty reception. Commander Speed, from what Johannes had gathered, would be on a casualty ward, so he should be reasonably easy to find. Already, following the corridor, ignoring the waiting sprains and gashes on the plastic chairs, he'd picked up Ferrow's scent, though he knew it to be about five hours old. It led him to a room with two uniformed constables outside and a plain-clothes officer beside the bed. Waiting until both uniforms were looking anywhere but down he followed the wall and slid into the room between them. The man in the bed and the detective superintendent were playing question and answer, and Johannes secreted himself under the bed to listen.

'. . . a little more complicated than it might have appeared at first,' the policeman was saying. 'One of the men we put on this room last night turned up drugged. The last thing he remembers was Inspector Ferrow coming to see you.'

'All very well, y'know,' came the reply. 'I was out cold at the time, so I can't really help you. Sorry to hear you've lost a man, though.'

'Commander, can you tell me what the intruders were after?'

'Hard to say. Probably they thought I'd stolen the mess plate. How should I know?'

Something in his tone suggested to the listening *glebula* that he was lying, though the policeman didn't seem to notice. Johannes snuffled at the floor, separating scents. The Magister's was still there, faintly, together with those of a man and a woman who'd been in the room more briefly. There was also another scent, close to where he was hiding, which was much stronger, as well as the policeman who was there at present and some other man-scents. The biggest puzzle, though, was the closest. It was a scent unlike anything in the *glebula*'s experience, seemingly part-human and part-animal. Whatever it belonged to was capable of being friend or enemy with equal ease.

And yet . . . there was something about it which *was* familiar. Not the scent itself, but something attached to the scent, traces of another, perhaps, which Johannes knew or, at least, had sometime experienced.

Something which said *Keeper*.

If he was right, if his koala-like nose hadn't deceived him, the forces of Thule were marshalling again for another assault upon the world of man. This time, though, Johannes had no misgivings about which side his Magister was on. This time, he knew, by instinct if by no other means, the conflict was about to be resolved.

He had to find Robert Ferrow. And fast.

The uniforms by the door saluted as the detective left. Above the *glebula* Commander Speed relaxed into sleep once more. This old man was going to be a problem, knowing more than he was prepared to say. So was finding Ferrow.

Johannes moved to a position beneath the head of the bed, screened from prying eyes by the chair and the bedside locker. This man in the bed, or one of his visitors, was probably the only remaining chance of finding the Magister. All he could do was wait and watch for, whilst he had scented Ferrow going into the hospital, there was nothing to say that he had emerged further than the doorway of this room. To all intents and purposes his scent had vanished from the face of the earth.

Time passed. A woman in her early thirties arrived and addressed the man in the bed as Uncle Chas. As she left another man entered, introduced as John Faber. This one also had traces of a familiar scent mingled with his own, though it was a different scent to the Keeper's.

'So it looks as if Inspector Ferrow had the plans?' Speed was asking.

'From what the police have told me, he must have done,' Faber answered. 'Fortunately I still have the set taken from Erzebet von Bamberg's caravan at the Circuz Ferencz whilst it was in Banff. Otherwise we'd have lost the machine altogether. It looks as if duClausky is progressing well with the prototype, even if the base concept is rather difficult. Alterjective reality isn't the sort of thing one gets used to easily, Commander.'

'Y'know,' Speed muttered, 'it's easy to dismiss all this as a load of bilge, John. Two forms of reality are enough for most people. This multi-dimensional stuff is rather hard to swallow, especially for an old sea-dog like me.'

'And yet it's as real, in its way, as capstans and foghorns, Commander. That's why we have to take the third reality seriously. Because it *is* the third reality.'

'Well, if duClausky's doing as well as you say, we've at least that much to be grateful for. Now, what about this chap Ferrow? D'you think he had some reason for hanging onto the plans?'

'He could have known what they were. After all, he's one of two, no, three people who saw a variant of the machine constructed near Fortstown. The other two were a Scots policeman called Harris and a reporter, a girl named Merry something-or-other. Chances are Ferrow noticed the similarity and pocketed them for reasons of his own. We'll find out for certain if we find him.'

'*If* you find him, John?'

'It's starting to look a bit doubtful. The police haven't any leads.'

'And if you don't find him?'

Faber shrugged. 'Then he's dead and out of it for good.'

Johannes suppressed a growl. There was a dismissiveness in that statement he didn't like. It hadn't rung true or natural to his listening ears. Either Faber was a particularly nasty specimen of the species *homo sapiens* or he knew more than he was prepared to say – even to a man he was obviously collaborating with.

'Anyway,' Faber continued, 'I've taken enough of your time for now, Commander. We want you well and out of here, so I'll make a move and not tire you any longer. We'll keep you posted on developments.' With that he shook the old man's hand and left the room.

Johannes waited until Faber was well-clear before he made up his mind. He could sit there and hope something was going to turn up to lead him to Ferrow, or follow Faber and see what happened. The choice came easily.

Not bothering to be cautious he emerged from under the bed and padded out of the room. One of the policeman at the door noticed him, but he was gone before the man could alert his colleague, and following Faber's scent out of the hospital. Trusting in his authority Faber had occupied a consultant's parking space, as Ferrow had done the night before. Ferrow's car was still there, though, even after its going-over by the forensic team once his absence had been noted. Before the spook could drive away Johannes sniffed the exhaust and tyres. For the *glebula*, cars, like people, also had their individual scents. The only real problem was to follow them without getting flattened by another vehicle. Some dogs didn't bother, chasing cars because they liked the smell of them. Most of them ended up squashed.

As Faber drove off Johannes followed, staying on the pavement except to check the scent at junctions, hugging the shadows as much as he could, though at that time of day the shadows were small enough to be considered next to useless. The car's scent would last for several hours before the smell of other traffic obscured it completely, and Faber was probably staying locally.

If he isn't, Johannes reflected, then I've got it completely wrong and the Magister is on his own. I don't think I have, though.

The scent eventually led to a local pub, the Dog and Hare, where the *glebula* found Faber's car in the car-park. It was less than five minutes' drive from the hospital so the chance was that Faber could be found quite easily.

A man with a German shepherd, the dog off its leash, walked past the car-park. The dog padded over to Johannes, growling menacingly, demanding submission. Its jaws widened and the ears flattened to the skull, then rose again as the *glebula* responded in kind. Whimpering softly the German shepherd returned to its master and continued its walk, somewhat abashed.

Johannes was following Faber's scent into the bar when he encountered a drunk reeling out of the pub. The drunk aimed a kick at his ribs. Johannes dodged just enough to allow a slight and painless contact and yelped convincingly. He needed to find Ferrow, not trouble, and that meant not tearing the human animal's foot off. The drunk smiled smugly and staggered past, singing.

'Have you ever made love to a seagull . . .'

Faber was sitting at the bar drinking whisky. Johannes hid himself beneath a wall-mounted bench-seat and watched in silence. Eventually time was called and Faber, instead of leaving with the others, made his way up to his room, the *glebula* following silently, sneaking in past the intelligence officer when he opened the door.

Faber lay down on the bed and closed his eyes. Johannes stayed hidden, following his instincts, feeling that somehow this man was going to lead him to his Magister. He wasn't disappointed.

Sometime after four one of the staff knocked on Faber's door, waking him up. He opened it and was told that a young lady was asking for him downstairs. Wondering if his luck was in, the spook spruced himself up and wandered down, failing to notice the peculiar shape which was shadowing him. Young lady was right. Light brown hair, hazel eyes, good figure, wide and inviting mouth. She introduced herself as Ylena Hahn.

'And what can I do for you, Ylena Hahn?' Faber inquired, leering.

'I'm the personal secretary of a Dutch businessman, Commander Faber,' she replied. 'My employer, Mynheer van der Taxl, wishes to speak to you about some plans we hold a mutual interest in.'

Faber's eyes narrowed. There were more players in this game than he'd suspected.

'We have a car waiting, Commander,' Ylena pressed. 'I think this visit will be worth while, if you'd care to accompany me.'

Her phrasing was deliberately vague. Intrigued, incautious, Faber assented.

Johannes followed the scent of the vehicle east along the A427. Before it reached Weldon it branched off south, then turned right into a private drive. The house at the end was essentially Jacobean with later additions. Ylena and the giant driver escorted Faber through the main entrance, their shadows long in the afternoon sunlight. Several minutes later Johannes was about to follow when he scented the Magister.

Faber could be left to his fate, whatever it might be. The priority was to find Robert Ferrow and get him out of there. He was near enough for Johannes to sense the disturbance of his thoughts sufficiently to realize he was in some danger. Rather than following the others inside he decided to make a circuit of the building, trying to locate that familiar mind. He was passing a small, ground-level window on the west side of the house when he sensed the Magister's proximity and moved closer to the glass to confirm his impression.

It was only a small window, and the glass was quite thin. Moving away he determined to crash through it. Before he did so he called a warning to the prisoner within.

Stay clear of the window, Magister, he instructed.

Inside his cellar prison Ferrow grinned and rubbed harder at the adhesive tape which bound him. OK, Johannes, he thought back, wondering just how the *glebula* had managed to find him. Then he heard the approaching footsteps on the other side of the bolted door, footsteps that could only belong to Grost.

The tape parted and Ferrow's wrists finally came free. Keeping himself against the wall beside the window-chute he forced his tingling fingers to peel away the tape which bound his ankles. He was doubting his ability to stand when the first of the bolts shot back. Moments later the bottom bolt was removed and the door began to swing inwards.

For fuck's sake, Johannes, he ordered, get in here fast.

Patience, Magister, came the reply.

Grost's massive shape appeared in the open doorway, leaving Ferrow nowhere to go. Grunting his displeasure, the giant, enormous and powerful hands outstretched, lunged for his throat.

As the glass shattered Grost, distracted, turned his gaze towards the chute, hesitating in his stride as he did so. The sharded window was followed by a flying shape, eyes blazing, teeth glimmering in the electric light from the doorway. A streak of deadly, clawed and slavering fur hurtled down onto his chest. Howling with rage and surprise he brushed it away, pawfuls of his flesh tearing with it.

With a brief 'Oh, shit!' Ferrow hurled himself against the big man's legs, knocking them from under him. As the giant crashed down onto his back Johannes went for his throat, performing the rapid, bloody, deadly work for which the *glebulae* had been bred. Grost's scream became a gurgle before he relaxed and lay still, the life-blood spilling out of his gigantic frame in a jetting fountain.

For once Ferrow nodded his approval as he stumbled uncertainly out of his prison, forcing the circulation back into his constricted limbs. 'Now for the others, Johannes,' he muttered grimly. 'But I want them alive, if we can manage it. I have to know what's going on.'

They passed the wine-racks and mounted the curving stone stairway. In the kitchen Ferrow took his bearings, though Johannes' senses had worked out which way they should go ahead of him. Moments later they burst into the room where Faber was seated before Ylena Hahn and Mynheer van der Taxl. Ferrow's eyes widened in recognition as he saw the man who'd investigated the Fortstown affair with his captors.

'Ferrow!' Faber exclaimed. 'Thank Christ!'

'Just hold them back, Johannes,' Ferrow ordered. 'No killing.'

Van der Taxl wheeled himself to a far corner of the room, Ylena moving with him. Johannes, snarling and – had the *glebula* been a dog – rabid, pinned them there with an overt display of naked savagery. Faber leaped from his seat and pointed to the doorway.

'You've only just got free in time,' he grunted. 'Quick. They left the car outside when they brought me here. Let's make a run for it.'

They headed for the entrance whilst Johannes contained the wheelchair-bound Mynheer and the terrified Ylena. Outside they found the Granada, the keys still in the ignition, in which Faber had been taken to the house. Once inside, with the engine running, Ferrow thought to Johannes: We're clear. Get out of there.

With a rear passenger door open he waited until the *glebula* bounded into the car. Then he reached back and slammed the door shut, gunning the engine and speeding down the drive. It was only when they hit the main road that he began to wonder why two men and a *glebula* hadn't been able to keep an old cripple and a young woman under restraint and ring for the police.

And by then, of course, Ylena and van der Taxl were on their way clear.

'So where am I supposed to be going, Mr MI6?' Ferrow demanded, pulling the Granada into the side of the road and turning to look at his passenger.

'Somewhere that they won't be looking for us,' came the reply. 'At least, somewhere that they won't see us, even if they do look.'

'You think they'll be looking? With the kidnapping and attempted murder of a police officer hanging over them they'll hang around here looking for us? If there was a radio in this thing I'd have roadblocks out already in every direction round that house. *And* the SAS in through the windows if I could swing it. That fucking giant of theirs wanted to kill me!'

'And how do you propose to explain away Johannes killing him?'

'How the fuck do you know about that, Faber?'

The spook shrugged. 'You'd never have got me out of there if he hadn't.'

Ferrow's blue eyes narrowed. 'Come off it. You could have walked out of the house whilst Grost was finishing me off. Neither of the others had a gun. You weren't bound, or drugged, like I'd been. What was stopping you?'

'I needed to know their involvement. After all, they've got that plan, haven't they?'

'Not from what they were doing to me to find out where it was, they haven't.'

Faber's brow creased. 'You mean it really is missing?' he scowled.

'Just like the lost chord.' Ferrow slid the Granada back into gear. 'We're wasting time. I'm heading back to the nick. I've enough explaining to do as it is, and I want those bastards tidied up.'

Patience, Magister, Johannes cautioned from the rear seat. There are still some questions to be asked.

'I wouldn't advise you to go back just yet,' Faber told him. 'We may have forced Mynheer and Ylena into flight or hiding, but they still have resources they can control to send against us. They could take you out of the police station as easily as they took you out of the hospital. And the same is true of your flat. It also goes for me. They need those plans. They'll do anything to get hold of them. Hold off for a while, Ferrow. Give them some rope.'

'And who the hell are they going to hang with it, if they can find us as easily as you say?'

'They can't, if you do what I tell you to. I know somewhere that they won't be able to find us.'

'So the man from MI6 and the missing police inspector go into hiding like shit-scared rabbits?'

'Not quite. Bear with me for half an hour, Ferrow. That's an order.'

Do it, Magister, Johannes confirmed. We only have a few fragments of the puzzle so far. This man can help us piece more of it together.

Do we really want to know, Johannes?

The time has passed when what we *want* counted for anything, Magister. We both know that the game belongs to the Keeper, now.

The *glebula* was right, Ferrow reluctantly admitted to himself. Ptythonius had used Speed's body to speak to him in the hospital, and Ylena, he remembered, had mentioned the *Landgravine*. That could only mean that Erzebet von Bamberg was both still alive and somehow involved in whatever was going on.

'You're military, Faber,' the policeman said slowly. 'You're in no position to order a member of a civil force in peacetime.'

'Not directly,' came the smirking response, 'but my initial reason for being here was to have you seconded as my assistant. I have the paperwork back in my room, approved by the Chief Constable. You may not like it, Ferrow, but you're working for me now. And it's my orders you have to take. We'll get where we're going and you can ring the CC to confirm, if you wish. Then we'll call off the search for you and concentrate on the matter in hand.'

'Like briefing me, for instance?' Ferrow sneered. 'Telling me who that so-called Dutchman and his nurse really are?'

'I think I can manage that. Shall we drive as we talk?'

'If you tell me where I'm supposed to be going.'

'Head for the Rockingham road. There's a turning just past

Commander Speed's house that leads up to some abandoned farm buildings. Take that and pull up at the first barn.'

With a reluctant sigh Ferrow indicated and moved the car back out into the traffic. Somehow he'd always known that he hadn't done his last dirty job for Ptythonius, yet at the back of his mind the fear nagged on that this was to be more dangerous, more *permanent*, than any of the conflicts he'd lived through so far.

'Ylena Hahn is a Bolivian national,' Faber began, inwardly smiling at Ferrow's compliance. 'She was born in La Paz 22 years ago. Her pedigree is quite impeccable and her education, whilst informal, was extremely thorough. She has detailed medical knowledge and a complete mastery of small arms and hand-to-hand combat techniques.'

'She doesn't look like she has a drop of Spanish blood in her ancestry,' Ferrow remarked. He had another thought as well, but he reserved that for Johannes and felt the *glebula*'s unqualified agreement.

'She hasn't,' Faber replied. 'Her mother was Maria Hennendaur, daughter of Ilsa Hennendaur who was a theatre sister at Auschwitz, working with Mengele and others on their grotesque experiments on human guineapigs. Her father is still alive, and was the official representative at the secret funeral of Rudolf Hess, after his suicide in Spandau . . .'

'Official representative? Of what?'

'The abortive Fourth Reich. The Nazis still nourish the hope, albeit in exile. But so much for Ylena. Mynheer van der Taxl, as you probably suspect by now, is, of course, German. He replaced Standartenführer Hans-Heinz Gudenheim as head of the white files section of Deutsches Ahnenerbe A M T V II in the early days of the last war. His real name is Heinrich Volker. So you see, their search for the plans could be construed as merely a natural desire to have their property returned to them. In actual fact, of course, it is something much more sinister.'

They passed Speed's house and Ferrow swung the Granada onto the dirt track leading towards a cluster of tumble-down farm buildings. 'Keep talking,' he told Faber.

'They want to duplicate certain research that we are undertaking into a concept known as the third, or alterjective, reality, and for that they require a machine very similar to the one you saw at Fortstown, which Erzebet von Bamberg was using to summon

Pudendagora. Ah, pull over here and park with the car away from the road, behind the barn.'

Leaving the car they entered the barn, empty except for a few bales of rotting straw. An ancient wooden door to one end corresponded with one Ferrow had seen securely nailed up on the outside. Faber, however, produced a key and opened it easily, sliding a piece of wood back to show a modern Yale lock. Only when they were upon the staircase which led down beneath the barn did Ferrow realize that the inner wall and the outer door were both dummies.

Faber closed the door behind them and clicked on the light. Their descent was down a flight of broad concrete steps lit by electric bulbs encased behind glass and wire covers. At the bottom a wide underground corridor led off in both directions. Faber turned right, taking them further towards the abandoned farmhouse. The floor and walls of the corridor were remarkably dry, despite the recent heavy rain, though patches of an odd greenish mould stained the walls.

Any ideas, Johannes? Ferrow asked the *glebula* padding along beside him.

This kind of structure is beyond my experience, Magister, came the reply.

Looks like it's left over from the last war, Ferrow thought back. Probably an underground communications bunker. There'd have been fewer houses around in those days, though Speed's would have been there. Certainly there's a room of some kind up ahead.

There was. A heavy metal door with a wheel at its centre blocked their progress, reminding the policeman of old U-Boat movies. On the wall beside it, however, was an ultra-modern electronic combination lock that took both a security card and an entry code to operate. Ferrow and Johannes waited as their companion slotted in his ID and punched up a number. Then he twisted the wheel, which turned easily.

The door swung inwards with little resistance and a total absence of the anticipated creaking metal hinges. Ahead of them, brightly lit, was a large room with concrete supports sloping inwards from the base of the walls every few feet. Everything, floor, walls, ceiling and fittings, had been painted white and appeared clinically clean. Two men at a bench against the far wall had turned to look at the newcomers, alerted to the door's opening by a light on a wall-panel. One of them, the taller, started forwards. The other, short and almost completely bald, turned his lab-coated back to the visitors and continued with what he had been doing.

'We hadn't expected to see you today, Mr Faber,' the tall man began, coming up to the intelligence officer.

'Circumstances alter, Dr Gunndner,' came the reply. 'Meet Robert Ferrow, policeman and now my official number two.'

Gunndner and Ferrow shook hands. The scientist had thin features, like Faber, but his eyes were somehow wider and more innocent. His nose was straight and the upper lip above his narrow mouth was quite short. His chin receded badly, giving the impression that his face was falling away into his neck. Not a handsome man, Ferrow decided, though he'd learned a long time ago not to judge by appearances in his job. Handsome men could as easily be psychopaths as film stars.

'My name is Nils,' he informed Ferrow. 'Since we shall be working together the formality of titles would be quite out of place, do you not think?' His English was perfect. Too perfect, Ferrow thought, for it to be his native tongue.

Gunndner looked down at Johannes, sitting dog-like by his master's side. 'A strange animal,' the scientist remarked. 'It must be a *glebula*, I believe.'

Ferrow peered intently at Gunndner, both concerned and intrigued that the scientist should have recognized Johannes, and puzzled that no fear accompanied the recognition. If Gunndner knew Johannes to be a *glebula*, then he must also know what the *glebulae* were, and what they were capable of. Yet the remark was almost as casual as it would have been if Johannes were a Boston Terrier or a Springer Spaniel. Before he could comment, however, Gunndner took him gently by the arm and led him along the room towards the bench where his less sociable colleague was still working.

As they drew near to the far wall Ferrow noticed the banks of electronic equipment, linked to a computer console, which were ranged along one side of the room. The other side consisted of a small chemical laboratory and what reminded the policeman of the metalwork room at his secondary school. The only difference was that the machines, mostly lathes and grinders, were all hooded with extractor shields to minimize swarf and filings.

Johannes stayed close to Ferrow, sensing the Magister's thoughts and impressions of their new surroundings. The policeman's unease was increasing as they came closer to the end bench where the shorter man was working. Something about the half-seen configuration of the gleaming machine, crafted from brass and stainless steel with extreme precision, was distressingly familiar.

'Let me introduce my colleague,' Gunndner said. 'Robert, this is Professor Edvard duClausky. Edvard, can you spare a moment to be polite?'

The little man turned, reluctantly, from his work. He was a little over five feet tall and his bald pate was fringed with white hair like an ancient monk's tonsure. If Ferrow had thought Nils Gunndner unprepossessing to look at, duClausky was downright ugly. His features, prematurely lined and seamed for a man in his early forties, were basically plain, with the one good eye clear and piercing, yet somehow remote in its ice-blue depths. The eyebrow above it was bushy and a yellow-white beard struggled to cover his chin. But the entire right side of his face, including the eye and much of the nose, was crossed and recrossed with the most appalling scars, some of them deep enough to lose a small coin in. From the small areas of flesh which weren't scar tissue stubble grew in unshaven patches, creating the impression of a Hollywood werewolf on the change. A gleam of dull white showed between the horny flesh of the eyelids, and the scarring continued well up onto the wrinkled forehead.

DuClausky declined to shake hands, his good eye studying Ferrow's reaction to his features, his expression challenging an unspoken what-do-you-think-of-that, Mr Policeman? In the next second or so the scientist was going to decide whether or not this good-looking newcomer was worth knowing or not, and the decision would be made on Ferrow's reaction to his face, as it always was.

Johannes read the stance and expression. Insult him, Magister, he advised. Something mildly insulting and dismissive. It doesn't have to be amusing.

Ferrow grinned. 'Let me guess,' he began, sneeringly. 'Trouble with the pressure-cooker, Professor?'

The good half of duClausky's face grinned back and the little man held out his hand for Ferrow to shake. 'Maybe I give the lid extra turn, next time,' he said. Then he noticed that the policeman's gaze had gone past him to the construction on the bench. 'Ah, yes,' he continued. 'You Fortstown Ferrow. Like my little toy, Robert?'

Ferrow was scowling. 'I didn't like the first one I saw, Professor. Why the hell should I like this one?'

'You know what it is?'

'Sure. It's a scaled-down replica of the one Erzebet von Bamberg used to summon Pudendagora.'

'Full marks right, full marks wrong. Yes and no, policeman. Yes and no. The Lady Erzebet use it for that, not us. We take it, examine it, refine it. This I dismantle. Over there,' he gestured towards the lathes and grinders on the side bench, 'we make more modern escapement. Nils is horologist specialist, you see?'

'I see. And what's your speciality?'

'I nuclear physics. But that not important. We fit quartz movement, do away with spring mechanical drive. Reduce size, increase potency.'

'Can I ask what for? Some kind of weapon?'

DuClausky sighed, then shrugged. 'All things weapon to friend Faber over there. Science always work for gunsmith in the end. Gunsmith have the money. But not at first, Robert.'

'Then what do you intend to do with it? And how the fuck did you manage to build it? I thought Speed had the only plans.'

'Not exactly,' Faber told him. 'Speed had the Deutsches Ahnenerbe plans, but we constructed this from the ones I took from McAllister at Fortstown, the originals that Erzebet von Bamberg created hers from. We checked the one against the other and came up with a compromise design that could be suitably modified. That's what the professor is building down here.'

Ferrow began to wonder whether it was worth pressing on, but it didn't stop him saying: 'That's all very well. So you're not going to use it for another go at Pudendagora. You're carefully not telling me what you *are* going to use it for, though. Is this on your need-to-know basis, Faber?'

The spook studied Ferrow's expression, noting degrees of annoyance and . . . fear? Well, that was understandable. Ferrow had seen the original machine and knew what it could do. Faber replied: 'You will need to know. The problem isn't so much what to tell you as *how* to tell you. Do you want a crack at explaining it, Professor?'

'I try. You know any physics, Robert?'

'Not much. I'm not one of those types who can cook up an A-bomb on a gas stove, if that's what you mean.'

'Then we go to basics. I keep it simple. Atom is smallest portion of an element, yes? Molecule is smallest particle of matter composing a compound. We made up of molecules. Bench made up of molecules. Floor is molecules. All things molecules. Like bricks in house. Molecules are building bricks of matter. You with me?'

Ferrow nodded. 'So far. Something tells me it's going to get harder, though.'

DuClausky's good side smirked. 'Much harder. Now, all molecules vibrate. All different things have own rate of molecular vibration. Sound also composed of vibration. When high note shatter glass sound vibration align with molecular vibration of structure of glass. Still here?'

'Still here, Professor.'

'Good. We take step further. Machine you see at Fortstown create sound vibration which act to summon monstrous something from other place. This other place contiguous with our place, real but not apparent. Vibration attuned to bridge between molecular structures of objective and alterjective realities. Ah,' he exclaimed, noticing Ferrow's expression begin to cloud into bewilderment, 'now I begin to lose you. I try explain alterjective reality.

'We have at least three realities. You know two of them, objective and subjective. Objective what you see, subjective what you feel. Roots of words from Latin, thus, *Ob* mean in way of, *sub* mean under. *Jective* come from *jacere*, mean to throw. Objective, throw in way of, like you walk into tree is objective. Subjective, throw under, throw inside you, not outside. *Alter* is Latin for make change, as in English. Alterjective is third reality, beyond other two, yet may also embrace other two. I try make example.

'Think of onion. Peel outer layer off, onion different but still onion. Change made. In this case onion smaller. Can make more change, peel off other layers, until only little middle bit left. All peeled off layers still exist, though different. Yet they same as when part of original onion, except they *somewhere else*. Whole onion make one person cry, maybe not another. That is subjective. Pick up onion, feel weight, is objective. Whole or dismembered onion embrace these two but is also something more. This is alterjective. Not so easy, heh?'

'Look,' Ferrow replied, 'I can't say I understand what you're telling me, but I think I can see some of what you're getting at. Supposing I say I can accept a third reality, beyond the other two. How does this tie in with the machine?'

'Simple,' duClausky told him. 'No, Robert. I not tease. It *is* simple. We discount subjective reality for now because it not vibrate. Objective and alterjective vibrate. Machine create vibrations, empathize with vibrations of objective and alterjective realities, create bridge between them. Now you know as much as duClausky, yes?'

'No, but I'll settle for what I've got.'

'Good. I stick with physics, leave hard part to you. I not make joke. Nils and I make and operate machine. You work with machine.'

A familiar feeling, like an injection of ice-cold water, was creeping through Ferrow's body. The scientist's last statement, made with such matter-of-fact acceptance, was chillingly suggestive. 'And just *how* do I work with the machine?' the policeman demanded. 'Not to mention *why*.'

DuClausky shrugged. 'Other tell you that, like Faber, perhaps? I just make and work, I hope. We test soon. Oh, not on you, Robert. Not yet.'

Ferrow turned to Faber, standing beside him with Nils Gunndner. 'How about it, Mr M16?' he asked. 'I think it's time you told me what's really going on.'

'Me?' Faber feigned surprise. 'No, not me, Ferrow. Commander Speed's the best person to do that. He'll be out of hospital tomorrow. I'm not much more than an innocent bystander, innocently standing by. I just screw the funds out of the MOD and keep an eye on things. This whole scheme is Speed's doing, not mine.'

'You mean I have to wait until tomorrow for the answers?'

'Some of them. In the meantime we'll find you somewhere to bed down and see about a meal. And I don't know about you, but I could do with a drink. Oh, and there's something you might want to read while you're waiting.'

Faber reached into his pocket and removed a hand-bound book, the spine blank. Without even opening it Ferrow recognized *The Last Voyage of Martin Fallenberg*. 'Where the hell did you find that?' the policeman asked.

'I didn't,' Faber replied. 'When I visited Commander Speed earlier today he gave it to me. Somehow it had found its way into his bed.'

# THE LAST VOYAGE OF MARTIN FALLENBERG

## Chapter 12: Final Hours

Throughout the previous chapters of this work I have endeavoured to reconstruct the events of Fallenberg's ill-starred expedition from the log and from the accounts provided by the few survivors. Once they had abandoned the Swede to his fate, however, all possibility of finding a witness for the last tragic hours of the voyage disappeared. For that reason I can do no better than reprint Fallenberg's own entries in the log by means of explication. That they are obviously the work of an unhinged mind the reader will quickly discover for himself.

This account so far has dealt with the conception, outfitting, departure and conduct of Fallenberg's expedition to discover the lost continent of Thule, known to the classical world as Hyperborea. We have seen that the woeful navigational failure of its leader led the schooner *Harfanger* into the sub-polar ice-desert beyond Svalbard, hopelessly trapped by floes solidifying for the winter and without even the slender hope of forcing a return to Spitzbergen. That any should have survived at all is remarkable in the extreme.

Perhaps the single good thing which may be remarked of Martin Fallenberg at this stage is that he chose to remain on board the *Harfanger*, remaining with his ship to face the inevitable and deadly conclusion which his folly had brought upon him. Yet even in mitigation of that I must postulate the mental disturbance evident in the following entries, taken directly from the *Harfanger*'s log, discovered six years later in October 1895 by members of the crew of the Arctic survey vessel *Tannenbaum*, who also provided the account of Fallenberg's condition appended to this chapter.

Without further preamble I refer the reader to the log of the *Harfanger*.

Thursday 31st October, 1889. Dawn.

I say it is dawn, though at this latitude, at this time of year, dawn is little more than a formality. My pocket-watch was left out on my desk last night and has frozen solid. I have little idea of time left, as, I suspect, I have little enough of life. My extremities have now given in to frostbite to a greater or lesser degree. The hand that holds the pen, despite my mittens, is blistered and red and beginning to swell. My boots have had to be abandoned as they could no longer be made to fit over toes swollen like small party balloons, despite the fact that the small toes on both feet have amputated themselves, so I have wrapped those parts loosely in strips of torn blanket.

There is ice everywhere. The world I now inhabit glistens like diamante. Pain and tiredness are my constant companions and hunger is making its bid for a position in their company. My ship will not move, and there is no-one left to move it even should some miracle free it from the embrace of the surrounding ice. Only the fungi remain as my companions now, and they say little enough, contenting themselves with the same phrase over and over.

'The Keeper is coming. The Keeper is coming.'

Later.

I forced myself to go on deck when I finished the above entry. It was more difficult than it has ever been before, though the pain has now begun to subside through familiarity. They say that hope remains whilst there is yet life, though what life may remain to me, even were I to be rescued at this moment, would be crippled and deformed by my ordeal. Both physically and, I suspect, mentally. My hunger is robbing my body of the last small vestiges of heat, but the effort of finding my way to the galley is now beyond my small abilities. I have opened the portholes to either side of my stern cabin in the hope of seeing some rescuer approach and, should I not, to hasten my end by removing my last shelter from the fierce white world outside. This may well be my last entry.

Later. (Probably late afternon, from internal evidence – Author.)

The fungi are triumphant. The cold doesn't seem to worry them, or to affect their voices. They dance about me, shouting out their news. 'He is almost here,' they tell me. 'The Keeper is almost here.' But they do not tell me what the Keeper may be, or what he, she or it intends to do. They simply tell me of the Keeper's impending arrival and urge me to look out and see for myself. Well, I shall spite them, for they do not think me capable of humouring them any longer. I shall force myself from this chair and look out of the portholes, though my limbs snap off with the effort. And I shall warm my revolver over the stub of candle yet remaining to light these efforts of mine. I do not trust the fungi, and I will not trust the one they call the Keeper, if he comes. A bullet, though, is a fact of death, if I am able to unfreeze the firing mechanism.

I have made my way to the porthole and looked out. The fungi are right. The Keeper, or someone, is advancing across the ice towards the *Harfanger*. There is a pale figure out there, coming closer. They say that Death rides a pale horse, so perhaps he is a pale rider himself. Certainly even Death's horse would be unable to survive out here, so he would come for me on foot, as this one comes.

Is there some significance about the date? This is the eve of All Saints, I recall, when the dead come back to comfort the living. Only my own death will bring me comfort now, and it advances with every beat of my heart, with every ice-stilled tick my watch might have made if I had only remembered to sleep with it in my armpit, as I had learned to do, I thought. Who are you, stranger who comes to speak with me? What can I tell you? And what can you tell me?

He is here. I know he is here because I have heard his footfall upon the planks of the deck above me. He is seeking the entrance to the companionway, the steps that will lead him here to my cabin. He must be Death. No living thing remains now. Even the fungi have gone, have left me here alone in this icy silence which only the advance of the Keeper breaks. No albatross or gull may fly above. No other creature, seal or polar bear, would trek across the white fastness of despair beyond this vessel. It cannot even be some lost and forlorn member of my crew, unless he be naked, for they all wore darker clothes than this stranger. Besides, they could not come back naked. They would be dead if they came back naked. Even I, clothed as I am, am freezing.

I have warmed my gun just in time. I hear his footsteps outside. I hear them cease. Yes, I hear nothing. I do not even hear the accustomed creaking of the door to my cabin as it swings open.

He is here . . .

*

Fallenberg's log terminates at this point. Nearly six years to the day later, on Monday 28th October, 1895, Lieutenant Hans Kikkener and two other members of the *Tannenbaum*'s crew sighted and boarded the *Harfanger*. They found the body of Martin Fallenberg, preserved beneath a crusting of ice, still seated at his desk in the aft cabin, his revolver on the floor beside him. One round had been fired from the 7.6 calibre Mauser Zig-Zag. It had entered his right temple and lodged in his brain, the point of entry brown with crusted blood. There can be little doubt from the evidence of his log that the hallucinations his madness had brought about were responsible for the merciful suicide which terminated his suffering.

It really wasn't terribly satisfactory at all, Elspeth decided.

She'd borrowed her uncle's Porsche to drive into the hospital for her evening visit, and her reflection on the road home had nothing to do with either the vehicle or its performance. It was, however, relative to her uncle's.

Elspeth had sat beside his bed for the better part of an hour, armed with flowers and grapes for the dear old chap. He had been pleased to see her but rather reserved, and his reservation had strengthened rather than given way before her questions.

'Did you know that your Mr Faber was the man who took Noel out of the sanitorium?' she'd asked. 'Dr Rosenblum didn't say anything, but I could tell by his manner he was upset about it. And you should have seen the state Noel was in when they brought him to my flat, Uncle Chas. Who is this man? And what's he got to do with you?'

Commander Speed reached over and patted her hand reassuringly. 'He's just an associate,' he replied. 'We have a small project we're working on together.'

'You're not still involved with those people from NATO, are you? I thought you'd given that up. Honestly, it's time you settled into your retirement gracefully, you know. I'd have thought there was quite enough to keep you busy around the house and garden, not to mention all those things you keep tinkering with in your study. I don't like that man Faber, Uncle. I wish you wouldn't have anything to do with him.'

The old man held his tongue. Better to let Elspeth have her head and get on with it. Visiting hours would be over soon and, if he was discharged in the morning, as he expected, he'd be back on home territory and Elspeth could return to Kensington and her beloved Noel once she'd collected him.

As for Faber, well, he wasn't too fond of the spook himself. But the project had to be carried through, and if that meant working with Faber, then he'd work with the man. If only Elspeth would stop going on about it.

'So, what are you doing with him?' his niece inquired persistently.

He forced himself to wink and tap his strong nose with a finger. 'Need to know, m'dear,' he told her. 'Nothing terribly sinister. At base we're simply doing a quiet sea trial on a new machine, when its finished. Sort of chronometer chappie.'

'You *are* still working for N A T O, Uncle Chas.'

He shrugged. 'M O D actually, though I 'spect there's a N A T O link somewhere in the pipeline.'

'And is that why you were attacked? Because some wicked men wanted the plans for it?'

'Not at all. The plans they tried to steal were old ones left over from the war. But that's quite enough,' he added firmly. 'I shouldn't be talking about my work, to you or anyone else.'

'Then Mr Faber's from the Ministry of Defence?' Elspeth pressed on.

'Damn it, girl, he is. And there's an end to it. Now, how are you getting on at the house? Mrs Clarke looking after you? Has she got the men to fix that damn window yet?'

She had to answer him to put his mind at rest, and he knew it. For the rest of the visit he kept firing questions of a purely domestic and social nature, firmly ensuring that she didn't return to the subject of the machine. When they parted she kissed him goodbye and began the drive back to the house on the Rockingham road, not much the wiser about what he was doing or exactly what John Faber had to do with it. Not very satisfactory at all.

How was she supposed to look after him when he wouldn't give her even an inkling of how to do it? she asked herself, turning the Porsche into the driveway. The question remained unanswered as she entered the house and found Mrs Clarke's note on the hall table, telling her that there was a tray in the kitchen when she felt like something to eat.

She didn't feel hungry. What she really wanted was someone to complain to, but the note made it obvious that Mrs Clarke had retired for the evening to the granny flat at the back of the house, and probably wouldn't welcome Elspeth's disturbing her. Ignoring the tray she went into the lounge and turned on the television, seating herself in front of it with a hefty and consoling vodka and tonic.

Using the remote control, she flipped from channel to channel as she sipped her drink, wondering how Noel was managing without her that evening. When she'd emptied her glass she phoned his home to see how things were going, but received no answer. Obviously the silly boy felt he was off the leash for the night and had gone out to do something stupid. With a loud sigh Elspeth helped herself to another v and t and went back to the television. Irritated, drinking more than she usually did, she fell asleep.

Elspeth surfaced again in the middle of the late-night re-run of *The New Avengers*. Now that the commercial channels had gone 24-hour, at least there wasn't the cruel hissing of a snowstorm on the screen to wake her up. Instead, Joanna Lumley in black boots was kicking guns out of naughty hands.

Her mouth felt unpleasant and her tummy was rumbling faintly to itself beneath her twin-set. She remembered the tray Mrs Clarke had left for her in the kitchen and decided to examine its contents. The hall light was still on, illuminating the nearer end of the passage leading to the kitchen, so she didn't bother with any more lights. Seconds later she wished she had.

She opened the kitchen door and stepped inside. Moonlight illuminated the area outside the kitchen window, silhouetting the frame and curtains and shining off the edges of the stainless steel double sink beneath it. To either side were units with cupboards above and below. Straining to reach into the right-hand upper cupboard, obviously searching for something, was a shape that definitely wasn't Mrs Clarke. With her heart pounding, Elspeth clawed her hand out for the light-switch, but not knowing her uncle's house that well, her searching fingers missed it altogether.

The shape had heard the door open. It turned hurriedly, startled, and some of the illumination from the hall reached its features.

That was when Elspeth began to scream.

Ferrow closed the book and looked at Johannes, curled on the floor beside his bunk. The *glebula* had been sharing his master's thoughts as Ferrow read, and now felt that some comment was required.

Do you think that Mr Faber and his companions are after the Keeper, Magister? Johannes asked.

I wish I knew, Ferrow replied mentally, preferring to keep their speculations private in their new and unknown situation. I rang the Chief Constable and Faber's credentials check out with Renfrew, so he's real enough. As to what he's up to, I can't make much of a guess right now. What worries me more is that Nils Gunndner knew you for a *glebula*.

That's not so surprising, Magister. They have the Landgravine's papers. I expect her experiments are detailed amongst them. Certainly they had her plans for the machine to add to the Commander's.

Yeah, the policeman agreed. And there's another problem. From what duClausky was saying they want to use it to explore something called the third reality, as if we didn't already have enough problems with the first two. What really puzzles me, though, is why they wanted me to read this book on Fallenberg. There has to be a tie-up between Fallenberg and the machine, a link between them that we don't know about yet. Maybe Speed will have the answers. There again . . .

He broke off his speculation and looked about his surroundings. The quarters at the opposite end of the underground corridor to the workroom were spartan but adequate. Divided into two rooms, the area was roughly equal in size to the other part of the bunker, a rough partition splitting the area into two. On the corridor side was a kitchen and mess room, equipped with running water and Calor gas heating and cooking facilities. A small refrigerator was powered from the same source and, whilst there was obviously electricity available, there was neither radio nor television. Behind the partition a sleeping area contained eight bunk beds and a linen store. Including Ferrow's, five of the beds were made up, suggesting that Commander Speed sometimes joined his associates overnight. Outside, in the corridor, was a door which led off to toilet and washing areas. Beyond these an inner door, regularly used by the look of its hinges, opened into an underground passageway which Ferrow hadn't yet explored, preferring to wait until the opportunity to do so unobserved presented itself.

It was late evening. They'd eaten well, albeit on tinned food, and Faber had been quite generous with the litre bottle of cheap scotch from his locker. The spook had firmly declined any invitation to explain further why they were there, so Ferrow had given up, filled his glass and retired to his bunk, with Johannes, to read *The Last Voyage of Martin Fallenberg*. Nearby Nils Gunndner was fast asleep, both he and duClausky having been called from the workroom to eat the meal Faber had prepared. The tall horologist seemed exhausted and was snoring gently, stretched out fully-dressed. His colleague, however, was a bundle of energy, rattling round in an effort to finish his turn on the washing-up rota and get back to work. Johannes had reluctantly settled for a can of beefburgers, wolfed down raw. Or as raw as canned beefburgers ever were. Return to the surface that night seemed out of the question, so Ferrow improvised a litter box for the *glebula* out of an old wooden case and some newspapers.

Faber was sitting in the mess reading his way through a stack of comic-books when Professor Edvard duClausky returned from the workroom and rattled the kettle to the tap. 'I make coffee,' he grinned lopsidedly. 'More to do. Test tomorrow.'

He pulled open a cupboard and reached inside for the instant coffee. When the jar came out, clutched in his stubby fingers, the little man grunted disgustedly on finding it empty. Then his eye brightened as the solution to his problem came to mind.

'Charlie have some upstairs,' he stated. 'I go steal some off Charlie.'

Faber looked up from his reading. 'OK, Professor,' he assented. 'Be careful, though. The Commander's niece is staying in the house, so no noise or lights, right?'

DuClausky faked up an English accent. 'Right on, old chap,' he responded.

He left the mess and went back down the corridor into the toilet area. Passing through this, he opened the further door and started along the passageway. Its walls, unlike those of the bunker proper, were damp and slimed with leprous fungi, and he picked his steps carefully along the puddled floor, trying to keep the soles of his shoes as dry as possible. Mysterious footprints in the Commander's kitchen would be a certain giveaway if the intruders returned. Ascending a short flight of steps he came out through a concealed door in the Commander's cellar and went up to the kitchen.

The scientist had located a jar of coffee, in a cupboard beside the sink unit, when the kitchen door suddenly opened, spilling light from the hall towards him. Startled, he turned, revealing the scarred side of his face. The woman silhouetted in the open doorway began to scream.

'Ach,' duClausky grunted to himself. 'Ich grosse schwanze!' Then, taking the coffee with him, he darted back into the cellar, leaving the screaming Elspeth to calm down as best she could.

As the professor returned to the mess his expression and the rapid breathing generated by his flight told Faber something was wrong. 'You were spotted,' he snarled. 'Somebody saw you up there.'

DuClausky nodded. 'Niece, I think. She make great screams.'

Faber weighed the situation. The choice was whether to haul Ferrow out to play policeman investigating the intruder or leave it to the local men and sit tight. Recalling Elspeth's recent requirement for psychiatric care he decided to ignore the situation if he could. After all, finding the scientific equivalent of the hunchback of Notre Dame in your kitchen wasn't going to sound very likely.

'You closed all the entrances behind you? Nothing left open?'

'No. I shut all up.'

'Then you'll have simply vanished into thin air when the police open the cellar to look for you, if she calls them. That ought to make you a figment of her imagination. End of problem,' he smirked, returning to his comics.

It was the logical course of action to pursue and Faber felt that he had reasoned it out most efficiently. His mistake, however, had been in assuming that whilst everyone else might accept the fact of duClausky's presence in the kitchen as delusion, Elspeth wasn't going to. She knew reality when she saw it. She'd seen reality at Wegrimham and she'd seen it again in her uncle's house.

And she wasn't going to let the matter drop.

Orford in Suffolk consists of several features, some of which conspire to provide its unique character. To list only a few there is the parish church of St Bartholomew, the most interesting features of which are in ruins, an excellent seafood restaurant called the Butley Oysterage, a castle which is unique in being the earliest for which any kind of building record survives (begun Michaelmas-ish 1165), and a location on the Suffolk coast (almost) within 20 miles of the *Fine Lady*'s departure on its last ill-fated voyage to Denmark. Its early-closing day is Wednesday.

The inland approach to Orford is along roads lined with conifers planted by the Forestry Commission, then past expensive-looking houses set back from the highway and screened by trees and high hedges. The drive from Corby takes about an hour and a half, depending on traffic and the vehicle making the trip. For Ylena Hahn, driving a Volvo estate with Mynheer van der Taxl and his wheelchair in the back, the overland journey was slightly shorter, being completed just after sunset.

Whilst Robert Ferrow was reading *The Last Voyage of Martin Fallenberg*, Ylena was parking the Volvo outside one of the more imposing residences on the landward side of Orford and helping her passenger out into his wheelchair. Neither she nor the erstwhile Standartenführer Volker were looking forward to entering the house and explaining their arrival to its beautiful occupant. In her dealings with them Erzebet von Bamberg had been noted neither for her tact nor her patience, and their failure to obtain Commander Speed's plans was unlikely to be appreciated. Even Ylena's search of Faber's room at the Dog and Hare, and the removal of certain items found there, was unlikely to placate the Landgravine.

Ylena wheeled Colonel Volker towards the arched double doors inside the porch and tugged at the wrought-iron bell-pull. After a short delay a servant, soberly dressed in a dark suit which emphasized his enormous and powerful bulk, admitted them. He was one of the largest men Ylena had ever seen, blond and blue-eyed with classically Aryan features. At nearly seven feet, he was both taller and broader than the late and unlamented Grost, whose body still lay in the cellar of the now abandoned house near Corby. Ylena found herself wondering if all the parts of the giant's body were in proportion. To her great disappointment that had not been the case with Grost.

Following Karsten, as she later discovered his name was, she pushed Volker through the hall and into a well-furnished drawing-room. Here she waited, standing, whilst Karsten fetched his mistress. The wait seemed interminable and Ylena was tempted to sit down. To do so without the Landgravine's express invitation, however, was to invite the lady's wrath, and that wrath, Ylena knew from experience, could be murderous.

Several minutes later a door at the further end of the drawing-room opened and the Landgravine Erzebet von Bamberg, her Titian-haired, brown-eyed beauty belying her age of 470, swept gracefully into her visitors' presence, the hem of her emerald green day-robe trailing behind her.

The ancient eyes, young-looking and bright with a fearsome desire, burned into Volker and Ylena in turn. 'If you are here,' she began, her voice pleasant, her smile deceptively gentle, 'you have the plans I require. Give them to me.'

Ylena felt her grip tighten with fear upon the handles of the wheelchair. She looked down at Volker, who slowly raised a hand and pressed the button in his throat to answer Erzebet.

'We do not have the plans, Landgravine. But,' he continued rapidly, sensing the response his words would elicit, 'we have the skull and the figurine for you. The plans, I regret, have vanished. We have interrogated both Robert Ferrow and John Faber. Neither of them knows what has happened to what we were seeking.'

Erzebet's lovely features clouded and transformed into a mask of snarling fury. 'The skull?' she snorted. 'Useless. It gave me its final service in Banff. Whilst it may yet have some purpose that purpose is not to my service, Volker. As to the figurine, that little obsidian monkey is also useless unless I have the machine to use it with. It might just as well be that standard lamp over there, or one of the turds you deposit in whatever commode this little whore lifts you onto. Useless, you hear me?

'This failure could have cost you your lives,' she continued. 'Yet there is still a way in which I may salvage something from this situation. Karsten will show you to your rooms and give you something to eat. You will need to be refreshed for what lies ahead of us tonight.'

'Might I ask what that is, Landgravine?' Volker enquired raspingly.

'A small experiment in necromancy,' came the reply. 'Ugo da Dondi built something into his original construction that has been imperfectly understood through the years. Now that I need to know I shall question the only person who has ever had the secret.

'Tonight we raise the spirit of Ugo da Dondi.'

With that she turned on her heel and swept out of their presence.

Volker looked up and patted Ylena's hand reassuringly. That they were still alive and unscathed by all but words was in itself a minor triumph. Whilst they might not know of Erzebet's role as the negative Keeper, whilst it was a role only imperfectly understood by Erzebet herself, they were both fully aware of what had happened to others who had incurred her fury. Many had died for less, and none of them had died pleasantly or quickly. One glance at Karsten's handsome, psychotic features was quite sufficient to dispel any hope of assistance from that quarter. He had doubtless been chosen to attend Erzebet for the same reason that she chose all her immediate household, and those who experienced her favours for the first time simply tasted a drug which would consume and destroy them as surely as any opium derivative.

'If you will follow me?' Karsten ordered them, unsmiling.

Ylena wheeled Volker along in his wake. One of the lesser reception rooms downstairs had been rearranged as a bedroom in consideration of the German's condition, and an adjoining room, even smaller, held a camp bed made up for Ylena. Karsten left them there to settle in and went to the kitchen to prepare a meal.

Not one of them felt the unseen, watching eyes.

Once they had eaten, Ylena helped Volker from his chair onto the bed. Within a few minutes the old man's stertorous breathing announced that he had slipped into an uneasy sleep. Ylena herself remained awake, watching her charge, her mind working around their current circumstances.

For Standartenführer Volker the choices were easier to make. He remembered the glorious days before the collapse of the Third

Reich. He had known, or at least met, the Führer on more than one occasion. Now his remarkable countrywoman, this Erzebet von Bamberg, had found a way to increase the presently limited potential of the Fourth Reich by means of techniques akin to those researched and sometimes employed by the Deutsches Ahnenerbe office of the SchutzStaffel. These techniques closely paralleled and even intermeshed with the acceptable occult philosophies indoctrinated into Himmler's so-called Black Knights, impressing Volker with a sense of the *nearness* of the Fourth Reich's achievement in the Landgravine's hands. Even the proposed act of necromancy was not so improbable if one recalled some of the lesser-known experiments performed in certain of the death camps. What a pity that those boorish and vengeful victors had executed Wolfram Sievers in 1948 after the Doctors' trial.

Even so, Thule was rising again, carrying the Fourth Reich to the new victory of world domination in its wake.

In Ylena's case their cause was not quite so clear-cut. Certainly her background and education had indoctrinated her thoroughly in both the ideology and requirements of their cause. Yet some of the views expressed by the rest of the world concerning the activities of Hitler's thugs inevitably filtered through, if only in a distorted form as evidence of the persecution of loyal Nazis. Whilst in England she had taken advantage of Erzebet's frequent absences on business connected with the Circuz Ferencz to haunt available libraries, devouring in secret works such as Brad Smith's *Judgement at Nuremberg* and Sklar's *Gods and Beasts: The Nazis and the Occult*. The taste which these books left in her mouth was one of a disturbing and unpleasant reality, despite her years of solid indoctrination. And she had also discovered, much to her own surprise, that killing and a casual approach to death didn't seem to come as easily as it should. Oh, it was no problem to use her training to inject narcotics or truth drugs, but there was something abhorrent about the torture and slaughter of human beings which both Volker and the Landgravine accepted so readily.

Ylena watched the sleeping Volker, suddenly wondering if there was anything more to him than a vicious, crippled old man who had survived throat cancer as well as World War II.

And the *other* eyes watched her, still unseen.

Towards midnight Ylena heard sounds which she interpreted as Karsten moving furnishings and dragging something heavy along the hall outside. The minutes dragged by, leaving her thirsty and curious, but unwilling to risk Erzebet's volatile nature by venturing out of the room before she was summoned. From the Landgravine's demeanour on this and previous occasions it was obvious that Erzebet disliked her, if only because her own good looks might rival those of her mistress in the affections of Erzebet's predominantly male vassals, possibly undermining her authority.

Volker finally awoke. Ylena prepared him and helped him into his wheelchair, ready for the approaching moment when Karsten would summon them to rejoin their mistress. A few slow minutes later that summons came, and he led them back into the room where they had reported before, finding it substantially transformed by the blond giant's activities.

It was no longer simply a room. It had become a temple of darkness. The comfortable furniture had been removed, together with the oriental rugs and carpets which formerly covered the polished wooden floor. The mirrors and other wall-hangings were also gone, with only the curtains, now firmly closed, remaining to suggest its former opulence. Yet it was a long way from being empty in terms of atmosphere.

Whilst the floor coverings were gone, the boards beneath them had been painted, obviously some time previously, with a variety of symbolic designs. The largest and most imposing of these was an outer square, the sides some twelve or thirteen feet long, exactly containing a double circle. In the space between the circle rims the legend *Revelabitur gloria Domini; et videbit omnia caro salutare Dei nostri* had been inscribed in a Gothic script. Ylena struggled to make out the unusual characters, mentally translating: *The glory of the Lord shall be revealed, and all flesh shall behold the salvation of our God.*

Salvation or damnation? she found herself wondering.

Inside the inner circle, the tips of its outer arms touching it and exactly aligned to the cardinal points of the compass, the remaining area was taken up by an outsize swastika.

The room seemed to shift and alter its dimensions from moment to moment in the flickering light from the candles set about the central design. At the compass points, fat black candles, all in heavy, high candlesticks, burned with dirty flames betraying the presence of something more or other than tallow in their composition, and at the corners of the square flamed slender red ones.

From the burning wicks issued an odour which lay somewhere between the heavy perfume of incense and the cloying, revolting stench of organic decay.

Beyond the square, on the northern side, resting lidless, almost upright against the wall, reposed an ancient, weathered wooden coffin. Inside, carefully set atop the fragments of bone and cloth and other unidentifiable human detritus, was a crumbling skull. If the remains exuded any odour it was faint enough to be masked by the stronger stench emanating from the burning candles.

'Not the most splendid chamber to use as a Thulean Temple of Necromancy,' came Erzebet's voice from behind them, 'but it will serve this once.'

She swept past them, dressed in a black robe of a sheer, clinging material which emphasized every curve of her splendid body. She wore no ornament, carried no grimoire or magical weapon, trusting in her own powers and the powers of the negative Thule to accomplish the task which lay ahead. Yet there were objects, very far from the traditional concepts of magical paraphernalia, which were required. These lay upon a small table in a window bay and Karsten moved to take them up at a nodded command from his mistress.

Beyond the house, deep in a tract of Forestry Commission woodland, the bloodless body of a young girl awaited eventual discovery and subsequent police investigation. Most of the missing blood was sealed in a large plastic freezer-bag, resting heavy and fragile on the surface of the table. With Erzebet's assent Karsten lifted it carefully and carried it across to the open coffin, placing it on the ancient skull. He then returned to the table and loaded the air pistol which had lain beside the blood-bag, tucking the weapon into his belt.

'And now we shall take our places,' Erzebet announced. 'We shall stand in the smaller squares formed by the arms of the swastika, facing north. Volker, you on my left. Karsten, my right. Hahn, behind me.'

They took up their positions as instructed. After a last examination of the room, Erzebet von Bamberg closed the open door and stood for some moments staring at the coffin. Then she walked unhesitatingly into the square and assumed the most northerly position, closest to the last mortal remains of Ugo da Dondi, stolen from the cemetery outside Karlstadt over 300 years before.

It paid to be prepared for *anything*, Erzebet had reasoned. There had been little opportunity for her to speak with da Dondi living. That, however, was no obstacle for one who had the power to speak with da Dondi dead.

The ritual began.

Ylena, standing behind the Landgravine, couldn't see Erzebet's face. By moving slightly to the side she was able to observe the open coffin, though she wondered if she really wanted to. Neither Volker nor Karsten spoke, remaining mute as Erzebet recited the opening invocation and progressed from Latin into a form of Old Norse.

This is insane, Ylena found herself thinking as the spoken ritual droned on. This is like something out of a cheap horror film. The woman's mad if she expects anything to happen.

She's mad anyway.

The invocation ended and a heavy silence descended around them. Erzebet held out her right hand to Karsten, who took the air pistol from his belt and placed its butt in her outstretched palm. Her fingers slowly closed about the weapon and her arm returned to her side.

The silence deepened and lengthened. Though the night wasn't particularly warm Ylena discovered that she was beginning to sweat. Fumes from the candles were making her head ache and her limbs were beginning to cramp from inactivity.

All that changed when Erzebet began the evocation. Ylena had read one or two books which mentioned Aleister Crowley, the grand panjandrum of modern magic, who claimed to have sent a copy of his creed, *The Book of the Law*, to the Führer before Hitler's rise to power. The book spoke of so-called *barbarous names of evocation*, syllables which might be meaningless in themselves, but when spoken in a certain fashion, affected the levels of reality experienced by those who used them ... as Erzebet was using them now.

She was speaking low, almost whispering, as she began. Her voice gradually increased in volume, becoming both louder and stronger as the gibberish spewed forth into the weighted, waiting atmosphere in the ritual chamber. Her tones became wilder, the sounds more guttural, less articulate, degenerating in places into howls and hisses and shrieks. With the increase in the overt barbarity of the sounds her stance broke, turning into a kind of wild, demonically choreographed dance. The air pistol was raised and lowered, swept about her, pointed in turn at all within the square, though mostly at Ylena. The girl's eyes widened as the gibbering Erzebet, features wild, hair matted with perspiration into dull, whipping rat-tails, robe rent and torn with her exertions to show the bare flesh beneath, steadied the air pistol with both hands and sighted along the barrel. The pellet wouldn't kill her, in all probability, but it could take out an eye or create some other disfigurement or disability.

Erzebet uttered five syllables more ... 'OOOOOOOOO-GOH ... DAAAAHHHH ... DONNNN ... DIIIII' ... before whirling suddenly and violently away from Ylena and discharging the air pistol. Sobbing with relief Ylena could only marvel at her antagonist's marksmanship as the pellet smacked firmly into and through the centre of the blood-bag.

The dead girl's blood spurted out through the punctures in the plastic, spattering onto the floor and the inside of the ancient coffin, flooding in eager rivulets over the skull, soaking into the jumble of rags and dust and sharded bones beneath it.

Erzebet flung the gun away and waited. They all waited. And watched. And felt fear's fingers tightening on their sanity.

Slowly, very slowly, in that silent room by the flickering light of those odd-smelling candles, a change began to take place in the contents of the coffin. The remains began to absorb the blood like a sponge, dry and compressed, absorbing water and expanding.

From a dark corner beyond the range of the candlelight other eyes were watching too, noting the way in which the remains of Ugo da Dondi were reacting to Erzebet's summons, marvelling at the way in which dust was becoming flesh once more, expanding, enlarging, reuniting.

The watchers within the square stared in helpless fascination at the horror being created before them. The blood and the alterjective reality created by the barbarous evocation had lent an unhallowed life to the dead fragments, slowly knotting sinews once more, recreating vital organs, presenting a semblance of the life they had once originally held. A parody of da Dondi's features formed about the skull. Dull eyes presented themselves, white and horrible, in the waiting eye-sockets. Yet the thing which was growing in the coffin was a long way from humanity, even in appearance. Flesh and bone there was, as there had been in life, but it was not positioned as it had been in life with arms and legs and body and head clearly defined, for that was not the way it had been positioned for the ritual.

Ugo da Dondi was reforming, but he was reforming as fragments of flesh around fragments of bone, with shreds of tangled, ragged clothing stitched through his shapeless body again and again. He wasn't man-shaped. He was a column of dismembered pieces bloodily joined, a tangle of organs and limbs grown up from the jumble which had slid down and rearranged itself when the coffin was stood upright. Fingers and toes projected from the central column at odd angles. The left hand, on the end of a short length of forearm, and a dangling loop of intestine were just recognizable as parts of a human being. And the head, the almost-fleshed skull which Karsten had so carefully arranged on top of the pile of human detritus, was vaguely human, though it lolled with one cheek missing and the tongue hanging through the gap to one side.

The thing stopped growing. Volker's eyes were riveted to it and his chest was heaving for breath. Karsten's mouth was open and his fingernails had cut the palms of his hands, bloodying his whitened knuckles. Ylena's legs were shaking and her bladder felt insecure. Erzebet, however, simply stood in haggard, unsmiling triumph before the monstrosity. Then she said: 'Can you hear me, Ugo da Dondi?'

The tongue wagged and a thick, inarticulate mumbling issued deeply from the remains.

Erzebet snorted disgustedly. 'Can you move?' she demanded.

Anything approaching a walk or a crawl was completely out of the question. The creature terminated in a cone-shaped projection which served to keep it upright in the coffin. The only part capable of any movement, the left hand, jerked spasmodically, the fingers distorting with effort into shaking claws.

Ylena's mind began to spin. 'Oh ... my ... god ...' she whispered, her legs giving beneath her.

Karsten caught her as she fell. Erzebet ignored the movements beside and behind her.

'Your right eye is lidded. Can you blink it?'

The eyelid flickered closed, then opened again. As it did so the black dot of a pupil, large and unearthly without an iris to surround it, formed on the dull white surface of the eye. It seemed to sweep about the room, focusing on Erzebet and then upon the unseen watcher in the shadowed corner.

'Look at me.' The eye obeyed. 'I have to know about the plans you drew . . .'

The eye returned to the watching shape. The watcher nodded gently.

'Will you look at me?'

The eye blinked. When it reopened the pupil had vanished. Slowly, as the blood congealed and dried, the monstrosity which had been formed by the remains of Uga da Dondi began to crumble and fall apart.

'Listen to me!' Erzebet shrieked. 'Stay. Stay, I command you!'

It was time. Their attention was distracted sufficiently. Exerting all the effort his small forelimbs were capable of, Toadflax slid the missing plans across the polished floor. They appeared, as if by magic to the preoccupied occupants of the square, in the area between Erzebet's station and the upright coffin, the folded surface yellow-white in the candlelight.

Erzebet looked down, as did Volker. Then the Nazi stared up at his mistress. 'Those are the plans!' he hissed. 'We have them, Landgravine. It worked!'

'Then back to whatever hell you came from, da Dondi,' she snarled to the dissolving creature before her. 'We shall have to do without your further assistance.'

It didn't hear. The skull was sinking down through the tangled torso. The hand, fingers crumbling and falling into dust, twitched slightly before it imploded, seemingly setting off a chain of small implosions as da Dondi became graveyard detritus once again.

'Karsten, get the lights,' Erzebet ordered, snatching up the plans from where they had so mysteriously appeared. 'And let some air into here. Open the door and windows.'

The blond giant obeyed. As the light snapped on and he opened the door Toadflax hesitated briefly, caught in the glare of electric light in the open, coverless room. For the duration of those few moments Erzebet's eyes burned into his own. Then widened.

'Night-mouse,' she whispered, as Toadflax leaped out through the doorway.

It was only with her uncle home from the hospital and seated with a rug over his knees that Elspeth finally made up her mind to mention the incident of the night before. She was about to do so when Commander Speed threw off the rug and struggled to his feet.

'Uncle!' she snapped. 'Sit down. Whatever you want I can get you. Now, what is it? Something to read? A cup of coffee?'

Speed raised his eyes heavenwards and sighed softly. 'I could do with a bloody big pink gin,' he growled. 'I've been in that bloody place through nearly forty hours of abstinence.'

'You know what the doctor told you. No alcohol with the pain-killers . . .'

'Bugger the bloody doctor, Elspeth. If you don't fix me a pink I'll fix one myself.'

His niece scowled, then acquiesced resignedly. 'Gin, bitters and water?'

'Like this. Two good shots of pink, left in, put in after you've filled the glass, that one there, with ice. Then gin over the top. To the brim. *No* water.'

'I'm surprised you still have a liver, Uncle Chas.'

The old man chuckled to himself. 'Hard livers have hard livers, m'dear,' he told her.

Elspeth's trip to the kitchen to fetch the ice was the first time she had set foot in that room since Mrs Clarke had found her there after her fright the night before. She entered from the passage carefully, surveying the daylit kitchen suspiciously before actually setting foot inside it and crossing to the refrigerator. Mrs Clarke, disbelieving, had checked the cellar and found no sign of anyone down there. Elspeth, furious at being disbelieved, had summoned the courage to go down after her and also found nothing. She had slept badly that night, despite a sleeping pill or three, and had been dozy when the time came to collect her uncle, driving the Porsche rather badly into Corby. Now, as she emptied ice into the ice-bucket from the drinks table, her eyes were darting about into every conceivable hiding place, expecting the miniature horror from the night before to jump out at her.

With a sense of relief she finished filling the bucket and made her way back to her uncle, preparing his pink gin exactly as instructed. She handed the completed drink to him and he managed a smile of thanks before taking a substantial pull at the only slightly diluted liquor.

'Have one yourself?' he invited.

She shook her head. This was going to be difficult enough without being accused of having drunk the experience. And it was better he heard it from her right then than later from Mrs Clarke.

'Uncle,' Elspeth began, 'there was someone here last night. I saw him.'

Commander Speed frowned. 'You mean an intruder, m'dear?'

Elspeth nodded. 'Here in the house. In the kitchen.'

'The kitchen? Not the study?'

'No. The kitchen. Short and ... hideous. And you're not going to believe this, but he went into the cellar and ... vanished.'

She studied her uncle's expression carefully. He wasn't laughing at her, though he did appear somewhat relieved. If she'd been Alice she would have thought it curiouser and curiouser.

He took another good swig and held the glass out to her. ' 'Nother dash of pink, m'dear, and up to the top with gin. No more ice.'

Startled by his reaction she did as he asked without objecting. At the very least she'd expected him to tell her she was seeing things, the way Mrs Clarke had carefully avoided doing. She gave him back his glass.

'Small, you say? And hideous? That mean short with a scarred face?'

'Um, yes. I suppose it does.'

The Commander's features relaxed. 'That was probably a fella called duClausky,' he remarked.

Elspeth felt her jaw drop open. 'You *know* him?'

'Uh huh. Works for me. Well, with me, as a matter of fact. On the project.'

'Here? In the house?'

'No, under it. There's an entrance through the cellar to an old

World War Two communications bunker. That's why I bought this place.'

'And this . . .'

'. . . Professor Edvard duClausky. Scandinavian Polish cross. Damn clever little mongrel . . .'

'Works down in this bunker place? But what does he do down there?'

After a solid day's abstinence the gin was beginning to bite. Commander Speed looked at his glass, thought of secrecy and reasoned what the hell. After all, the gel'll keep on until I tell her the rest in dribs and drabs, so I may as well get a refill and tell her it anyway.

He held out his glass for a third. Elspeth complied without comment.

'Edvard duClausky,' he began, 'is one of the top ten nuclear physicists in the western hemisphere. He's somewhere way past good and only just this side of Einstein. He freelances his talents on a contract basis to the NATO countries and he's able to pick and choose those jobs which attract him the most. If you can't get duClausky you can still get the job done, but it takes longer and will probably cost you more. Now . . .'

He paused and attacked the gin again.

'duClausky and Faber are working together with a fella called Nils Gunndner. He's a horologist . . .'

Speed noted Elspeth's expression. 'Clock specialist,' he explained. 'He and Edvard are working on the machine we're developing. In the bunker. Down there.' He stabbed a finger at the carpet.

'What does this machine do, Uncle?'

'Al . . . alters reality, m'dear. Bit like alcohol only different. S' not a weapon. Not yet. 'Spect they'll find a way to make it one, sooner or later. Not now, though. Have to see what it c'n do, first, and that means finishhing it.'

'But what would this duClausky fellow be doing here?'

The old man shrugged, slopping the gin in his glass. ''Shpect he ran out of coffee. Drinks a lot of coffee, does Edvard. Probably came up to steal some of mine.'

Elspeth assumed her firmest and most displeased expression in readiness for the reply to her next question. 'Are you funding this research, Uncle?' she asked.

Speed shook his head and began to wish he hadn't. He was drinking too much too quickly, and that bloody doctor had been right. Booze didn't mix well with the pills they'd given him.

'Not mee. Not ol' Charlie Speed. No, no, m'dear. Ministry of Defence. And I think there might be a grant from the bloody D o'D as well.'

'Who?'

'Bloody Yanks. Want to be in on everythin' these days. Should never have let the buggers into NATO.'

'So the entrance into this bunker is through the cellar?'

'Tha'sh right. Door to the left as you go down. Looksh like boxes stacked againsht the wall, but they're empty. Jusht pull 'em and they open up. Open sesamee . . .'

Elspeth raised a hand to her mouth to hide her grin. When it had subsided she gently prised the glass, now empty except for several half-melted lumps of ice, from her uncle's fingers.

'You have a nice sleep,' she told him.

'Goo' idea,' he mumbled. 'Could do with a nap . . .'

She tucked the rug firmly around him before she tiptoed out of the room, heading more confidently towards the kitchen and the cellar door. He'd be fine where he was whilst she did a little exploring.

Sure enough, there it was. A stack of boxes against the left-hand wall of the cellar as she descended the stairs. She tugged at them. They gave, swinging out towards her without leaving any sign on the tiled cellar floor, the lowest box carefully attached to the door a quarter of an inch above the tiles.

Beyond the open doorway was a dank-looking corridor. On the wall, just inside it, Elspeth saw an electric light switch. She pressed it and the corridor lit up.

'For what we are about to receive . . .' she muttered to herself, then took her courage in both hands and set off towards the bunker. As she reached the door at the further end she hesitated, hand on handle, then firmly pushed it open and stepped through. The washroom was unoccupied and in darkness, so Elspeth passed quickly through it to the entrance leading into the passageway which connected the mess and laboratory areas. Very slowly, very warily, she tried the handle and pulled it slightly ajar.

Johannes was lying dog-fashion with his muzzle resting on his crossed forepaws at the mess door. He sensed the movement, unable to see it by the thick wall which projected beyond the door, but remained where he was.

Magister, there is an intruder in the bunker, he called along the passage to the laboratory.

Ferrow heard him. He was standing with Faber and Nils Gunndner whilst duClausky explained the operation of the finished machine, describing the complex fuelling mechanism which he had just connected.

'But I thought you'd modified it to accept lithium battery power?' Gunndner was asking.

'For quartz crystal, yes,' duClausky told him. 'But that only replace drum-spring or falling weight for mechanical power. Make machine go, yes? Make machine *operate* is different. Machine go as useless super-clock. No hands. No tell time. No do anything but go. Now this,' he pointed to an object rather like an aqualung but screwed together and safety-clamped along its centre, connected by thin tubes to the machine at one end and, via an electronic control console, to a laser-like device at the other, 'make it work.'

Ferrow silently detached himself from the group and moved back down the laboratory to where the heavy metal door had been left ajar. For a secret operation the security seemed to have become extremely lax. All it took was someone to work out that the bunker connected to Commander Speed's house and there could be a squad of Erzebet's killers, human or inhuman, inside in nothing flat.

I hear you, Johannes, he replied mentally to the *glebula*. Can you see him yet?

Elspeth stepped quietly into the passage and glanced towards each end in turn. Johannes, in the doorway of the darkened mess, was almost invisible.

A woman, Magister.

Erzebet?

No, not the Landgravine. The one who visited the old man in the hospital whilst I was looking for you. She called him Uncle Chas and he called her . . . Elspeth.

Elspeth? That name rang bells. Ferrow hadn't known more than two Elspeths in his life and one of them had been an ancient aunt. The other one had been with him through the closing moments of that horrific mess at Wegrimham. Elspeth Coulston.

Elspeth Coulston began creeping towards the laboratory door.

In complete silence Johannes rose to his feet and started to follow her.

She's alone, Magister, he advised. Early thirties, perhaps. Brown hair. Dresses well. I believe you would find her attractive.

Right now I'd find Faber's mother attractive, Ferrow reflected. Since June and I broke up there's been fuck-all time to find anyone else. But the woman you've just described sounds like Elspeth Coulston, all right. So, she's Speed's niece? What the hell is she doing down here?

'Then if it's not drawing on the lithium batteries,' Faber was asking, 'how does it operate?'

Professor Edvard duClausky treated them to his one-sided smile and tapped his nose. 'A fragment of that figurine I examine is good to do it. Monkey figurine you show me what . . . two months ago? How long we work on this thing?'

John Faber frowned. 'That was in my room at the Dog and Hare. I went back there this morning to get my things. Both the figurine and the skull were gone from my luggage. Won't any piece of obsidian do the job?'

The professor shook his head firmly. 'Obsidian, you English say, no bloody good. Not work.'

'Oh, shit,' Faber groaned. 'you mean I have to get that figurine back? But what's so special about it? It can't be the shape or you wouldn't be talking about chipping a fragment off it.'

Elspeth crept nearer to the laboratory door. Ferrow, careful not to show himself, waited.

Tell me when she's in grabbing range, Johannes, he ordered.

'Ah, I not tell you everything, friend John,' duClausky confided in a conspiratorial whisper. 'Now this,' he continued in his normal voice, tapping the aqualung-shaped container, 'work like miniaturized atomic reactor, except break down atom more slowly, then distort rather than destroy nucleus. Big leap forward, eh? Equal power, greater control, smaller size. Not work with standard nuclear fuel, though.'

'Then what does it work with?' Nils Gunndner asked.

She's about six feet from the door, Magister. She's stopped to listen.

Then if I try to grab her now she'll run and it'll get messy. Especially as I have to open the door inwards before I can make a move.

'Sub-form of element atomic number 69,' duClausky replied. 'Unlike other forms, need extraction from euxenite ore, this occur naturally. Look like obsidian. Many think it obsidian. *Not* obsidian. Figurine not obsidian. I know this when I examine figurine . . .'

'Now hold it right there a moment,' Faber interrupted. 'What's all this about an element's *sub-form*? I may not be a scientist but I seem to remember something about an element being a pure substance that can't be separated into component parts.'

DuClausky gave Faber an approving look. 'You right. Element not break down into ingredients like cook-book formula. Yorkshire pudding not element. Sodium element. Copper element. Niobium, lanthanum and cerium elements. I try to explain.

'In genetics two parents of pure strain sometimes throw sport. Six generations both sides have blue eyes. Then child born with brown eyes. Who father? They ask. Father is father. Genes mutate, yes? Child is genetic sub-form.'

'Okay, but elements don't have genes. Do they?'

'Not genes, friend John. But sometimes number of electrons in quantum groups make variation like genes. In this case normal grouping is 2, 8, 18, 30, 9 and 2. Sub-form grouping is 2, 8, 18, 30, 8 and 2. This alter atomic weight from 169.4 to 169.1. Also serve to stabilize properties to suit our function here and mean element occur in pure sub-form naturally. So, we use.'

She's moving again, Magister. Nearer. Nearer. Almost touching the door . . .

'So which element are you going to use?' Nils asked.

DuClausky shrugged. 'For this project, nothing more appropriate. So-called obsidian monkey actually sub-form, and here I say inert until processed in the machine, of element called *Thulium*.'

Ferrow pulled the door suddenly inwards and leaped around it. His hands grasped Elspeth's shoulders and his eyes searched her face, widening in recognition. His grip held, but relaxed.

'Why, Mr Ferrow,' Elspeth began, 'I understood that you were missing. Have I really found you all by myself?'

As lunch ended Karsten helped them to coffee and liqueurs and then poured himself a large brandy and joined the group at the table. Ylena thought how placid and domesticated the giant appeared at this moment in his role as butler cum general factotum. There was no sign of his lethal potential, nor of his assistance at the raising of Ugo da Dondi the night before.

Ylena herself had struggled to consume a little food in an attempt to banish the memory of that dreadful ritual. She knew that she would never banish it completely, that it would return to haunt her, waking or sleeping, for however long she had to live.

Volker had told her of the conclusion of the ritual, of the return of the plans and the discovery in the room, believed empty of all but the participants and the principal in the necromantic rite, of something Erzebet had called a *night-mouse*. Volker himself was unable to describe it, falling back on a brief impression of something that was rat-sized but, in an inexplicable way, semi-human. As Erzebet had obviously mellowed with the plans back in her possession, albeit not da Dondi's originals, the ancient Nazi decided to venture a few questions that he felt required some kind of answer.

'Lady Erzebet,' he began, 'what was that creature that we glimpsed last night?'

Erzebet von Bamberg's brown eyes were lustrous and compelling, even allowing for a slight deviation in their focus after an alcoholically-indulgent lunch. 'The night-mouse?' she asked back. 'Ah, that is a part of a greater philosophy than that of Shakespeare's Horatio, Volker. It is a survival from vanished days. You know that they used to say that witches were served by imps which were called their familiars?'

Volker assented.

'Then know also that those familiars were not demons or supernatural creatures, merely a species of animal, a separate branch upon the evolutionary tree, which had evolved certain human characteristics but not others. The night-mice, or *familiares* as they are also called, were in tune with the old gods in the same way as the witch cult, and so they sometimes pledged their allegiance to humans they felt in sympathy with. Yet I believed that they had all gone underground during the persecutions of the sixteenth and seventeenth centuries. That was why the sight of that creature last night occasioned me such surprise.'

'But how did you know about them at all?'

Erzebet sipped a liqueur cognac, then set down her glass. 'I once told you my real age, Volker, and informed you of my role as a servant of Thule. Do not make the mistake of believing I am the only servant that Thule has had through the centuries. Before me there was my cousin, the Prince-Bishop Franz-Alberich Carolus von Bamberg, who was killed attempting a ritual at Karlstadt. It was the night-mice, working under the direction of the Keeper, who foiled that ritual. I know. I was there.'

Volker thought for a moment. 'Then . . . the night-mice are our enemies?'

Erzebet shook her head. 'They are neither our enemies nor our friends, though that one last night performed a brave and welcome service by returning the plans which Ferrow took from Commander Speed's house.' She noticed her subordinate's surprise. 'Did you think that grotesque column of reanimated flesh had anything to do with their appearance?' she demanded. 'The summoning of Ugo da Dondi was an unmitigated failure. Had the night-mouse not been here with the plans we would have remained as frustrated after the ritual as we had been before. Why it chose to help us, I do not know. I suspect that it was ordered to do so, for there are powers working around us that, by their very nature, must remain mysterious. But I do not yet know by what or by whom it was instructed. Until I can answer that question it will be unsafe to assume the creature's service was reliable. Though,' she paused, 'as you have authenticated the plans I think we may assume them to be genuine.'

Volker drank some of his coffee through a silicone plastic tube which Ylena had positioned in the corner of his mouth. They had managed to cut the cancer out of his throat but he had been younger and stronger then. Now, with the growths they had missed multiplying and securing a daily greater hold within his living tissue, he knew himself to be dying and would note the almost daily deterioration in his condition.

He pushed the tube out of the way with his tongue. 'You have not yet told me why you require the plans, Landgravine,' he persisted.

'Because they are a refinement of da Dondi's original, reworked as they were by some of the finest occult scientists in the Third Reich. You know that yourself, Standartenführer Volker. What you may not know is that Ugo da Dondi was in many ways the genius ahead of his time which he always claimed himself to be. In that machine he anticipated the modern understanding of the relationship between time and matter and reality. He found a way to gain access to that third reality in which the powers of Thule which I serve exist. That is why, on two widely separated occasions, the invocation of Pudendagora almost succeeded, and would have succeeded if not for the interference of the Keeper.'

'So you wish to attempt a third invocation?'

'More than that, Volker. My intentions go beyond the summoning of a single Thulean power. At Fortstown, in a moment of weakness brought on by the sight of one I loved long ago, I betrayed Pudendagora. Had the invocation been successful I would be more than simply dead today. That moment cost me both the trust of Pudendagora and, very nearly, my life. It will not happen again. It must not. Because of it I must make a terrible reparation. If I simply summon Pudendagora again he will chastise me for my failure at Fortstown in ways you would not wish to imagine. In order to avoid that I must effect his release, but I must do it either at the same time or later than I release the other powers of Thule. With their gratitude assured, and I do know how to assure it, I shall become their vice-regent upon this planet, and those who serve me will both share and enjoy my power as a result. You see, Volker, I do know how to be grateful.

'The machine, itself,' she continued, 'is the key which provides access to those powers. But I do not intend to build it myself. My informant, the one who told me of Speed's interest, which was how I knew to send you, Hahn, together with your late assistant, for the plans, also told me that Speed is having the machine constructed by one of the few men in the world who could refine it for the task I have in mind.'

'Then why did you want me to steal the plans in the first place,

Lady Erzebet?' Ylena asked, puzzled. 'If you're not going to use them they can have little purpose for you. And that ritual last night was without any kind of purpose whatsoever . . .'

Erzebet smiled. Her expression, mellowed by her lunch and her satisfaction with the progress of her operation, was relaxed and inviting. Her beauty, together with that invitation, brought stirrings in the flesh of the two men present. It also made Ylena wonder why she had never previously contemplated a lesbian relationship, such was its power.

Because she's too dangerous, hissed a voice inside her. Lovely, yes. But more deadly than a spitting cobra.

'Because the plans contain the keyword to whatever Faber and the others are planning,' Erzebet replied. 'No, I do not want to use them. But your friend Volker, here, as is often the case with the aged, and the sick, and let us not forget that he is both, has a deficient memory. Whilst he was responsible for the modified Nazi version of da Dondi's plans, he was unable to recall the codename given to the project which might have originated from them, had it not been for the diversion of resources resulting from the siege of Stalingrad. The codename, in itself, means nothing, but my informant told me that it had been used as the designation for the intelligence operation for which the machine is being constructed. He had not seen the plans in their original form, however, as Commander Speed had them redrafted and retained the originals in his own keeping. And the redraft did not bear a copy of the original Deutsches Ahnenerbe label. So, you see? It was only by obtaining those plans that I could see for myself what the codename is.'

She surveyed the others at the table triumphantly. 'Now that I have seen that label and know the codeword,' she added, 'I begin to realize that I should have known it all along. And, knowing it, I may now call upon other informants so that I can learn when and how it will be used.'

'What is the codeword?' Ylena asked, curious in spite of her caution.

'*Rückfahrkarte*,' Erzebet told her.

Volker frowned. 'Return ticket?' he translated. 'But . . . return to where?'

Erzebet beamed at him. 'To Thule, Standartenführer Volker,' she replied. 'Where else?'

Ptythonius von Meersburg was unsmiling as he sat in the ice-cavern. Before him the skyfires hovered and hummed, awaiting his assessment of the information they had brought him.

Yet that wasn't the only reason for the Keeper's grim expression.

He moved his position upon the chair slightly and reviewed the pulsing lights. 'Is there any amongst you who doubts or fails to understand my intentions?' he asked.

NO, KEEPER.

'Is there any who wishes to question me as to the methods to be employed?'

NO, KEEPER.

He bowed his head. No questions, simply the obedience he had always received from the skyfires, until comparatively recently.

Ptythonius hadn't entirely accepted Erzebet's emotional surrender to him at Fortstown. It had been too easy, too complete. Oh, she had meant it. He believed that much. Reviewing his own feelings he was very much aware that he had been tempted to a similar capitulation himself, a capitulation which would have permitted Pudendagora's unrestricted entry into the realms of man to prey upon them and summon his disgusting peers. No, Erzebet had acted genuinely, but her actions were only temporary.

Sooner or later she would wish to atone for her surrender and the failure of negative Thule which it had entailed. And there was, Ptythonius knew, only one way in which she could do that.

She had to restore the negatives to the world man inhabited, no matter what the cost.

Doubtless the entities were already in some kind of tenuous contact with her, directing her actions to the end of their liberation. The negatives were both subtle and powerful, working through their human servants with subliminal prompts and sleep-shrouded whisperings. They chose well and directed powerfully, as they had always done. Even Caillchen Mac Eamon, all those centuries before, had been told which scroll and figurine to take by them. He might have believed the choice to be random, but they had led him to the ice-cavern and then they had led him to the scroll.

And a skyfire had watched as he had taken the scroll and the monkey. A skyfire had permitted his service to the negatives.

So, Erzebet had recovered Caillchen's skull and the figurine. She also had the Deutsches Ahnenerbe plans for da Dondi's machine. That would tell her the codename for Faber's operation and enable her to interfere with the spook's plans. It had taken a great deal of careful manipulation to ensure the interest of MI6 and arrange for joint British and American funding for such a speculative, from their point of view, venture. The entire annual Secrets Vote for the year by the British Government had only been £120 million, officially. That had to cover GCHQ's staff of nearly 11,000, increasingly sophisticated and expensive equipment, MI5 and 6's 3000 employees and all required peacetime operations. The MI6 slice of the cake was comparatively minute, though much of the £16 million increase over last year was to fund ongoing operations in the Gulf. Yet somehow the arrangements had been made, complicated as they were by the American involvement which required that the Director General of MI6 should officially work through the Foreign Secretary's office.

The total cost of Operation Return Ticket was likely to be in excess of £8 million, most of which was going into the hardware. Decommissioning and refitting a Tenacity class patrol vessel didn't come cheap. The navy did nothing on the cheap, especially when the Senior Service had been told what to do by the spooks in Century House. Edvard duClausky didn't come cheap either. Nor did his machine. And sub-elemental Thulium was hardly one of the standard off-the-shelf pre-processed nuclear fuels, even if duClausky 'just happen to have bit.' All that really came cheap, Ptythonius reflected wryly, was his reluctant amanuensis, Robert Ferrow.

Additionally, of course, Erzebet von Bamberg had her own resources, which would also be put into Operation Return Ticket. Whilst they were more likely to be occult rather than financial, she would still have to spend a considerable amount from her secret funds. Certainly, if she succeeded, money would become a useless commodity in the restored nightmare world of negative Thule, a world where man would be simply the food and the amusement of the creatures Erzebet wanted to release.

He knew that his act of faith was going to cost him his existence as the Keeper. He also knew that, were it to fail, he would be the last to hold that office, that the war of the two Thules would resume, eventually consuming all life on this planet. And it could fail. Nothing was guaranteed. Nothing at all.

Especially now.

Ptythonius studied the skyfires carefully as they waited before him, his eyes darting from light to light. Counting, again and again.

There was no mistake. He had called them and they had come. Six of them. Six out of seven.

One missing.

Ferrow's presence was sufficient to calm Elspeth's immediate fears. He introduced the others and explained Johannes away by the funny-looking-dog routine. Gunndner and duClausky were treated to her smile and, as expected, were enchanted by it. Only Faber refused to respond warmly.

She was shown into the mess and made comfortable with a cup of duClausky's coffee, her alarm at his appearance quickly fading as she sensed an extremely clever and basically kind human being beneath the disfigured exterior. Whilst the others waited, Faber left the bunker via the farm buildings and called upon Speed by the front door, eventually rousing him from the effects of the gin. Mrs Clarke was out so the old man struggled through the alcohol and medication to admit the spook himself.

'You know that niece of yours is downstairs?' Faber snarled.

'Elspeth? Clever girl, eh?' Speed grinned, masking his discomfort.

'Clever, my arse! What the hell do you think you're playing at, Charlie?'

'Come now, Johnnie me boy. You don't know her like I do. Once she gets her teeth into a thing she don't stop until they meet in the middle.'

Faber's eyes narrowed. 'How much have you told her?' he demanded.

'Only about the bunker and the machine. If you'd kept Edvard in coffee properly she'd not have had occasion to worry that much out of me.'

Deflect the attack back on to the attacker. Your small flaw caused my bloody great big one. Think about that and maybe you'll get civil again.

Slowly Faber agreed. 'You all right now?' he enquired, more gently.

Speed shrugged. 'Few aches here 'n' there. Be right as rain in a few hours.'

'OK. Can you make your way down to the bunker when you're ready? I've got some shopping to do for the professor. Know any pet shops round here?'

Speed's eyes brightened. 'We're ready to test?'

'We will be, once I get duClausky's bunny-wunny.'

'Then we're set to go . . .'

'Hold on, Charlie. That gizmo could still have bugs to be ironed out. We're only at the test stage. I'm not going to action reberthing of P298 just yet. So duClausky splits up a rabbit. That doesn't mean he can split up a 160-ton patrol boat. The only thing I know so far that'll do that is an Exocet or something similar. Still, if the professor's cocked it that thing could well act like a nuclear bomb and do the job instead. Anyway, pet shop?'

'One on the market square. That's the easiest one for you to find.'

Faber nodded and turned to leave. At the door he looked back. 'Sorry I snapped, Charlie,' he apologized. 'It's good to see you up and about again, OK?'

He found the pet shop easily and bought a couple of Netherland Dwarfs. When he returned to the bunker Speed was already down there, sitting with Elspeth and Ferrow in the mess and listening to the first substantiated account he had heard of his niece's part in the Wegrimham affair. Faber went straight to the laboratory and deposited the rabbits in their wire cages on one of the work-surfaces. 'Reckon they'll do, Professor?' he asked.

DuClausky glanced up from the machine and briefly surveyed the caged animals. 'They do good,' he answered, then returned to the adjustments he was making to the timing mechanism with Nils Gunndner's help. Close by Johannes was apparently asleep.

The *glebula* had been instructed to remain unobtrusive whenever his Magister wasn't present and to keep Ferrow informed whenever practicable. Whilst Ferrow might be under orders to cooperate with Faber and the others, he still had his doubts about exactly what they hoped to achieve. The explanation promised from Commander Speed wasn't forthcoming, and he suspected that this had something to do with Elspeth's uninvited presence.

Faber himself had been working on that. It would be inadvisable to contemplate anything too drastic as he still needed Speed's cooperation. After all, he was no seaman, and someone had to captain the P298 once Operation Return Ticket was under way. There were, however, resources for him to draw upon which were denied to lesser mortals. Spooks, like criminals, were only answerable to the law if they got caught. Even if they did get caught there were ways of not coming to trial, in the national interest, naturally. And, to his credit, the course of action he eventually decided upon, whilst not exactly legal, wasn't particularly harmful either.

He joined the others in the mess and poured himself some coffee. Noticing that Elspeth's cup was empty he gallantly pressed another cup on her. Ferrow noted that the action was out of character but said nothing, neither then nor when Elspeth apparently fell asleep some minutes later.

'It's all right, Charlie,' Faber assured her uncle. 'Just a mild sedative. I've some people coming up with a private ambulance. They'll hold her in a private clinic for a couple of days. That's all. Good food and a few little pills to stop her worrying. Just until we're clear.'

Speed's threatening anger subsided. In his way Faber had acted correctly. Elspeth's presence was neither desirable nor necessary and the MI6 man had found the best of several far from ideal solutions. Ferrow's innate distrust of Faber left him doubtful, but he held his peace.

'C'mon, Bob,' Faber began, suddenly familiar. 'Let's get her upstairs and pack her things. The ambulance'll be here in about half an hour. Charlie, you go up ahead and make sure that bloody housekeeper of yours is out of the way.'

Speed shook his head. 'No need,' he answered. 'She's off until tonight. Don't think m'niece was exactly her cup of tea, y'know.'

Ferrow managed a smile. Despite Elspeth's attractive exterior he knew exactly what the commander meant.

With Elspeth safely sedated and on her way to a private medical facility near Harrow which was funded out of the Secret Vote, Faber and the policeman returned to the bunker. As a courtesy, Ferrow had checked Elspeth's address book and phoned Noel Jorisund, so that he could visit or vanish as he chose.

A beaming Edvard duClausky was awaiting them as they came back through the washroom. Without further ado he announced: 'Test set up. We try machine now, yes?'

Ferrow assisted Commander Speed, still a little unsteady on his legs, along the passage to the laboratory. He felt a strong liking for the old man, despite the briefness of their acquaintance, as he had done for Professor duClausky.

A lead crystal case had been positioned beside the laser assembly. Inside, one of the rabbits was nibbling a fragment of lettuce. The other, in its cage, was ignoring Johannes' hungry glances.

'Thulium in,' duClausky announced. 'Rabbit ready. We go, yes?'

Faber nodded. 'We go, Professor. Do we need goggles or anything?'

The nuclear physicist shook his head. 'No light. No radiation. All safe for bunny and safe for us. We next,' he added grimly, 'remember?'

'All of us?' Nils Gunndner asked nervously.

'All of us,' Faber confirmed. 'We all have a part to play. Yours, like the professor's, is to make sure that the equipment you've built between you works when it has to.'

'Enough chat. We go. Now, watch bunny.'

DuClausky tapped an instruction into the computer console. It flashed briefly on to the screen and was almost instantly replaced with a series of equations and formulae in rapid succession. The professor nodded, then pressed another combination of keys.

'Watch bunny,' he repeated.

They watched. The laser-like projection began to sweep the interior of the crystal case as if scanning the lines on a television screen. Once it had built up a series of faintly luminous, semi-visible lines horizontally across the interior of the crystal it began to criss-cross them with verticals.

'I slow this down so you understand,' duClausky told them. 'It work almost instant when we go.'

Ferrow felt beads of perspiration break out upon his forehead. When *we* go? he asked himself. Go where? Go why? All I know so far is the *how*, and that's enough to scare the shit out of me!

Johannes diverted his gaze from the other rabbit. I can monitor this for you, Magister, he mentioned casually.

Then why the fuck didn't you say so before? Ferrow snapped mentally. For Christ's sake do that small thing, will you?

The rabbit in the case continued to nibble its lettuce with surprising nonchalance.

Then it split.

The splitting wasn't the ghastly, messy business that was implied from the use of the term. No blood. No rabbit guts. Simply a multiplication of images that persisted briefly before fading, like the original creature, altogether. The lead crystal case was suddenly empty.

'You see?' duClausky grinned.

Faber assented. 'I see,' he answered. 'What I don't do is understand. Where the hell is it?'

'Elsewhere. Rabbit enter other reality. Third reality. Now I return it, yes?'

'You can bring it back?' Ferrow asked, incredulous.

The professor nodded. 'I bring it back. You see it again. No harm.'

He punched a code into the console. The multiplication of images flashed back inside the case, then solidified into the original, still munching, rabbit.

DuClausky removed the heavy case with Nils Gunndner's help, then picked up the animal, completely unharmed. 'You see?' he announced. 'What bunny do, *we* do.'

That *we* again. I'm going to take some convincing, Johannes.

A simple redistribution from physical to alterjective dimensions, Magister. I assure you that it appeared much more drastic than it actually was. The creature is totally unaffected and still quite edible.

But is it whatever passes for sane in a rabbit?

It is.

Hey, just hold it a minute, Ferrow ordered. I thought you could only tap into my mind. What's with this link to duClausky's rabbit?

Yours is the only human mind I can penetrate, Magister, came the reply. Animal minds are much easier. That is how I was able to monitor the creature's progress and condition.

'OK, so where did the bloody thing go?' Faber demanded.

'Nowhere. It remain here,' the professor answered.

'I thought the whole point of that machine was to get it into the third reality?'

'That is correct, friend John. But third reality is all around us. Only our limited perceptions prevent us acknowledging its presence. Machine simply alter our perceptions by adapting our molecular vibrations. Or attuning, I rather say.'

'And that will happen to us?' Nils Gunndner enquired. 'We'll still be ourselves?'

'Indeed. We still be us as bunny is still bunny, there as here. Yet we function in third reality, not here. We function where need is greater.'

Ferrow studied his companions closely. 'I think it's about time someone told me what's really going on. Commander?' he asked, settling on Speed.

'Y'mean they haven't told you yet?'

'We thought it would come better from you, Charlie,' Faber said. 'And I reckon Nils could do with hearing it again as well.'

'It would help,' Gunndner told him. 'Especially now I see what that machine can do.'

'Right, m'lads. Let's retire to the mess and I'll spell out Operation Return Ticket to you both. Professor,' he added, shaking hands with duClausky, 'you've done a remarkable job. Hasn't he, John?'

'Exactly what we need, Charlie.'

'You'll give the reberthing order for the P298 then?'

'As soon as I can get to a phone. Let's get this show on the road before that von Bamberg woman can find out what we're up to.'

Whilst Faber phoned through to Century House on an unlisted number, Ferrow and Nils Gunndner listened to Commander Speed's explanation.

'You've both read the account of Fallenberg's voyage?' the commander enquired.

They nodded. 'But how does it fit in with that machine?' Ferrow asked.

'Nothing simpler to tell, Robert m'boy. We're going to recreate it. I've been fascinated by Fallenberg for many years. The machine, as far as I'm concerned, is what'll make the difference between the two expeditions. And its potential as a weapon was sufficient to get the Whitehall boys interested. Just think of it. Enemies dispersed from the battlefield without a shot fired in anger. Brought back when they can be effectively contained. Whatever they say, the next war'll be conventional, not nuclear. And the third reality is what'll win it for us.'

'I still don't see how Fallenberg and the machine fit together.'

'T'do that we have to go back to the last thing Fallenberg was able to tell us.'

'The log of the *Harfanger*?'

Speed grinned and shook his head. 'A phrase in Swedish scrawled on a chart spread out in front of him. Translates into three words of English, don't y'know?'

'No, I don't know, Commander. What did he write?'

'*The third reality*, Inspector Ferrow. That's the legacy of Martin Fallenberg.'

Ferrow permitted himself a low whistle. Now it was starting to make sense. He still had some questions, though.

'So where does Faber come into it?'

Speed shrugged. 'Needed funds for the trip and to make the contraption. Best place I know is H M's Government. Contacted duClausky and promised them a new kind of weapon, so they laid on the boodle. Faber's officially in control.'

'And the ship? This P298 or whatever you call it?'

'Sea trials prior to land ops, m'boy. All very hush-hush. Got ourselves a Tenacity Class P B, y'know. Good fast vessel. Stay out eight or nine days at a good rate of knots if we have to.'

'So that's how you're doing it. Now, Faber mentioned Erzebet von Bamberg. How does she fit into this?'

'Don't know, m'self. Still, where there's ops there's spies, don't y'know?'

Visitors to Century House are not encouraged to penetrate far beyond the reception area. Usually it takes a ministerial pass to even receive serious consideration from the security station in the lobby, let alone get as far as one of the lifts and actually gain access to one of the twenty floors above ground and the others underneath. Yet sometimes it can be done.

A great deal depends upon the determination and technique of the visitor. This particular day, late in the afternoon with many of the civil servants already on their way home, the lobby was quiet and deserted, except for the duty staff. The security station was being manned by 347192 Willis, Richard H., Sergeant, Royal Marine Commando, and his corporal, 351143 Baxter, Jeremy R. (Jake), both of whom were involved in tallying the entry/exit log for the day and wishing that this particular piece of bureaucracy could be reassigned to the central computer.

The *stutter* in the sliding door mechanism, opening the main entrance a few inches before reclosing it, despite nobody going anywhere near the detector pads, went unnoticed. Sergeant Willis clattered his clip-board down onto the counter and stretched. His eyes swept the lobby and focused on the lift indicator lights. Coming down, he remarked mentally. Another one on the way out.

He glanced at his watch. The Director General was in today, so it could be the man himself. Unlikely, with no car waiting outside, but you never knew.

'Shape up, Jake,' he muttered. 'Might be the D G.'

Jake Baxter stood up and prepared to snap to attention, a courtesy that he was usually loath to bestow upon civilians. As an organization, MI6 officially didn't exist during peacetime. Neither did its personnel hold military rank, unless they had a service background which entitled them to retain a courtesy title. The Director General, though, was something else.

The lift settled and the doors opened, showing no-one inside. Both Willis and Baxter registered faint concern. There was, after all, no-one in the lobby who could have called the lift, was there?

'Watch that thing, Jake,' Willis ordered, taking a service automatic from a drawer beneath the counter. 'If there's a joker down here, I'll find the bastard.' He said this quite loudly, hoping to use the threat to flush any intruder out into the open, despite the fact that there was positively nowhere that anyone could be hiding.

He stepped out from behind the security station whilst Baxter watched the lift through narrowed eyes. With mechanical precision the doors began to close. As only an inch or so of lit interior remained visible, the corporal voiced an inarticulate cry.

Sergeant Willis turned sharply towards the lift, both hands holding the automatic, knees slightly bent, feet separate. The doors were now completely closed and a faint whirr from the mechanism, together with the indicator panel lights above, showed that it was now ascending again.

'What the hell?' Willis asked, relaxing and staring at his corporal. 'You see something, Jake?'

Baxter was sitting bolt upright in his chair, his hands gripping the arms with a strength which made his knuckles whiten. 'I . . . I thought . . . when the doors were closing, you know, like an arc.'

Willis put the gun away. 'No, I don't know. *What* like an arc?'

The corporal relaxed and shrugged. 'Probably looking too hard, Sarge. I thought I saw a sort of blue spark pass between the doors . . .'

They watched the indicator panel until the light stopped. Willis flipped over pages of an internal directory. 'Department 7,' he said aloud. 'Coughlin, Short and Faber's people.' He checked the names in the directory against the entry/exit log. Coughlin and Short had gone for the day, as had their staff. Faber's people had also left, and Faber himself was out of the office for a while anyway. So Department 7 was deserted. Officially.

He picked up an internal phone and dialled a two-digit number. 'Security mess?' he began. 'This is Willis. Two men to Department 7 for a check. And use the stairs. The lift could be playing up.' He put the phone down and turned back to Baxter. 'Could just be some kind of shorting out if you saw it sparking, Jake. Doesn't hurt to be sure, though.'

They settled back to wait. Less than two minutes later the phone rang and Sergeant Willis answered it, identifying himself. He listened for a moment, then replaced the receiver.

'The lads are up there now,' he said. 'Seven's in darkness and looks deserted, but they're sweeping it anyway.'

A few minutes later the phone rang again. Willis said: 'O K. Get the master key from the mess and stick it back in the files. Then make out the standard report on an S13A.'

He put the phone down and grinned at Jake Baxter. 'No problems,' he smiled. "Cept for young Jenny Crashaw in the morning. Looks like she was in such a hurry to get home she left an MoD Q-Directive file out. Silly kid'll get her arse paddled for that.'

Baxter frowned. 'Jenny? That's not like her. She's supposed to be one of the up-and-comers. Good attention to detail.'

Willis shrugged. 'The lads found it on her desk, Jake. And it was open. Doesn't sound like attention to detail to me. Hey, that lift's coming down again.'

It was. It stopped at the ground floor and the doors slid back. The light inside it wasn't the standard electric yellow, though.

It was blue.

SECURITY MEMORANDUM 256/3/11–Q  Date: 13.7.88

From: Chief Artificer, Royal Naval Dockyard, Chatham.
To: Department 7, MI6, Century House. Attn. JG Faber.

Ref: Received Request A3A5 dated 17.9.87.

In accordance with the Berthing Order issued under codename
RETURN TICKET and delivered by messenger this date I am
to advise you that P298 decommissioned Tenacity Class patrol
vessel is to ETA 0400 hrs HMS Scrabster 15.7.88.
I anticipate receipt of your A3A5 Completion Notice at your
earliest convenience.

Ylena couldn't sleep. It wasn't, she decided, simply the sound of Volker's stertorous breathing in the next room that was keeping her awake. It was something more insistent and, under the circumstances and considering her background, disturbingly worrying. There was a word for what she felt, but it was a word she hesitated to voice in case it gave strength to what it described. After all, she'd seen more powerful magics than that in this house at Orford.

The word was *doubt*.

Perhaps she might have been better able to dismiss her fears if she'd liked Erzebet von Bamberg better. Knowing you're working for a beautiful, deadly creature may have a certain fascination, but it's the fascination of the prey in the presence of the creature about to devour it.

She kept telling herself that the new Reich was important, was the purpose to which her life had been dedicated from the cradle. She even added that Erzebet embodied the most tangible hope of achieving that Reich in the spirit of its cruelly suppressed and dismembered predecessor. Yet men like Volker treated human life too casually, and women like Erzebet were even more cavalier about both the living and the dead. About those who stood in their way. And about those who served them, once their usefulness was ended.

That wasn't what the Fourth Reich should be. It should be an ennoblement of the Aryan race, an ennoblement which would point the way to a harmonious and glorious future. But from the few details she had been able to gather of Erzebet's intentions, the future was to be entirely different, with the entire population of the planet, not simply the *untermenschen*, subservient to the Thulean powers which Erzebet intended to release.

No, that wasn't the role she had foreseen for her persecuted people. Perhaps Hitler had been mad, but he had not betrayed the German people until the overwhelming strain of defeat inspired him towards the great myth of the Götterdämmerung. This one, however, this Erzebet von Bamberg, was starting where the Führer had left off, with fewer shreds of sanity remaining and the enslavement of all mankind as her purpose, including those who would help to build the Fourth Reich for her.

Those who betray her will die, Ylena thought. And even those who *could* betray her as well.

That means me.

When this is over I'm dead.

Ylena shuddered and pulled the bedclothes tighter over her body. Normality had long since crumbled away, being replaced with this nightmare servitude for which the only possible reward was death. And the nightmare kept deepening, increasing in intensity with every day that passed, every day which brought them nearer to the resolution Erzebet sought, the resolution which would finally release the nightmare horrors of Thule into the dimensions of mankind.

Sleep wouldn't come. Cold sweat left her limbs and body sticking to her nightdress. A couple of Volker's painkillers might make her drowsy, but a drink would work better, Ylena decided.

She threw back the covers and, not bothering with a dressing-gown, slipped out of her room and past the sleeping Volker. She thought briefly of losing herself in the powerful arms of the handsome Karsten, but she knew she'd find neither satisfaction nor an ally in one who had slept with Erzebet von Bamberg. Oh, Ylena was good. Ylena was very good, both in bed and out of it, but she couldn't compete with her ageless mistress, and the possibility of Karsten's rejection of her advances was a torment she wasn't prepared to add to her present despair. Besides, he'd probably be sweating under Erzebet even as she considered the possibility. Somehow she couldn't see the Landgravine in the missionary position. Rather she was the Whore of Babylon, riding whatever beast would slide between her thighs until the creature screamed with ecstasy or exhaustion.

She opened Volker's door and looked out. The hall was in darkness but a glimmer of light showed between the almost closed doors of the drawing-room opposite. A shaft of moonlight through a tiny window caught the face of a grandmother clock close by. The time was a little after three in the morning.

And here she was, in the middle of the night, seeing a light still burning?

Ylena crept across the hall in her bare feet. Her hair was wild and tangled with her thrashing about on the camp bed, adding to rather than detracting from her natural beauty. Her lips were slightly parted as she breathed silently through her mouth, wishing that she'd opened Volker's door more quietly. Carefully, stealthily, her bladder suddenly prickling with a hitherto unsuspected need, she approached the drawing-room doors and peered inside.

Erzebet, naked, was sprawled upon a sofa, displaying those charms which should have atrophied centuries before. She was speaking softly, coaxingly, staring across the room towards the curtained windows. Ylena struggled to follow the line of her vision, to discover to whom she could be speaking. It couldn't be Karsten. She was cajoling in her tone, in her expression, inviting in her posture. Karsten wouldn't have needing persuading. Not like that. Yet that only left Volker, and Volker was struggling to live another day in the room she'd just left.

With infinite caution she opened the doors a fraction more. Then she looked. Her right hand flew to her mouth, her teeth biting hard onto the knuckles to prevent herself from crying out. Erzebet, she saw, was alone in the room.

In human terms.

Ylena might have expected to see the creature which Erzebet had called a night-mouse. More probably she would have anticipated the presence of some as yet unknown male assistant. Yet what she actually saw was neither.

Opposite Erzebet, hovering some four feet from the floor, was a tiny globe of blue light about the size of a golf-ball. It seemed to pulse, to vibrate, to be speaking in some fashion to its appreciative mistress, whose hand was trembling towards her exposed sexual orifice.

The fingers sought and found the clitoris, teasing it out like a *langue du chat*, gently rubbing until it moistened and threatened like a tiny penis.

The blue light buzzed. It began to expand and contract. It vibrated, wavered, but held its position.

Ylena bit deeper.

'You don't want your reward?' Erzebet whispered. 'Is life, then, so very different in the Kingdom of the Keeper? Are you so ethereal as to have no desires? But that is sad, my little skyfire. So sad. Let me teach you about the desires of humans. Let me show you what even humans of the same sex may aspire to. Join me, Ylena.'

Of their own volition the doors swung open, leaving the surprised Ylena Hahn standing exposed in the sudden flood of light from the drawing-room. There was nowhere to flee to, and no time for her to flee even if there had been somewhere. With limbs that denied her resistance, helpless and exposed, she found herself walking towards Erzebet.

'There's a good girl,' Erzebet whispered. 'A pretty girl. A *loving* girl.'

Ylena's mind raced back to that moment after lunch when she had wondered about just such a moment as she was now experiencing. Perhaps Erzebet wasn't going to kill her. Perhaps Erzebet needed more love than she could derive from any man. Perhaps there was a way to stay alive, to serve, to lose herself in a service which was both life and worship. Or, at least, a means of self-preservation.

'Take off your nightdress, my dear,' Erzebet coaxed, her eyes darting from Ylena to the skyfire. 'That's it. Let it fall. Step out of it. My, but you have such fine breasts. Doesn't she have fine breasts? Small, perhaps, but so firm, so jutting. And do you see, little skyfire, how her nipples are standing up for me? You've never been with another woman, have you, my Ylena? You shall now. You will show our guest the pleasure you are experiencing for the first time. That's it. Closer. Come closer.'

Her free hand reached out, the fingers flickering about Ylena's pubic bush, parting the labia, exploring. Ylena thrilled with a sudden and unnatural pleasure, suddenly more vulnerable yet more alive than she had ever felt before.

Alive, she reasoned afterwards. That's the keyword. Alive. I have to stay alive.

Erzebet drew the girl towards her, kissing those parts of her body which came closest in the approach. Her tongue lingered over each breast before reaching up and forcing its way into her mouth, exploring her teeth, seeking her own tongue's hypnotized response.

Their mouths slipped wetly apart. 'My Ylena,' Erzebet whispered, feeling the response.

They clung together, fingers moving, passion mounting. They slipped and slithered like one amorphous, erotic creation, finding a unity Ylena could never have even suspected. It intoxicated and sickened her at the same time, leaving her helpless and yielding in the predatory grasp of her mistress. She felt the strength of Erzebet's manipulations and the Landgravine's eager response to her own.

The skyfire pulsed. It reached out, expanding, to embrace them both.

Ptythonius von Meersburg shuddered.

They lay languidly together, bathed in an afterglow which was more than their own individual efforts could have achieved. Around them the blue light wavered for an instant, then was gone.

Ylena opened her eyes and looked at Erzebet. Both their expressions showed echoes of the pleasure they had found together, a pleasure that mere men could never have supplied. Slowly Erzebet drew away and rose to her feet, crossing to a table beside the door. From a drawer she took a broomhandled Mauser and screwed a silencer to the muzzle. Then she turned back towards Ylena, holding the automatic.

'A broomhandle is for house-cleaning,' she smirked. 'Our moment has passed, little girl. Our audience has tasted the joys of our flesh and departed. Now we must return to business.'

Ylena's eyes widened in terror. Erzebet raised the gun, sighted along the barrel and pulled the trigger.

The Mauser clicked, emptily.

'Did you think I would surrender your pleasures so easily?' Erzebet demanded. 'This isn't for you, my Ylena. This is for your master.'

She reached into the drawer and pushed a full clip from the metal loader into the magazine. Pulling back on the slide she fed the first round into the breech. 'Come with me, love-child,' she ordered.

Ylena, her limbs tingling, fear and pleasure suffusing every inch of her being, followed Erzebet across the hall and into Volker's room. She stood in the doorway as her lover of a few moments before emptied the contents of the automatic into the sleeping Nazi. The weapon chugged, its barrel spitting flame, as the bullets did their deadly work.

Erzebet allowed the empty weapon to slip from her fingers. Then she turned.

'He was dying anyway,' she announced. 'You, on the other hand, have only just begun to live. Now, come here and listen to me.'

She took Ylena's hand with the same fingers which had both explored their intimacy and held the gun within the past few minutes, leading her to the edge of the bloodstained bed and seating her there. Ylena shuddered at the touch, though whether with pleasure or revulsion she was too confused to know.

'You want to know why I killed Volker,' Erzebet began, stating rather than asking the question. 'The answer is that his usefulness, as you might have suspected, was at an end. His disabilities were not in his favour, either. It takes two lives, his and yours, to preserve his one. That, my lovely child, is inefficient in our present circumstances.

'Doubtless you're wondering why Karsten didn't come running at the sound of the shots. Silenced though they were, they will still have echoed about the house at this still time of night. The answer is simply that Karsten isn't here. There are so many details to be arranged, Ylena . . .'

She broke off, still holding Ylena's hand, and stared vacantly at the riddled bedclothes, red stains spreading across them, which shrouded the unfortunate Volker's body. Her features began to crease with strain, to develop unsuspected lines more appropriate to her real age. Her mouth hung slightly open, the lower lip quivering, and a single tear developed at the corner of her left eye.

In that moment Ylena came closer to understanding Erzebet von Bamberg than she had ever done before or would ever do again. Erzebet served, and her life was dedicated to that service alone. There was so little time she could permit herself for ordinary human emotions, for genuine love, or hatred, or even pity. By her own admission she had surrendered once to an old love, and must now make a dreadful reparation for that surrender.

Ylena reached up and took Erzebet's other hand. 'Do you want to tell me about it?' she asked gently.

Erzebet sighed and looked down. 'Do you know what the skyfire is?'

Ylena shook her head, her eyes wide and puzzled.

'The skyfires are the servants of the Keeper, my old lover and my greatest adversary. There are seven of them all together, embodiments of the essence of the old powers of positive Thule. Seven blue lights, all the same. And yet they are not all the same, though they are impossible to tell apart. One of them, the one you saw a few moments ago, has decided that the time has come for the Keeper to be replaced. Not by another Keeper as such, but by someone, or something, which will reconcile the warring factions instead of simply maintaining a balance between them.'

'You mean . . . that blue thing . . .'

'. . . is on our side, Ylena. By now the Keeper must know he is being betrayed, but he will not know by which of the skyfires. They may not agree with the actions of this one, but they will support its right to those actions. You see, my old love Ptythonius is practically helpless, for whilst he is their master they are also, in their own way, his masters. They created the office of Keeper thousands and thousands of years ago. They taught the Keepers all they knew. But this one, at least, has grown tired.'

'And the night-mouse?'

Erzebet shrugged. 'The night-mouse is as a rat before a python when compared to the skyfire. A thousand night-mice could only obey if a single skyfire ordered them to drown themselves. Even the Keeper would be helpless if the seven turned against him.'

'Will they do that, Lady Erzebet?'

'Turn against him? Perhaps. One already has . . .'

She dropped Ylena's hands and half-turned away. For a moment there was only silence and death in the room. When she looked back there were fresh tears in her eyes.

'I have to beat him, Ylena,' Erzebet whispered. 'I have to defeat him to preserve myself. I may even have to kill him. But I don't want that, Ylena. I don't seek his death. How could I? I've loved him for centuries. I could love him for centuries yet unborn. I want to spend whatever time remains to me in his arms, feeling the warmth of his love enfolding me. I need him, whatever his name, be he Johannes Faust or Ptythonius von Meersburg. I love him . . .'

She wiped her eyes on the backs of her hands and forced a smile. 'I've never spoken to a living soul like this, Ylena,' she continued. 'I've never been able to before. It's only now, now that I know the end is approaching, now that I can feel my final victory, that I can confess the price I may have to pay for it.

'So, now perhaps you know why I take my pleasure so ruthlessly, why I snatch these moments out of whatever time I can make for them. You won't want to finish the night here, Ylena. Not with that . . .' she gestured towards Volker's corpse. 'Come with me. Spend this night with Erzebet von Bamberg.'

She stretched out her hand to the seated girl. 'Please?' she asked. 'I've been alone so long, Ylena. Be with me this once. My nights are so dark, so lonely. No man has ever stood comparison with Ptythonius for long.'

# PART THREE

## Acts of Faith

'One last test and then we all at go,' duClausky announced.

The others looked doubtfully at one another. 'The other rabbit?' Nils Gunndner asked.

DuClausky shook his head. 'This time man,' he replied. 'I make calculations as to power increase, bunny to man. I need to check accuracy. Man go this time, yes?'

'You mean I gave the berthing order and you're not ready?' Faber scowled.

The physicist shrugged. 'We ready. Machine work. Only check on calibrations remain. That what I do now.'

Ferrow felt his legs weaken. Oh, shit, he thought. This means me. He forced a grin. 'OK, Professor. Let's get this show on the road.'

'You be OK, friend Robert. You all right. Wait and see.'

'Not too long on the waiting, if you don't mind,' Ferrow answered. Then, mentally: If I don't come back, Johannes, for better or for worse you find Ptythonius, get it? Find the Keeper. I don't know what all this has to do with him, but he's in it somewhere.'

You'll be back, Magister, Johannes assured him.

'Wish I had your confidence,' Ferrow replied aloud.

Nils Gunndner looked at him probingly. DuClausky simply said: 'Confidence proof of pudding. I confident you find pudding OK.'

You weren't talking to us, were you, Robert? Gunndner thought. You made a slip. You were communicating with the *glebula* mentally, as you have done all along. But for once you slipped up and did it out loud.

Johannes studied Gunndner's stance, read the lines across his brow, and knew.

Cylindrical sections of heavy crystal had enlarged the case used for the rabbit. Gunndner and duClausky removed all but the bottom section on the floor of the bunker. With a grin which was far from what he actually felt, Robert Ferrow stepped inside and waited whilst the others replaced the sections which enclosed him.

'On open sea we no need these,' duClausky explained. 'In bunker for test they essential. Contain and minimize effect of machine. You set, Robert?'

Ferrow gave him the thumbs up, reluctantly.

'Then we go. Fine man. Full speed this time.'

The laser snaked out its pattern faster than the eye could follow. One moment Ferrow was there, encased in crystal in the bunker. The next he was . . .

His ultimate expression, the one reserved for those moments *in extremis*, was 'fuck a duck.' Now he saw.

'Fuck a duck,' Ferrow breathed.

Nobody heard him. Nobody saw him. Yet he was still there. It was the others who had disappeared.

He looked out from the crystal prison he reasoned still enclosed him, although he couldn't see it, at the empty bunker. The work-surfaces had taken on a faint greenish hue and nothing was exactly the colour it had been before. Once in his youth he'd looked at things around him through the edge of a clear plastic ruler and seen how they took on tints of prismatic colour. Now it was as if he was doing the same thing. Reality was still there, but it had somehow tilted upon its axis, taking on subtly different colours and perspectives. Reality was apparent in everything he saw, yet it wasn't the same reality he'd grown up with. It was another, strange reality. Yet despite its initial peculiarity he knew that eventually, were he to remain where he was, he'd become used to it and work with it as he had done in his previous plane of existence. Oh, he'd be clumsy at first, as a child is clumsy and hesitant and falls over things when it is learning to walk, but that would pass. It was becoming more familiar with every passing second, if seconds were truly what they were . . .

Then, as suddenly as they had altered in the first place, his visual and sensory impressions altered back again. He was looking through the walls of the crystal surround, his mouth open with the gaping wonder of the shift. Faber and Gunndner and duClausky and Johannes and Speed were all there, smiling, nodding, congratulating one another. Even the *glebula* was panting, dog-like, and wagging its unearthly lack-of-tail.

You see, Magister? Johannes thought to him. I told you you'd be back.

DuClausky and Gunndner removed the casing. They all clustered around him. 'How was it?' Faber demanded.

Ferrow shook his head, as much to clear it as for any other reason. 'Like . . . being somewhere else,' he replied. 'It was all real enough, but somehow different. And none of you were there with me. It was as if you'd all ceased to exist . . .'

DuClausky beamed. 'But we *had*, friend Robert. We had ceased to exist. We were no longer a part of your reality, for you had entered the third reality. You had experienced alterjective reality. Yet we, for our part, were still only objective, and thus, as you put it, we had ceased to exist.'

'How d'you feel, m'boy?' Commander Speed demanded, his expression anxious.

Ferrow forced a conciliatory expression. 'A little confused,' he answered. 'If I'd been there longer I'd have got more used to it. But basically I'm the same now as I was before I went.' Anyone do anything unusual, Johannes? he inquired.

'So it's safe for the rest of us?' Nils Gunndner asked.

Not exactly, Magister, but this one knows how we communicate. I'm sure of that.

'Perfectly safe, I'd say.' He can hear us?

Not hear us, but he knows *how*. That makes him dangerous.

Come on, Johannes, the whole fucking shooting match is dangerous. *How* does this make Gunndner different?

I wish I knew, Magister. So much of this is beyond my experience.

'Right,' Faber announced. 'The truck'll be here in an hour or so. Let's get this box of tricks dismantled and ready for shipping. Bob, you come with me.'

He led Ferrow back along the corridor to the mess. There he unlocked a wall cupboard and took out two Skorpion 7.65mm machine pistols and two 20-round magazines for each.

'You've had firearms training, I expect?' Faber asked.

'Not with anything like this. Police training doesn't run to Czech machine pistols.'

Faber grinned. 'This is one of the wickedest weapons in the world, Bob. Forget everything you may have read about size of round not equating with stopping power. These buggers could fire a thousand rounds in a minute, if there wasn't a reducer built into the action. Here,' he added, reaching back into the cupboard after he'd handed Ferrow the Skorpion and two mags, 'you'd better have one of these as well.'

He tossed over a silencer which Ferrow screwed to the end of the barrel before checking the safety and loading a magazine into the weapon in front of the trigger-guard.

'So what're we going to need these for?' Ferrow demanded.

Faber shrugged. 'You never know. It's a bit better than riding shotgun when we accompany duClausky's machine, though.'

'Riding shotgun? Where the hell are we supposed to be taking it, apart from Thule, that is,' he sneered.

'Ever heard of Scrabster?'

'Some kind of seafood?' Ferrow quipped.

'*Funny.* It's a naval base on the Caithness coast, just west of Thurso. That's where we take the gear and get it installed in the P298.'

'Which is?'

'Our equivalent of Fallenberg's *Harfanger*. Three Rolls-Royce Proteus turbines, each on a separate shaft. Two Paxman Ventura six-cylinder engines on wing-shafts for manoeuvrability. Bloody fast. Bloody tough. Stay out ten days if it has to, and then it'll do it at 20 knots.'

'Doesn't sound like old Martin's schooner to me, Faber.'

'It isn't. It's better and faster. And it's small enough for du-Clausky to project into alterjective reality. He wants Thule, I want a weapon. World of difference? Maybe not. Who knows? I might even find both, and that'll make everyone happy. For now, though, we've yet to get underway. You and I both know Erzebet von Bamberg's likely to be after us before we can finish this little jaunt, so the Skorpions keep her away.'

'Or sting her stone dead, for once and for all.'

Sounds like a good idea to me, Ferrow thought. Then he began to wonder. That's at least twice Faber's mentioned Erzebet von Bamberg in connection with Operation Return Ticket. OK, so I told him about her at Fortstown. So he knows what she tried to do there and obviously believes in the two Thules. He wants her dead, and that's as good a way as any of stopping her. But if he's MI6, which he is, and he can put together an expensive job like this, why hasn't he simply had Erzebet disposed of?

Answer: it's a bluff. He wants her to stay alive. This hardware isn't going to be used. She's not going to attack us on the way to Scrabster and try to take the machine.

Question: why does he want Erzebet alive? Answer . . . How the fuck should I know? Maybe he's in with her, the way McAllister was. And yet, and yet he was active at Fortstown before the machine was assembled there. He slapped that D-Notice on the press to hush the whole thing up. If he was in with Erzebet he could have helped the whole thing through. Even if she did give up her own attempt at summoning Pudendagora he could have ensured that McAllister's worked.

Any answers, Johannes? he asked the *glebula*.

Nothing valid, Magister, came the reply. It would be as well to keep an eye on John Faber, though. Something about him makes me question his motives. From what Elspeth Coulston said, he interrogated Noel Jorisund to learn about the Wegrimham affair. I find it odd that he didn't do the same to Elspeth. After all, she was the one who helped you. Noel was simply Williamson's tool in the summoning of Velaeda.

Hey, that's right. And he got the monkey back after I threw it away. And speaking of Noel Jorisund, there's something that's always puzzled me about him. When I spoke to him on the phone and asked for his address he told me he was in the book. I checked that later. He wasn't. I got the address from directory enquiries after identifying myself as a copper, but why should he have lied about that?

'You still with me, Bob?' Faber demanded.

'Hm? Oh, yeah. I was just thinking something through.'

'Like what?'

Ferrow took his courage in both hands. Better to know now than to get shat on later, he reasoned. 'Like why you want Erzebet von Bamberg alive,' he answered.

Back in the laboratory Gunndner, duClausky and Speed were busy crating the equipment ready for transport. Here, in the mess, Faber slammed a mag into the Skorpion he was holding and pulled back the cocking buttons. 'I said I wanted her dead,' he snapped.

'Maybe a bit too much for me to believe you,' Ferrow pressed, aware that the silenced muzzle of the machine pistol was wavering towards his chest.

Johannes read his magister's fear. He padded down the corridor towards the mess. Silently. He tensed for a killing attack.

Faber nodded slowly and lowered the Skorpion. 'OK,' he admitted. 'Maybe I should have told you this before. You're right. I want the woman alive. There's more to Return Ticket than anyone knows, including Charlie Speed. I want both Erzebet and the Keeper, this Johannes fella. There're two things can come out of this job, Bobby. One's the third reality, and we've got that already, thanks to Nils and the Professor. The second's one of man's oldest dreams. Immortality. I want Erzebet von Bamberg *and* the Keeper alive long enough to get them tested in one of our facilities. If they've really lived as long as they claim to have done we're half-way to cracking an immunization system second to nothing we've already got. Just think what that could do for our armed forces and leading politicians. Good government and superior firepower for ever.'

Ferrow scowled. 'You mean we've got both now?'

'You're a cynic, Bob. Show a little optimism once in a while.'

I don't trust him, Magister. Say the word and he's dead.

Not yet, Johannes. We need Mr Faber a while longer. At least until we know how to find the Keeper again. There's no other way we can stop Erzebet von Bamberg.

'Coppers live on cynicism, Faber. It keeps us alive.'

'Maybe. But a blood culture from the Keeper's veins could keep you alive much longer. You may not like it, Bob, but them's my orders. And you take your orders from me until Return Ticket's over. Clear?'

'Looks like I don't have any choice,' Ferrow muttered, eyeing the loaded Skorpion in Faber's grasp.

'That's fine, then.' Faber slid the safety on and put the machine pistol down on the table nearby. 'Now let's help the others pack the machine up for travelling.'

They walked back to the laboratory, Faber leading. Johannes was nowhere to be seen. You here, still? Ferrow asked.

Still here, Magister. Are you sure you don't want me to kill him?

Yeah. Let's give the bastard a bit more rope and see who gets hung. You know anything about Jorisund?

Only a guess. From what I've gathered he was an absent-minded sort. He probably thought he was in the book. I don't believe there's anything sinister there. Perhaps he simply didn't want his life cluttered up with policemen?

Ferrow grinned. Now you're thinking like a human, he responded.

Not at all, Magister, Johannes answered him. Now I'm thinking like a policeman. The breed appears as unpopular amongst humans as we *glebulae* are amongst other animals. We both disturb lives that believe themselves best left alone. Might I offer an observation?

Fire away. Where the hell are you, anyway?

In the mess, under the table with the guns. I was going to ask your opinion regarding a mention of fungi in *The Last Voyage of Martin Fallenberg*. The man seemed to think they were *speaking* to him.

Maybe they were, Ferrow replied. After what I saw at Wegrimham I'd believe anything of toadstools. If they can poison a man's body, why shouldn't they be capable of fucking his thoughts up as well? There's quite a few hallucinogenic varieties.

Indeed, Magister. But from his log, Fallenberg hadn't eaten them. That implies a more indirect form of communication than ingestion, don't you think?

You mean he actually *heard them speak*?

That's what I'm asking you, Magister.

Lieutenant Harding was doing all right for himself at RAF Dunnet, he decided. His work on FTS was well-regarded and the CO had even hinted that there might be a promotion in the offing. He'd given up all thoughts of sneaking into flight training, having found his *metier* on simulation work. Even so, it didn't get him out of those niggling little chores which junior officers got themselves assigned to, and this week he'd been lumbered with night duty as Officer of the Watch.

It wasn't so bad, really. He'd get the occasional drink or something to eat sent over from the mess whilst he went over the results which the others on what the FTS detail had generated. And somehow between the efforts of NATO and the Yanks there was always an interesting selection of missiles awaiting assessment. Right now they were working on the Swedish Saab-Bofors R/BO6–E, a high-subsonic air-to-surface missile being produced to rearm the modified SH37–F Viggen, essentially a sea surveillance fighter. SHAPE had also managed to wangle the loan of one of the STOL craft for the duration of the tests, reducing the intensity of flight and target simulation exercises required.

Life at RAF Dunnet would have gone beyond the not-so-bad into the positively-bloody-perfect, if it hadn't been for those odd compulsions Harding experienced occasionally. At present they didn't seem particularly unnatural or disturbing, and they were often very brief, sometimes so brief that he was simply left with the feeling that he'd decided to do something and now couldn't for the life of him remember what it was. The only fortunate thing about them was that they encouraged him to find out more about the running of RAF Dunnet, about the computer codes for launching test craft and arming their missiles. He'd already learned almost all there was to know on the subject, and he'd occasionally reflect rather ruefully that he almost knew enough to start World War III if he ever felt inclined. Not bad for a First Lieutenant, eh?

One of the most puzzling aspects, though, was the way in which his superiors seemed only too happy to breach security regulations and provide him with the information he felt compelled to acquire, information which in less sympathetic surroundings might easily have led to a suspicion of espionage activity on his part. Sometimes, especially this week of night duties, he'd sit and try to puzzle it out. Now and then a little voice inside him would give him some kind of answer, but it was almost always vague and immediately forgotten.

Still, it was nothing to see the MO about, and he certainly wasn't going to risk his career by volunteering for a psychiatric check-up.

Sit tight and ride it out, he told himself. It can't go on for ever. Sooner or later, at this rate, I'm going to know all there is to know. It'll have to go away then.

Won't it?

They made the trip to Scrabster in a battered, S-registered Ford Transit with a souped-up engine under the cab. Gunndner, Ferrow and Faber drove in turns, one sleeping, one riding shotgun, one driving for four-hour stretches. Speed and duClausky, in the back, took shifts at watching the crated equipment.

The Transit travelled fast, making what time it could on the faster roads. On the A1 outside Nottingham a police patrol vehicle pulled them over for speeding but Ferrow and Faber showed their IDs. The policemen were obviously unhappy with the situation, especially as Ferrow was holding a non-standard issue machine pistol at the time, silenced and obtrusively ready for use. It also galled them to have to give up a court-appearance offence (the Transit had been doing the better part of 110 mph) in a county noted for its crack-down on offenders, but they had no choice but to back away and leave the occupants of the van in peace. Even so they radioed ahead to their colleagues in the South Yorks force to hassle the Transit, but questions as to the identities of the occupants only served to clear their way north.

Leaving the A1 at Newcastle they cut across and up to cross the Forth Bridge and pick up the A9 near Perth. The road meandered through Pitlochry to Inverness, past the Moray and Cromarty Firths, then followed the Caithness coast to Latheron, where they took the 895 across to Thurso. A little over twelve hours after leaving Corby they were following the line of Thurso Bay through Scrabster to the naval dockyard which supplied target vessels to RAF Dunnet, arriving at the harbour late the following morning. They checked in at the gate, where Faber identified himself, and were issued with passes permitting free movement about the base. Contrary to his expectations Faber was delighted to see that P298 had arrived and berthed before them.

'There she is,' he announced proudly. 'Look at the bows, Charlie. There's a little touch I think you might appreciate.'

Commander Speed's eyes followed the line of Faber's pointing finger. Despite the fine drizzle which was making HMS Scrabster an even more depressing place than it normally was, he read the legend painted on the bows.

*HARFANGER II* it said.

'Had it named for Fallenberg's schooner, eh?' the commander asked. 'Good show, Johnny m'boy. Good show.'

Ferrow grabbed the spook's elbow. 'Don't you think it's time you levelled with him?' he hissed.

'And spoil the old boy's illusions? Come off it. That'd screw the whole job up. Don't forget we still need him to sail the bloody tub.' Then, to Nils Gunndner: 'Bring the Transit up. I'll see the CO and scout up a couple of fitters to do the exterior installation.'

Ferrow looked over the *Harfanger II* carefully. He'd never been a particularly good sailor and the thought of a voyage through the rough waters of the North Sea was sufficient to bring a prickling to the hairs on the nape of his neck. Yet the vessel Faber had managed to acquire seemed about as good as anything, for all his doubts. Front and rear armaments had been removed and an extra antenna tower, skeletal in structure, was welded to the superstructure aft of the forward radar. The vessel's sleek lines suggested speed and manoeuvrability, which could be better than simple stability in rough seas. *Harfanger II* was nearly 150 feet long and over 26 feet across the beam. The Tenacity Class had been initially purchased by the Royal Navy as a counter-missile and fishery protection vessel. Theoretically, fully armed, it could engage and destroy much larger fighting ships. Demonstrations of the original, P276, had led to an order from Venezuela. All in all, Ferrow decided, Faber could have come up with something much worse than this for Operation Return Ticket.

Faber was as good as his word. The CO provided fitters and soon the laser-like alterjector had been fitted on a remote-controlled turntable atop the extra antenna mast. A cable fed down the centre of the structure to the machine which duClausky installed inside the marine laboratory created from a rearrangement of the crew berths. With a sweep of the turntable, once the device was working, it would be possible to place the entire vessel and its contents within the third reality.

So we're all going, Ferrow mused. Not just me. Well, misery loves company, they say.

And at least I've got something of an edge, having been there already.

They ate a hurried meal in the mess and were assigned visitors' quarters where they relaxed and slept after the long drive. For Gunndner and duClausky it was almost enough just to have seen daylight again after their weeks of work in the bunker. Eventually Faber was respectfully roused with the news that the fitters had completed their work and all was set for the *Harfanger II* to sail whenever they were ready. Commander Speed checked his notes and decided that the most propitious time for the expedition to begin was when the dawn tide began to ebb. Before then duClausky and Gunndner went aboard and checked the equipment, both satisfying themselves that it would perform as expected when the time came. Ferrow took his ease, leaving Johannes to keep an eye on things whilst he did so.

The hour for departure approached. They roused and dressed, were drilled by the commander in what he would expect of his makeshift crew, and prepared to commence the final stage of Operation Return Ticket. Having familiarized themselves with the vessel they returned ashore for a final briefing from Faber and Commander Speed, Ferrow observing and noting the subtle differences in approach manifested by the two men.

He almost expected Faber to tell them to synchronize their watches, but the marine chronometer aboard *Harfanger II* removed the need for that. Instead they simply packed their gear, left their quarters and went aboard.

With Nils Gunndner, who was a qualified engineer as well as a horologist, in the engine room, they sped out of Scrabster into the Pentland Firth, setting a course past the Faeroes towards Hornafjödhur in southern Iceland. Speed had delegated the navigation to Faber, who had already demonstrated a certain competence in that direction, and firmly believed that the *Harfanger II* was sailing east of the Faeroes towards Svalbard and the sub-polar ice desert, following Martin Fallenberg's original route. The discrepancy in bearings had been pre-calculated and the bridge compass adjusted to conceal it from the commander.

DuClausky ran a trial on the turntable mechanism and pronounced himself satisfied. Return Ticket was off and running, Ferrow grinned, without Erzebet von Bamberg or her henchmen anywhere in sight.

He was wrong. *Harfanger II* had barely come to full speed when the previously closed door to one of the redesigned aft berths opened. Ylena, armed with one of the Skorpions which Faber had stowed carelessly, took control of the marine laboratory and the machine. Karsten, armed with the other Skorpion, swept through the crew quarters and, finding no-one there, proceeded to the bridge. There he surprised Ferrow, Faber and Speed. Once they were covered he stepped aside to permit Erzebet von Bamberg to gloatingly take control of the bridge, broomhandled Mauser cocked and ready.

'Jenny Fellowes, I believe?' Ferrow sneered with a contempt he was far from really feeling. 'Or is it Erzebet von Bamberg?'

'I thought I'd see you again, Mr Ferrow,' Erzebet smiled. 'You caused me some problems at Fortstown. Doubtless you intend to again, given the opportunity. I must assure you, though, that the opportunity will not arise this time.'

Ferrow scowled. Johannes? he demanded. Where the hell are you? If you want someone to kill then here's your chance.

My apologies, Magister, came the reply. You forget that the Landgravine gave me life through her experiments. I regret that I must offer my first loyalty to her, apparently. Is this not the case, Lady Erzebet?

'That is indeed the case, Johannes,' Erzebet responded aloud, her eyes meeting Ferrow's in an unwavering challenge. 'You see?' she added. 'I have each of you exactly where I want you. I now control this vessel and all aboard her. I also control the machine which Professor duClausky has so ingeniously created for you, Faber.'

'It's a long way to where we're going,' Faber snarled back. 'A lot can change before we get there.'

Erzebet sighed. 'It's always been a long way back to Thule,' she told him. 'Yet we shall maintain our present course. Which incidentally, Commander Speed, is not the one you plotted or even the one the compass is showing you. Faber has betrayed you, Commander. And now John,' she walked over to Faber and gently stroked his face with the barrel of her pistol, 'I believe it's time for our little masquerade to come to an end. Robert Ferrow here has always suspected that you were in this with me.'

Faber scowled. 'What the hell are you talking about?' he demanded.

'Oh, very well,' Erzebet said dismissively. 'Keep it up if you must.'

'Keep it up?' He started forward but Karsten's Skorpion waved him back. 'You've got a bloody nerve, woman. This is piracy. Yes, it's still on the statute books, and, by Christ, HMG's going to throw them at you before this is over. Do you realize you're fucking up a multi-million-pound operation? Do you?' His sharp chin and thin lips were flecked with spittle from the vehemence of his outburst when he finished.

'And you thought I would spoil it for you?' Erzebet smiled. 'Dear John, this little demonstration was simply to let you know that I have resumed overall control, as we agreed. Operation Return Ticket will proceed as planned. *Exactly* as planned. You forget, I want to find the Keeper even more than you do.'

'If you two have finished your lovers' tiff,' Ferrow began, eyeing Faber with overt hostility, 'will one of you tell me what's happened to Nils and Professor duClausky? I take it they're still alive?'

'But of course, Robert,' Erzebet replied. 'I could hardly dispose of the one man aboard who knows how the machine is calibrated. They're below in the laboratory in the company of a young lady I believe you've met.'

'Ylena Hahn? She had to be working for you. Where's the Dutchman?'

'The Dutchman was actually an SS colonel, Robert. I'm afraid he didn't feel he'd travel very well. Men in wheelchairs don't sail easily without help.'

'You killed him, right? Like you'll kill all of us once we find the Keeper. *If* we find the Keeper.'

'Oh, we'll find him, Robert. Don't waste time thinking we won't. And don't waste time trying to devise some way to warn him. There isn't one. And now it's time for Karsten to take the wheel, or whatever you call steering this thing. He does know what he's doing, by the way. He used to pilot one of these things for the Venezuelan Navy, before they cashiered him for carrying unauthorized cargoes, like cocaine for the CIA. The Americans kept him out of prison, even though they declared him *persona non grata*. The rest of us will go below and experience a small reunion. After all, you've met Ylena before as well, haven't you, Faber?'

Have you really changed sides, Johannes? Right now, when I need you like I've never needed you before, not even with Grost?

Lady Erzebet will not wish to harm the Keeper, Magister, came the reply. He is in no danger from her, providing he complies with her requests.

She can pick up your thoughts, *glebula*. Can she pick up mine through you? If she can't, show yourself.

Johannes padded on to the bridge and went straight to Erzebet, licking her hand. You called me, mistress? Ferrow heard him ask.

'A clever beast,' Erzebet said gently. 'It is intelligent as well. No, Johannes, I hadn't called you, but I was about to. You anticipate your mistress well.'

At that moment a thought came into Ferrow's mind. At first he thought it was his own, a simple instance of memory generating an idea. Only later did he realize that, soft as it was, it was a message from Johannes.

Remember, the *glebula* told him, that in emergencies we may whisper to one another by an effort of guarded will.

They descended to the laboratory at the point of Erzebet's pistol and found Gunndner and duClausky, covered by Ylena's machine weapon, waiting disconsolately. Johannes' teeth patrolled their ankles threateningly as the original crew of *Harfanger II* submitted to their present circumstances. Once they were all assembled Erzebet motioned for them to sit.

'John's original plan,' she explained, 'was to sail this vessel to latitude 64° 37′ north, 15° 49′ longitude east and anchor there, almost within sight of Hornafjördhur, whilst you, Professor du-Clausky, alterjected both the ship and all aboard her . . .'

'Y'mean we weren't heading for Svalbard? The compass really was wrong?'

'Be quiet, Commander. I know you to have been a brave man. You are now, however, an old man, and old men are frequently foolish, not brave. I know a great deal about age, as Robert could tell you, if this were the time. It is not the time, though. Now, our course will remain as it was. So will the assigned point of alter-jection. Nothing has changed except the leader of this expedition. No, Commander Speed, you were never in charge of it. Rather it was in charge of you. My dear friend John wants a weapon and the secret of eternal life out of Operation Return Ticket. Don't you, John?'

Faber maintained a sullen silence where he sat and offered no reply.

'As I have told you,' Erzebet resumed, 'the only thing that has changed is the person actually in charge. I have even brought the obsidian monkey . . . I'm sorry, the sub-elemental Thulium monkey . . . and the skull aboard, so that every part of your intended operation may be completed, John. You see? I have forgotten nothing. I control the bridge, through my dear Karsten, and the area below deck through my beloved Ylena and this dear killing machine beside me.'

She reached down and stroked Johannes' head. The *glebula* made a good show of enjoying the attention.

Just whose side are you on, Johannes? Ferrow demanded.

The winning side, Magister, Johannes whispered back.

'Forget any ideas you may have about thwarting me,' Erzebet told them. 'Obey and you live. Disobey and you die, horribly. There is only one man living who has ever known me show mercy, and he is not aboard.

'And now the day is late and there is rough weather forecast ahead of us. Something to eat, I think, and then you get some sleep.'

DuClausky moved to stand up. Ylena threatened him with the Skorpion. The professor smiled. 'You need me to work the machine, yes? So. I go to galley. You search galley for hidden guns? I cook food. We do as you say and eat. Shoot cook, no pudding to prove.'

He stood up and walked from the laboratory. Johannes watched him, snuffling unpleasantly, but let him pass.

Erzebet smiled, displaying her perfect, sharp white teeth. 'A clever man, the professor. A practical man. I like that. He knows when he's bested. Learn from him, the rest of you.'

Edvard duClausky took advantage of the fresh vegetables aboard to prepare a ham salad for prisoners and guards alike. Erzebet and Ylena set theirs aside and watched the others eat. Once they had finished Ylena took them, one at a time, to their berths and shut them in. Johannes prowled along beside her. Eventually only Ferrow and the professor were left sitting in the laboratory, awaiting their turns, with Erzebet watching them.

'You like food when you eat,' duClausky told Erzebet. 'I good cook. Scrape fungus off.'

Scrape fungus off? Ferrow was about to challenge that statement when Ylena returned and Erzebet designated him next to be taken to his berth. He stood up and bade duClausky a good night, glared at Erzebet, who smiled pleasantly back like a hostess at a society soirée, then sullenly obeyed the point of Ylena's Skorpion and Johannes' tooth-stuffed jaws.

Later, as he struggled to get some sleep, turning the events of the day in his mind and trying to make some sense of them, he referred that brief reference to mould on fresh food to the fungi in Martin Fallenberg's log. Once that was done, however, further speculation along that line became unprofitable, so he tried another.

Erzebet claimed Faber was working with her. Faber denied it. Well, naturally he would. Yet if he wanted Erzebet and Ptythonius for his people to study, why didn't he bag the Landgravine when he had the chance, rather than leave it until she'd got the drop on him? It was simply one more thing that didn't make a great deal of sense to the policeman.

As his tired brain began to shut down towards sleep he reviewed his circumstances. Wet middle of nowhere. Prisoner on a boat. Can't trust Johannes. Can't trust Faber. Be a fool to trust any of the others too far. No gun. Nothing to do but get some sleep and play the waiting game.

But waiting for what? For the Keeper? For one of those blue lights to come down out of the sky and tell him what to do?

Ferrow glanced towards the night outside the porthole. It was both too dark and too light to make out sea or sky or stars. And yet he'd put the light out, hadn't he? So why was his world bright blue?

Few today recall the name of Sarah Doudney, despite her having spent a total of 83 years upon this planet. Yet in her poem *The Psalm of Life* she provided a frequently paraphrased and regularly abused couplet which can frequently be heard in hospitals, dentists' waiting-rooms and on station platforms:

> But the waiting time, my brothers
> Is the hardest time of all.

Ptythonius von Meersburg could only agree with her. All that he could do by way of preparation had already been done. All that remained was to wait.

He spent most of his time now in the records, a gaunt, pale figure in a library carved out of ice by hands perhaps even Anhuk had never seen. Occasionally he would seek out a figurine and take down the scroll it guarded, spreading it open on a plain wooden table and consulting its contents. Now and then he'd jot a comment into a small notebook, then read it back to himself in the context of the comments and observations which had preceded it. Mostly, though, he stood or sat and waited.

They'd be coming soon. All of them. Even Erzebet von Bamberg and Robert Ferrow would be coming, the one to assist in, the other to witness, his act of faith.

It was a gamble, naturally. Everything was a gamble. Yet he knew the game and was good at playing it. He'd played it at Wegrimham, gambling that Williamson's summoning of Velaeda would coincide with the Vernal Equinox. He'd played it at Fortstown, gambling that Erzebet would behave as she had, designating McAllister to complete the summoning of Pudendagora rather than do it herself and confront him directly. If she hadn't, if she'd taken the relic in her hand, she'd have known that it wasn't the tiny masturbating monkey she'd last seen in 1540. Then the play might have had a very different ending.

He'd gambled and won many times before, but he was far from over-confident. Every time was different, and this time, coming so slowly, was the most different of all. This time, if he lost, the game was over for ever. Even if he won, it would be over for him. No-one, not even the Keeper, could do what he intended and not terminate.

He wouldn't die. Keepers never actually died. But there were worse things than simple death, and he'd seen too many of them to be casual about the possible fates he might have to face. The negatives hated the Keepers more than anything, more even than their original defeat, for the Keepers were the ones who kept them always in check, ever bound and sleeping, never permitted to act directly but only through the workings of those humans they had managed to enslave.

'I should have told you more, friend Robert,' he whispered to himself. 'I should have told you not to trust the fungus. I should have told you who the other servant of Thule is, besides Erzebet von Bamberg. And I should have told you about the seventh skyfire, Robert. I should have done that much at least.'

Yet there were things I didn't tell you before, he thought. Things I should have done. The first time I didn't tell you because I wasn't certain I could trust you. The second time I didn't tell you because I trusted you too well. You've done all that I asked of you and more. It would be a pity if you failed now because I've kept my cards too close.

Yes, you've been a good friend to me over these last few months. A better friend to me than I have been to you. Could ever be to you. And now we both face our greatest tests and our greatest dangers, because you permitted yourself to be my friend.

In many ways you have played this game for me. I have remained here, preparing the final moments of my act of faith, whilst you've been foundering in the world outside, the world I may not touch this time. If you have a talent, friend Robert, it is for muddling through, for surviving. That is the talent I'm counting on this one last time. You worked with me before, now work instead of me. I think of this as your last test and my last gesture to mankind. Beyond it lies an ending, one way or the other . . .

He broke off his thoughts and drew the fur cloak closer about himself. The cold didn't come from the ice. He was used to that. It came from something much more powerful, something that he was reluctant to admit even to himself, though the centuries of wisdom behind his office forced the admission.

What if I really do fail this time? the Keeper wondered.

It was possible, even probable, that he would. The games played at Fortstown and Wegrimham had been as nothing compared to this. Pudendagora and Velaeda were comparatively puny as individuals to defeat. But the whole of the perverse and deadly Thulean pantheon was something much more dangerous, much more terrible in its implications than any single negative.

Somewhere beyond him, beyond the Kingdom of the Keeper, *Harfanger II* was approaching through the second reality. Doubtless its own small dramas were being played out aboard, life-and-death dramas which were of greater consequence to their actors than any nebulous occurrence on the alterjective plane. Sooner or later Ferrow was going to discover Erzebet's informer amongst the original members of Operation Return Ticket. Then he'd be forced to act.

Let's just hope he doesn't obey the fungi, Ptythonius reflected. I should have told him. But I didn't.

Then I have to do something to help.

*Harfanger II* sailed on, its speed calculated and maintained to reach the designated bearing for alterjection early the following evening. The rough weather predicted hit about midnight, but fortunately the *Harfanger II* was heading into it, rather than having to keep its course riding it broadside. For all its speed and manoeuvrability the patrol boat had a shallow draft and would not have fared particularly well at even 40° to its present course.

Ferrow lurched from sleep to wakefulness as a buffeting from the sea outside threatened to hurl him from his berth. The stifled cry from his companion did as much as the weather to restore his senses.

The blue light was gone. In its place was the occasional thin shaft of moonlight, when earth's satellite wasn't obscured behind scudding rainclouds. The ham salad wasn't staying down particularly well, and Ferrow wondered if this was due to nerves, weather or those peculiar chunks of apparently pallid green pepper diced into it. All speculation on that subject took second place, though, compared to what was going on beside his bunk-bed.

He sat up, gripping the sides of the bunk for stability. His life had taken many strange turns over the past few months, he decided, but none as strange as this was. Standing close beside him where he lay was a naked and, he was pleasantly surprised to admit, attractive woman – holding a Skorpion machine pistol.

'We have some unfinished business, Mr Ferrow,' said Ylena Hahn.

Despite himself, he felt stirred by her presence. 'I take it the missionary position's out?' he inquired. 'Unless I want that thing stuffed up my nose?' He gestured towards the Skorpion.

Ylena smiled, surprisingly pleasantly, and set the weapon down. Then she stood back as far as the narrow cabin allowed, hands on bare hips, and studied him where he lay.

'If you call out we're both dead,' she told him quietly. 'Erzebet would not expect to find me here.'

'You've a hell of a way of introducing yourself,' Ferrow muttered. 'First I get two of your pricks, now you want one of mine. Do you always behave like this?'

She drew closer and took his head in her hands, kissing him lightly on the lips. 'Listen to me,' she whispered. 'I have to prove something to myself and I need your help to do it. Will you help me, Robert Ferrow?'

He reached over and ran a hand from her waist to her shoulder. 'Help doesn't come cheap on this ship,' he grinned. 'So how come you're offering me some additional therapy?'

'I want you to make love to me . . .'

'No, really? Come on, kid. Don't play with a frustrated copper unless you've something to offer. OK, the light's not good, but I'd crawl across duClausky to get to you. But that doesn't tell me *why*. You going to?'

She pulled back the covers and slipped into the narrow bunk beside him. The perfume of her body, young and strong, filled his nostrils. She leaned over him, then felt the strong grasp of his hands about her shoulders, holding her off.

'I don't mix business and pleasure,' he hissed. 'Rather, I can't afford to, right now. Talk first, Miss Hahn. Then, if we've anything in common . . .'

He released one of her arms and stroked her hair, more conscious than she was in the darkened cabin of where she'd left the Skorpion.

She sighed and went limp in his grasp. 'What do you want to know?' she asked, pouting at him.

'We could start with why you're here, Ylena. And why that von Bamberg bitch would kill us if she knew. How about it?'

Because she loves you, said a voice inside him.

Johannes? Is that you?

The darkness volunteered no answer.

'If you have to know,' Ylena sighed, 'Erzebet has made me her lover. I need to prove to myself that I'm not, not really.'

'You mean . . . Jesus! You're a lesbian?'

'No,' she snapped, rather louder than she'd meant to. The silence settled in about them again. Then she added: 'I don't want to be. That's why I came to you. Yes, she's beautiful, but . . .'

'But I'm even lovelier? Come on. You'll have to do better than that.'

Ylena sighed deeply. 'I don't want to be her lover. I do it to stay alive. She's mad, Robert Ferrow. She's mad enough to kill any or all of us. I don't want her love. It's too dangerous. The first time I saw you I knew you were a *man*. And a man is what I need. Can we share some moments together? Just tonight?'

Ferrow relaxed. To his male mind it all made sense. Besides, if he did a good enough job of making love to this woman he had at least an ally he could half count on. Like Johannes. Like Faber. And one out of three might just come good when he needed help the most.

'OK, Ylena,' he grinned in the thin light of the moon through the porthole. 'Climb aboard.'

In the uncertainty of their world their lovemaking was fast and desperate, each smothering the other's cries, each finding what pleasure there was and, in it, a release from their separate prisons. Ylena was everything Ferrow might have expected, determined and efficient, yet somehow cold and almost mechanical.

She'll warm up next time, he reflected afterwards. If there is a next time. We could both be dead this time tomorrow.

As they lay together afterwards, Ylena sleeping, Ferrow struggling not to, a faint click sounded above the rough sea outside the cabin. His eyes darted towards the door, but it remained firmly closed.

The click repeated.

Very slowly, careful not to wake Ylena in the narrow confines of the bunk, he turned his head to look at the Skorpion. And froze.

'Say nothing, Mr Ferrow,' Toadflax hissed.

He could just make out the small shape of the *familiaris*, its grey eyes glittering in the faint light. The small hands had managed to remove the magazine from the machine pistol and were now releasing and removing the rounds it held, one by one.

'I can do nothing with the round in the breech, Mr Ferrow,' Toadflax whispered. 'These weapons are made to kill in bursts, though. If that first round misses you will have an advantage, I think.'

'Why . . . are you doing this?'

'Because I've been instructed to,' came the reply.

'By the Keeper?'

'The Keeper is nothing to me, Mr Ferrow. I take my instructions from my Venerable.'

'You mean Pyewacket?'

The *familiaris'* features crumpled into a parody of a human smile. 'That is a name from our history, Mr Ferrow. The Venerable Artisson is in charge of the colony I belong to. We left England over 400 years ago.

'But enough. There, the magazine is empty and replaced. I have to dispose of the bullets now. Perhaps I shall see you later, Mr Ferrow.'

'Toadflax ... wait ...'

'Shhh. Answers come later. If you live to hear them.'

The moon vanished behind a cloud and the *familiaris* seemed to vanish with its light. For some moments Ferrow heard faint sounds as it removed the bullets to a hiding place, then there was only the sound of the sea outside and the rhythm of Ylena's breathing. He turned his head back to its former position and stared at the ceiling. Some minutes later Ylena murmured in her sleep and then woke up. She struggled to make out his features in the darkness and saw that his eyes were open and looking at her.

'You didn't move,' she whispered. 'I'd have known if you moved. Why didn't you try to take my gun, Bob?'

Ferrow struggled to restrain a chuckle. Take the gun? If only she knew. Toadflax had as good as done that for him. Instead he answered: 'Is that what this is all about, kid? You want me to help you fight Erzebet, or to put you out of your misery? Well, maybe I'll do both. But I'll do it in my own time. And this isn't it, Ylena.'

'You know that I tried to save your life back in Corby, don't you? I did the first time. Volker wanted Grost to kill you before the drug wore off. I talked him out of it.'

Ferrow nodded. 'I remember. Want to tell me why?'

Ylena sighed. 'Death is too easy and too frequent an answer. It seemed a waste ...'

'And if Erzebet tells you to kill me over breakfast? What will you do then, Ylena?'

'I ... don't know.' She kissed him, then stared pleadingly into his eyes. 'Take the gun. I can open the other berths for you and free your friends.'

He shook his head determinedly. 'I need some answers first. I'm willing to believe Erzebet's got a spy in our camp, but I'm not over-convinced it's Faber. If I try anything before I know for certain, it won't work. And you think I can just creep up on that big bastard on the bridge and knock him on the head? Forget it. He's built like a brick public loo. Shoulders like he eats cornflakes in their packets.'

Try a little humour. Defuse her. Get her to see it your way. Buy time. And don't trust her too quickly, either. Erzebet's devious enough to have set this whole episode up. Use the advantage Toadflax has given you, when the time's right.

Faber is the traitor, Magister.

Johannes? Speaking to me openly?

Do what Ylena says. Take Faber prisoner with the others. Then you'll be safe.

'I have to go,' Ylena announced. She climbed over him, lingering for a last kiss, then slipped out of the bunk and began to dress. Ferrow sat up and watched her, wondering if perhaps he was making a mistake in not doing what she suggested. As she finished putting her clothes on, she picked up the Skorpion and turned to look at him.

'Thank you,' she whispered.

'For what? For a quick fuck? Listen, kid, you have to make up your mind. If you kill me you're stuck with Lady von Bamberg until she tires of you and says bye-bye in the only way she knows. Remember that. Besides,' he added, his tone growing softer, 'I reckon I could get quite fond of you, given a better set of circumstances.'

Ylena nodded. 'That's what I was thanking you for,' she said.

He watched her open the cabin door and step out. As she did so her hand touched the metal surround. She drew it back quickly and looked at it.

'Problem?' Ferrow asked in a whisper.

She shrugged and wiped her hand on her skirt. 'Some kind of mould,' she told him. Then she closed the door behind her and he was alone again.

He found it as difficult to sleep after she'd gone, as he had done before she came. His eyes kept searching the darkness, looking for anything within or without that could provide an answer to any one of the many questions he was struggling with. Especially he felt he needed to know more about this latest one.

You've lost your chance, Magister.

Johannes? For fuck's sake, *is* that you?

The fungi spoke to Martin Fallenberg. How? Toadstools don't have mouths. Mould is a fungus. That doesn't have mouths either. 'I good cook. Scrape fungus off,' said duClausky.

A mould that grows on *metal*?

Harding scanned the test schedule again. Sure enough, there it was. SH 37–F foul weather test on RBO6–E ASM from maximum launch height.

It was a recent addition to the schedule and had been pencilled in. True, it had been on the cards for some time, but the Met boys had only just come up with a reliable low-pressure front in the target area, so the test details and strategy hadn't even been logged into the computer yet.

He checked the wall-clock in the duty office against his watch. It was just coming up to 6 am and time for his duty to terminate for the night. During the day someone would log the TD&S and order up a target vessel out of HMS Scrabster. He'd be asleep though, and it would all be over by the time he came on duty the following evening.

Pity, he thought. I'd have liked to have had a hand in this one. And a night take-off with the SH37–F Viggen is so much more impressive with that wide afterburn. And that computer track from max launch height should be fascinating.

So why don't you reschedule before you go off duty, George? Go on, give yourself a treat.

He thought about it for a moment. It wouldn't be all that difficult to arrange, with what he knew about the workings of RAF Dunnet. And there wouldn't be any comeback if he was careful about how he did it. All it took was a quick recalculation, a check with the Met boys to make sure the low-pressure area was still on, and a call to Scrabster to set up the target. After that a note on the day log with details of the change and reason (delayed low-pressure area – when in doubt blame it on the weather) would take care of everything else.

Clock ticking away, Georgie. Now or never, you know.

He rang the weather station, noting the call, and checked that the situation wouldn't have changed radically by that evening.

Then he rang Scrabster to check on target availability, speaking to his bored and weary opposite number.

'Half a mo', muttered the navy man. 'Slight problem with your test area. Got an old Tenacity Class tub on course for 64° 37' north, 15° 49' east. Don't want you hitting that by mistake.'

Harding's eyes narrowed. 'You sure that isn't our target ordered up early?'

'Doesn't seem to be. Hang on, I'll check the crew manifest . . . Mmmm . . .'

He could almost see the navy man's hand waggle from side to side down the telephone. Then: 'Well, there's no crew listed, so it must be on auto. Yep. That's it. No navy personnel aboard. Decommissioned P298 out of here. That's your tub, Dunnet.'

'Can you give me speed and E T A, Scrabster?'

Harding took down the details, logged as a formality in case of difficulties by Faber before *Harfanger II* had left the dockyard. That was all he needed. Weather was right. Target was right, though he couldn't help wondering if maybe he ought to check on who had ordered it up early. Didn't really matter too much, he decided.

Right. Note for the day log, then off to the computer to make the test entry. Ought to be a good show to liven up the next spell of duty, Harding grinned.

The Venerable Artisson scowled with a black intensity which exactly matched both his eyes and his fur. His life, he admitted, had been both long and eventful, filled with dangers that were mere legend to the younger members of his colony. Yet somehow he felt that the present, for him and his, was likely to be equally, if not more, perilous than the ill-fated voyage aboard the *Fine Lady* which had originally brought them to Iceland.

Somehow he'd retained control of the colony after that particular fiasco, though there had been many ready to challenge his leadership. The safe, easy voyage to a new life in Denmark which he'd promised had degenerated badly in the face of wicked weather at sea. The ship had broken up in sight of land, forcing them to swim for their lives through the icy waters around Hornafjördhur. They'd come ashore wet, cold and hungry and had then been forced to pull down a sheep for some desperately-needed nourishment. Not the most auspicious of beginnings, Artisson had to admit.

Yet he'd held on. They'd made their burrows, with difficulty, seeking out and lining fissures in the volcanic rock. They'd found service with many of the native population, a population ready to attempt even witchcraft to show its displeasure at the foreign domination imposed by Iceland's Danish overlords, a domination which included the Reformation and the suppression of the old, magical runic script.

The *familiares* had maintained their secret life through the centuries, watching the times change about them, remaining a part of the sub-culture of their new home. Threats had come more from nature than from man, with volcanic eruptions menacing their homes on more than one occasion. It was a young land and its geology was still vigorous, but it made them a good home for all that.

And then, after all those years, when their home was secure and their lives quietly settled, the skyfire had come to them.

They'd seen the skyfires before, lighting the brief nights of summer and the longer, darker nights of the lengthy Icelandic winter. They'd even glimpsed the Keeper on occasions, that white-clad figure, as old and infinitely wiser than they were, walking the shore or setting off to travel no-one knew where. He'd come and gone, seeing them more than they liked to be seen, knowing of their presence even when they were certain they'd hid their presence from him. He'd smiled and spoken to them on occasion, though Artisson discouraged his colony from responding. Basically, though, they'd left the Keeper and the skyfires alone, as they, in turn, had remained essentially undisturbed.

But now the skyfire had come to them, and things could never be the same again.

Even in their burrows they weren't safe from the strange blue light. It had followed them underground like rainwater, flowing through their chambers and passageways, seeking them out. Only one of the seven, but, Artisson was sure, always the same one of the seven.

It told them what they must do.

Artisson continued to scowl. It wasn't right. Nothing told the *familiares* what to do. Nothing ordered their lives except the hierarchy of the colony, which he headed. Yet the skyfire told them and, somehow, they discovered that they were left with no choice but to obey it.

The skyfire had told Artisson to send Toadflax abroad, and he had obeyed. It had even taken Toadflax, immersing the tiny creature within itself as it expanded and solidified. Now Toadflax was gone, and not even the Venerable Artisson knew what had happened to him.

No, it definitely wasn't right.

And now the skyfire had come to them again, telling them it required a further service from them, compelling their obedience. Artisson had detailed the most skilled amongst his number to the task, feeling all the time that he should have gone himself to look after them. Yet how did you accomplish that when there was no choice but obedience? He was better where he was, with the others, waiting and watching for the absent ones to return.

Somehow he knew that it wouldn't be over then. The skyfire would demand something else of them, something more dangerous. All its commands pointed towards fragments of some unknown plan, an overall scheme which in time would trace out a grand design which they might or might not be allowed to discover. It really wasn't good enough. Not at all.

BE READY, the skyfire told them. THE OTHERS WILL BE BACK BEFORE NIGHTFALL. THEN I SHALL ASK ONE MORE SERVICE OF YOU.

One more? *Only* one more? Perhaps there was an end in sight after all. Perhaps it would be all over by the morning. All done. Then they could retire to their burrows again and go on with their lives undisturbed by the intrusive blue light.

Perhaps.

Yet in its way it had been 'perhaps' that had brought them to Iceland in the first place, and it was 'perhaps' that now placed them in servitude to the skyfire.

And it was 'perhaps', the Venerable Artisson reflected, still scowling darkly, that could get them all killed very, very soon.

With the coming of day, as the prisoners aboard *Harfanger II* were released from their cabins, Ptythonius von Meersburg checked through the list which he had spread out across the table in the records. He counted slowly, marking off the list, checking that there was nothing missing, that the chronology was complete.

He had to be certain. He had to know that nothing would go wrong. Everything, down to the smallest detail, must be completely accurate.

'Deguir de Meaux,' he read. 'Ilona Yuvicz, Marcus Flavius Tuvianus . . .'

All there. He smiled at the observation. All there. Yes, that was how it should be, how it had to be.

'. . . Ibrahim ben Kaffiz, Telemon of Samothrace, Vistigula, Tiamata . . .'

This was the only thing left to check, and he had deliberately left it until last. The skyfire had worked together on its compilation, centuries before. All seven of them. It must be right, Ptythonius found himself thinking.

Check it all the same, he told himself. Every entry. Check them all.

'. . . Tendobath, Trobiathian, Grimada ab Viszen, Poteth, Sendathion . . .'

Check them all. Be ready. Be *ready*.

And if something goes wrong? If *Harfanger II* fails to alterject? If it does, but Erzebet has complete control, or the fungi have whispered their lies? It mustn't matter. There is no choice left for anyone any more. They will do what has to be done, as I must.

'. . . Chandique, Sestrigoveth, Tultha, D'vyuq, Relemonath, Tragan, Wintegostro . . .'

No choice at all.

Ylena didn't shoot him over breakfast. For the most part her expression remained suitably severe, though she did manage to offer Ferrow a quick smile when she was certain no-one else was looking. He flashed a wink back, then swore at himself for doing so.

Johannes had been watching.

Erzebet was on the bridge, watching Commander Speed who had relieved Karsten. The blond giant was snatching a few hours' sleep in the berth where Ferrow and Ylena had made secret love a lifetime of speculation ago. Nils Gunndner, Faber, Ferrow and duClausky, who seemed to have taken the role of sea-cook upon himself as a matter of course, were eating the condemned man's traditional hearty breakfast in the laboratory, under the watchful gaze of Ylena and the fearsome, open jaws of the *glebula*, now no longer dog-like.

It would have been a good time to seize his advantage, Ferrow thought, if only he'd known whose side Faber and Johannes were really on. Still, maybe it was as well that he didn't. He'd slept badly and was still trying to work out exactly where he stood in this bloody awful mess. And that, he decided, was next to fucking impossible.

Life aboard the patrol boat was growing more confusing with every passing second. Their meal consisted of bacon, eggs, tomatoes and mushrooms. Not field mushrooms, Ferrow noted, but something similar yet with a more subtle flavour and a faint greenish tinge even to the fried flesh of the fruit-bodies. It was a hue which might well have been the same, in its original state, as the outbreaks of mould which had sprung up in the companionways overnight.

Mould that grew on metal.

He frowned and pushed his plate away, looking around him to see how the others were enjoying their meal. Faber and Gunndner had finished. The professor had cut the white away from his one remaining egg and eaten it. Now, his features suffused with pleasure, he lifted the yolk on the blade of his table-knife and slid it into his mouth whole.

Somewhere, at the back of Ferrow's mind, an extra niggle took hold and began to worry him. It was so vague that he couldn't even identify it properly. Not yet. He shifted his gaze to Nils Gunndner, studied the horologist's plate, then heard the voice inside him speak again.

*Nothing to worry about, Robert. You're making mountains out of molehills. Seeing ghosts where you ought to just be seeing shadows.*

He sighed and sat back. His eyes flickered to the doorway, to the small patch of mould which had formed beside it whilst they had been eating.

'Now what?' Faber demanded irritably.

'We wait,' Ylena told him.

'What the hell for?'

'Lady Erzebet will tell you, when she's ready to.'

'You mean she doesn't trust you enough to let you in on her plans?' the spook sneered.

Ylena gave him no response. She simply tightened her grip upon the Skorpion, unconscious of the mould intensifying beside the doorway behind her.

*She loves you, Magister.*

Ferrow stared at Johannes. The *glebula* growled threateningly back at him.

*So it isn't you,* he thought. *It calls me magister, and it sounds like you. But it's not. So what the hell is it? Where's it coming from? It sounds as if it's inside me . . .*

*It is, Magister.*

*Was that you? Growl if it was. I only just heard you . . .*

Johannes moved closer to the seated Ferrow and drew back his lips to offer a formidable and threatening snarl.

*Then you* are *still with me, on the quiet.*

The *glebula* growled again.

*One down, one to go. Faber.*

*Two to go, Magister. If the traitor isn't Faber, it's one of the others.*

*You're getting stronger,* Ferrow told him. *Aren't you worried Erzebet will hear you?*

She's out of range on the bridge. That's why I growled so loudly. I was testing for her response. We have to be quick, though, in case she comes closer. Now, listen very carefully, Magister.

I don't know what the other voice is that you hear, but I suspect it has something to do with the mould that is growing in more and more places around this vessel, if anything Martin Fallenberg said is to be believed. In time it may grow in strength, as the fungus grows in size, until it is indistinguishable from and even supplants your own thoughts. Be wary of that. As for Faber and his involvement with Lady Erzebet . . .

The *glebula* broke off suddenly.

Johannes? Ferrow demanded.

Quiet, Ferrow. My mistress will be here soon. Then you'll suffer.

OK. I get the picture.

No, you don't Robert. The *glebula* is lying to you. It's not your friend. It never has been. Don't trust it. For God's sake don't trust it! It's only served you this far to lull you into a false sense of security!

'Hey, Professor, just what were those mushrooms you served up?' Ferrow asked duClausky.

The physicist shrugged. 'They come out of freezer. I defrost in microwave and serve. OK to eat, yes?'

'And the peppers in the salad last night?'

'Same as mushrooms.'

Pop.

Pop, pop.

Ferrow turned at the sound, which seemed to come from the entrance to the lab. The patch of mould beside the door had expanded and begun to bubble. As the bubbles formed they broke open, revealing jutting caps on coiled stalks that sprang out of them.

'Like those?' he demanded.

DuClausky gasped. He nodded, fervently.

'Better keep 'em off the menu from now on . . .'

Ferrow's voice tailed off as the door to the laboratory opened and Erzebet von Bamberg ushered Commander Speed through it. 'Given up trying to keep us on course?' Faber growled.

Erzebet blew him a pouted kiss. 'Why, John,' she said, 'you know very well this vessel has electronic steering.'

'So why did your giant pet spend the night up there?'

'He didn't, silly.' She looked at Ylena. 'He was with me. I took the commander up there this morning for a little chat, that's all.'

Ferrow had to admire her. As divide and conquer went, she was doing a first-class job. Now Speed had to be added to his list of suspects. It was hardly credible that the old boy was in with her, but it would be foolish to gamble his life against that slender credibility.

'Now,' Erzebet continued, 'if we're all comfortable, Karsten will join us shortly and then I shall explain what we're going to do. *Exactly* what we're going to do.'

Pop.

Erzebet turned at the sound. From a simple mould, the fungus was quickly developing into a cluster of toadstools growing out and up from the wall. Ferrow noticed her features whiten as she watched another cap shoot outwards on its stem.

The *familiares* had begun by approaching the tumbledown stone hut with extreme caution. The work required of them by the skyfire was simple enough, if rather time-consuming. Take one pile of old bones and put them back together. Then go home.

Artisson had chosen well. He'd put Beanharvest in charge of the work because Beanharvest had the best knowledge of the complexities of human anatomy. Artisson was quite well-versed himself, but he still had problems telling carpals from tarsals and identifying the order of the vertebrae. He preferred coccyx and innominate bone constructions, if given the choice. Beanharvest, however, knew the lot.

The main form of the skeleton was little problem, its original crouching form supporting much of the structure by balance alone. The hardest part, which required them to fabricate some vegetable glue and spend ages balancing the components exactly whilst it hardened, was the outstretched arm and hand. Even that would come right eventually, though it would have been much more satisfying if the skull had been there so that they could have completed their task with it.

They finished work on the bones and began trying to piece the shreds of brown material together. The *familiares* did their best, though time and weather had destroyed much of the raw material they were trying to work with. Still, Beanharvest admitted, standing back with the others to admire the finished specimen, it wasn't bad.

Headless, fleshless Irish hermit-monk stretching out an empty, bony hand that had once held . . . what?

Maybe the skyfire knew the answer. The *familiares* certainly didn't. Nor did they care particularly. With their work over they could return to the colony and whatever else the skyfire had in store for them.

The others set off. Beanharvest took a last look at the fruit of their labours. They'd done well, he decided. It wasn't just anybody who could have put Caillchen Mac Eamon back together like that.

'. . . Reshomath, Pyutim, Vastagoraminoth, Gurith, Fistem . . .'

Nearly there. All checked out so far. No unaccounted dates. Final preparations all in hand.

He thought back to another of his favoured poets, a demented Englishman called Aubrey Melech. He quoted:

> Eternal eyes that search for imperfection seek me out
> And find me wanting . . .

Not this time, he thought. It shall be my credo, until this is over, but I shall not let it be true. I dare not.

'. . . Tlalath, Forgisac, T'regishem'z, Kythuq, Holomeneth, Tiveras . . .'

Only four left. Numbers 126, 127, 128 and 129. So very nearly there.

And when I am there? When I have them all by rote? Can I *use* them? Will they permit themselves to be used? I have no choice. I know that. But do they?

It was growing colder. It had been growing colder since that time the previous night when he had summoned the skyfires. They had come, but once again only six had answered him.

If only he understood them better. If only he knew more about their lives and powers. Then he'd be more certain of them. Probably.

Ptythonius von Meersburg sighed and resumed his work with the scroll. Nothing let slip. Nothing left to chance. Not this time.

A gamble is a gamble is a gamble.

He growled to himself. Not if you load the dice in your favour, he reasoned. Not if your planning is as meticulous as mine has been.

'. . . Segemon, 126. Vigirac, 127. K'thanes, 128 . . .'

One left. As the Gospel according to St Matthew said: 'But many that are first shall be last; and the last shall be the first.'

Many a true word spoken in jest? Not when he was citing Christ. He had no sense of humour where his Master was concerned. Not that he had much of a sense of humour anyway.

The Keeper studied the last name on the list. He knew it well, as all who had gone before him knew it well. Last it was, but also first and, being first, possibly the greatest. And the most difficult? '. . . 129, Anhuk,' he read aloud.

Ferrow noted Erzebet's expression. He grinned. For some reason she appeared to be afraid of the fungus.

He wasn't exactly unconcerned about it himself, wondering as he was whether it somehow connected to the promptings he kept hearing inside. Yet the effect it was having upon his captor was more dramatic and visible.

The colour drained from her cheeks, leaving her face a pale, ghostly thing framed by her bright red hair. 'You,' she ordered Nils Gunndner. 'Get rid of it. Scrape it off and throw it overboard. Then wash down the walls with undiluted disinfectant. Now!'

'Something the matter?' Ferrow inquired with feigned innocence.

'Don't talk. Just do it. The rest of you, do the same in the other places. Anywhere you can find it, get rid of it.'

'Is no good, yes?' duClausky asked.

'Do it!' Her voice had taken on a high, almost hysterical note. The muzzle of her machine pistol wavered threateningly.

Well, it gets us out of here, Ferrow thought. Probably she's already swept up anything that could be used as a weapon, but at least we've got a bit more liberty. Maybe I can get to the radio . . .

They took buckets and scrapers from the galley and began the long job of scouring *Harfanger II* for patches of the greenish mould and fungus, working in groups of three scraping and two washing. Ylena supervised Speed and Gunndner, Erzebet preferring to watch Faber, duClausky and Ferrow. The supervision was thorough, no tiny visible spore-culture being permitted to remain alive. Nor was there any chance for discussion between the prisoners.

They laboured through the morning and into the early afternoon. Karsten joined them, taking filled buckets and emptying them over the side into the rough, grey waters through which their journey was carrying them. When they eventually broke for lunch not a single fragment of the mould remained to be seen. *Harfanger II* was, it seemed, clear once more.

The meal was taken in silence, Erzebet violently discouraging any enquiries regarding her knowledge of the fungus. She gave the impression of wanting to erase its memory from her mind as thoroughly as she had wanted it removed from their environment. Their course remained constant, as did their speed, and the designated hour for alterjection of the boat and all aboard steadily drew nearer. In silence.

Erzebet's constant presence prevented any possibility of contact between Ferrow and Johannes. The *glebula* lay in a corner of the laboratory, eyes closed and breathing regular. Not asleep, Ferrow noticed.

It was Faber who eventually broke the silence. 'You were going to explain the object of this farce to us,' he stated. 'Now that we're sitting comfortably, do you feel like starting?'

'We simply do what you had originally planned to, John,' Erzebet began. 'At the appointed location this vessel and all on board enter the third reality, with Professor duClausky's assistance.'

'Why?'

The question obviously took her aback. She stared at Ferrow, as if attempting to determine if he was being facetious or simply naive. At length she answered: 'Because there we will find the Kingdom of the Keeper. Only in the third reality may we come face to face for the last time.'

The last time. The words hung in the air like the tolling of a death knell.

And then a surprising thing happened. Erzebet's features softened and relaxed, allowing the full power of her beauty to manifest. 'Fetch your medical kit, Ylena,' she said gently.

Ylena obeyed, setting the bag down on a bench-surface and opening it.

'Be so good as to take a blood sample for John.'

Faber looked at her quizzically. 'You're giving me a sample of your blood? Why?'

'Because you want it, John. You want both mine and the Keeper's. Well, you shall have mine at least.' As she spoke she set down the Mauser, releasing her hold upon the weapon. Ylena, preparing the hypodermic, had already let go of her own machine pistol.

'We cannot work together without trust,' Erzebet announced.

'This is my gesture of trust towards you. Karsten, give your gun to Robert Ferrow.'

Karsten's eyes narrowed as he glared at her, challenging the order. As Ylena pushed the needle into a vein inside Erzebet's elbow he nodded and reluctantly handed his Skorpion to Ferrow, who immediately checked the clip and levelled the weapon at the giant and Erzebet.

'That's not necessary,' Erzebet told him.

'Yeah. It feels better, though. O K, what's the game you're playing this time?'

'No game, Robert.'

'That's as may be. Faber, get the other machine pistol.' We'll leave it with just the one round in the breech until I know if I can trust you, he added inwardly.

Ylena finished taking the blood sample and emptied the contents of the hypodermic into a test-tube, which she stoppered and handed to Faber. The spook, his eyes firmly fixed on Erzebet, handed it to Nils Gunndner. 'Put it in the fridge for now, Nils,' he told him. 'Now, Lady Erzebet von Bamberg. Let's hear it, shall we?'

Commander Speed was edging towards the Mauser. Johannes growled threateningly and the old man froze in his steps.

'Then listen to me very carefully,' Erzebet replied. 'We have to enter the third reality in order to approach Thule. Thule isn't *in* the third reality, but it is available *through* the third reality. It acts as a sort of contiguous dimension, if you like. The Keeper serves to hold the two Thulean factions apart. That is why his kingdom is separate from both of them. You, Robert, believe me to be completely committed to the negatives. You are wrong. Ptythonius and I were lovers, once. We shall be again. That is why I have to go to him.'

'Simply renewing an old friendship, are we?'

'You have no reason to disbelieve me. I rejected the negatives at Fortstown in favour of Ptythonius. You believe me to be evil because I have killed and caused others to be killed. Didn't Ptythonius destroy McAllister? Did the Keeper cause no deaths at Wegrimham? Are we so very different, he and I?'

Ferrow didn't answer her. It was Faber who told her to continue.

'You want the secret of my longevity, John. That, and to test duClausky's new machine for weapon potential. The sample of my blood will tell you anything you need to know about the one. The other will go ahead as scheduled without my interference. All I really needed was to come with you. I regret that I was forced to make you all my prisoners, but I had to ensure that we had come too far for you to turn back before I surrendered. You may still thwart me, if you wish, by setting us adrift. You would be foolish to do that, though. You see, I *know* the third reality. Robert has spent mere seconds in it. I have spent decades, through the centuries. I can guide you. More than that, I will take you to the Keeper.'

Ferrow and Faber exchanged glances. 'And the fungi?' Ferrow demanded. 'What about the fungi?'

'They are a negative manifestation. They thwarted Fallenberg's original expedition by subverting his crew. They would have subverted us also, had we not disposed of them. That is why this vessel has been set on electronic steering. Machine intelligence is beyond their power to subvert. Only humans can be affected by them.'

'You mean we're safe, now? Or as safe as we'll ever be until all this is over?'

'Not quite, Robert. The fungi can be far-reaching and subtle in their efforts. It's always possible that they have some pawn ashore who could find a way to stop us. That is another reason for my surrender to you, a practical reason. We must all work together in order to achieve what we have set out to do.'

'And when we reach the Keeper? What happens then, Erzebet?'

'That is for him to determine, Robert. I am going to him voluntarily, without malice or evil intent, to find the man I once loved over again. That is all.'

Ylena had been listening open-mouthed to Erzebet von Bamberg's explanation. It contrasted so strongly with the one she had received herself. And there was no mention of the night-mice, or the skyfire. Or of Erzebet's intention to release the negatives in order to effect her own ambitions.

'And now I think it would be wise if Professor duClausky made a final check on his apparatus,' Erzebet added, 'and if two people manned the bridge to observe the instrumentation up there. I suggest Karsten and Commander Speed, as they both have substantial sea-going experience.'

'It makes sense,' Ferrow agreed. 'Ylena, pick up that Mauser by the barrel and bring it here to me. Faber, hand me your gun.'

Faber glared as Ferrow levelled the Skorpion at him, then reluctantly handed over his own weapon. Having done so, he slid his hands nonchalantly into his pockets, hiding his smugness as he touched the gravity knife which none of the others knew about. Sooner or later he'd have a use for that, he thought. A good use.

'This lot goes overboard,' Ferrow informed them, still keeping his own weapon at the ready as he backed towards the laboratory door. 'Trust is one thing. That much I'm prepared to try for a while. But I've made enough mistakes already, and leaving guns lying around whilst we trust each other isn't going to be my next one.'

Harding stood in the control tower, watching. Dusk had fallen and the runway beneath him was bright with the glare of artificial lights. On it, some distance from the tower, stood a Saab fighter of F13 wing, Norrköping, an R B O 6–E air-to-surface missile mounted beneath each wing. Only the test missile, however, was armed with a fragmentation warhead.

All details had been locked into the onboard computer, including estimated maximum launch height for the given weather conditions. As soon as he'd seen the bird take off, Harding was going over to F T S to watch the trace on the computer console.

Nobody at R A F Dunnet seemed particularly concerned about the test being rescheduled. The pilot had moaned a bit, but they always did.

The Viggen's low hum became a whine, which in turn slowly magnified into something approaching the scream of an Irish banshee. In the dark the brilliant orange afterburn became an elongated pyramid of flame jetting from the rear of the fighter. Then almost in the blink of an eye, as take-off clearance was radioed from the tower, the S H 37–F leaped forward in a fiery streak and roared skywards.

Lieutenant George Ratcliffe Harding smiled happily. Now off to F T S, he told himself. That old Tenacity patrol boat won't know what's hit it. Wheee!

Professor Edvard duClausky swivelled his chair away from the console and beamed at his companions, one-sidedly as ever. In his right hand he was holding a small key.

'Machine all check,' he announced. 'Calibrations check. Now I set timer.'

He swung back to the console and punched in a series of coded messages. A digital clock appeared, static, in a corner of the faintly-glowing monitor. With a flourish he inserted the key into a small lock on the side of the power unit and turned it. The clock began to run backwards in a countdown.

08.00 ... 07.59 ... 07.58 ... 07.57 ... 07.56 ...

Still beaming, he removed the key and dropped it into a glass bowl partly filled with clear liquid. As the key hit the surface the liquid began to hiss and bubble and fume. Then it clouded and subsided.

'No-one change mind now,' duClausky announced. 'Key gone. No stop machine. We all go soon, yes?'

'Supposing I take out the lithium batteries?' Ferrow asked.

'Not stop, Robert. Sub-elemental Thulium take over as back-up. You no stop that either. Clock locked in, power locked in. All go.'

Erzebet nodded. She was standing with the others, one arm about Ylena's shoulders. She had no doubts about the effectiveness of the machine and now, with the timer running, there was no possibility of it failing to operate.

The power of her triumph thrilled through her. At last her scheming and plotting and treachery were about to pay off. She'd beaten them all. She'd even, somehow, managed to defeat the fungi.

... 07.09 ... 07.08 ... 07.07 ... 07.06 ... 07.05 ...

In the companionway outside the laboratory something made a gentle popping sound.

'Give the bridge a call, Nils,' Faber muttered. 'You'd better let Speed and Karsten know we're on our way.'

Feeling the butterflies in his stomach begin to emerge from their chrysalides, fighting to keep a growing feeling of panic in check, Nils Gunndner reached out for the wall-mounted phone and rang the bridge. Karsten answered.

'The timer is set,' Nils announced. 'Time to alterjection now . . . 6 minutes. 50.'

On the bridge Karsten set his watch and relayed the information to Commander Speed, who appeared not to hear him. Instead he was studying a radar screen intently.

'Tell them there's something approaching,' Speed told him. 'And the damn thing's coming bloody fast, don't y'know. Aircraft, I'd say.'

. . . 06.02 . . . 06.01 . . . 06.00 . . . 05.59 . . . 05.58 . . .

The mycelium, the web which bound the separate fungi together, reached its tendrils into the communications system. Karsten rattled the handset rest as the phone died away.

The Viggen swept past overhead on its target-identification run. Pilot Officer Terry Redmond hit the radio button as he climbed back towards 18,000 feet.

'Lapwing this is Hen-bird,' he snapped. 'Are you receiving?'

The radio crackled.

'Receiving you strength five, Hen-bird. Target identified?'

'Yeah, Lapwing. Bloody thing's got lights on. Looks as if it's crewed. Over.'

'Checking with duty officer, Hen-bird. Stand by.'

A corporal in the duty office told them Harding was over in FTS. They called him there. For a moment he felt a sudden surge of panic as he realized he should have checked the target order. Then the fungi took over.

'Tell Hen-bird no problem,' he said calmly. 'Lights on timer for visual identification. Crew dummies. Repeat, any crew seen are dummies. Complete test.'

Lapwing told Hen-bird. Terry Redmond didn't like it, but orders were orders. Besides, it was logical enough, and his pass overhead had been too high and fast to see anyone actually moving on the bridge of the *Harfanger II*.

He levelled out at test height and waited for the computerized sighting to tell him to launch the RBO6–E.

Artisson wished that he could share Beanharvest's satisfaction. Even Beanharvest was less sure of himself at this moment, though.

The *familiares* had assembled as instructed. Before them the skyfire, tiny but immensely powerful, hovered, blue and brilliant. It began to grow.

IT IS TIME, the skyfire announced.

They felt its power embrace them as it expanded. They felt its strength lift them, gently, from the ground. It pulsed. It whirled.

It carried them with it.

... 04.41 ... 04.40 ... 04.39 ...

Karsten gave up on the phone and slammed it onto its rest. Beneath him, in the lab, they had to be aware that something was happening. They must have felt the power of the Viggen's pass, even if the bad weather outside had prevented them from hearing it.

*Harfanger II* rode the storm at anchor at its designated location. Nothing it could do would take it out of the path of the RBO6–E.

Breathing a Germanic oath, Karsten grunted that he was quitting the bridge to report to the others assembled in the laboratory. Speed nodded, his eyes not leaving the radar screen.

Pop. Pop, pop, pop.

His feet squashed toadstool caps as he fought through the fungus underfoot. His expression was determined as he reached out for the lab door.

... 03.51 ... 03.50 ... 03.49 ... 03.48 ...

The timer, relentless, governing those last few minutes and seconds before they alterjected, counted steadily down.

Commander Speed kept his eye on the blip.

Karsten touched the handle, then stopped. Around him his world had become a fantasy of pallid green fungi and conflicting mental statements.

... 03.09 ... 03.08 ... 03.07 ...

Soon be over, Erzebet thought. Soon be there. Ptythonius, you're mine at last. It's all mine, at last.

Karsten opened the door and stepped into the laboratory. He was grinning.

He could tell by the faces turned towards him that they hadn't heard the aircraft, nor sensed the presence of the fungi. He was delighted.

Six of the skyfires awaited their orders. About them the shadows were beginning to take shape.

Human shape.

Ptythonius von Meersburg shuddered. There was nothing left for him to do, except what he was doing.

' . . . Vandagina . . . Corobantius . . . Hamitho . . . Demogonac . . .' he recited.

They came as he called them. Formless at first, they gradually assumed their accustomed outward aspects. Beginning as little more than wisps, they grew into nebulous representations of what they once had been.

'. . . Vigirac . . . K'thanes . . . Anhuk . . .'

Two began to manifest. The third lingered, elsewhere.

'Anhuk,' the Keeper repeated. Then again.

'Anhuk!'

He had to have them all.

The skyfire swept them along, not knowing, not seeing what was happening. They could only wait, held powerless in its enormous and powerful grip, for whatever it intended to do to them.

Aboard the *Harfanger II* one of their number was rending and tearing with its teeth, fighting a hopeless battle against the ever-multiplying growths. However many Toadflax tore up and spat out, that number and still more sprang up around him.

Nothing seemed to kill the fungi. They grew and multiplied. One begat two. Two begat four. Four begat eight . . .

Terrifying in their refusal to abate they towered above the *familiaris*. They covered him with their caps. They pulled him down, still biting, still fighting, still hoping for a deliverance which probably wouldn't come.

Not in time, anyway.

The signal came. Terry Redmond jabbed the fire-button with his thumb. Beneath the Viggen the R B O 6–E A S M juddered and shot forward from the wing, locked on to *Harfanger II*.

It left a fiery trail behind it in the sky from its British-pioneered two-stage motor. With mechanical efficiency it began to close the distance between itself and its target.

On the patrol boat's bridge Commander Speed watched horrified as the main blip of the Viggen developed a smaller, faster offshoot. It was impossible not to know what was happening.

*Harfanger II* was doomed. As soon as that missile hit it would be blown out of the water.

And so would all aboard.

... 0.58 ... 0.57 ... 0.56 ... 0.55 ... 0.54 ...

'*Anhuk!*'

Karsten fumbled with the catch, and failed. Behind him the door swung open. The fungi surged into the lab.

He opened his mouth to speak. His tongue and teeth were green. His eyes were green. His flesh was taking on a similar hue.

The skyfire faltered. For a moment Artisson thought he was going to fall. Beanharvest also.

Toadflax fought on, hopeless, helpless against the toadstools which had possessed the *Harfanger II*.

'You've served me well, Professor,' Erzebet was smiling.

Ferrow remembered. When they'd had breakfast there had been no mushrooms on duClausky's plate.

Why the fuck had he thrown those weapons overboard, unless the idea hadn't been his own?

Harding tracked the missile on the computer screen. It was running true.

Karsten's flesh erupted. The open doorway filled with green. The vegetable which had been a man lurched forward.

Johannes growled. Then sprang at the giant and began to rip him open. Spurts of greenish ichor burned into his fur. Howling, he struggled on.

Terry Redmond followed the trace on his controls. Below the clouds, invisible to his searching eyes, the missile slowed as it was enveloped in blue light.

... 0.14 ... 0.13 ... 0.12 ... 0.11 ...

Atop the antenna mast the laser began its sweep. On the bridge Commander Speed crouched on his knees, his hands above his head, waiting for the RBO6–E to strike the vessel.

Toadflax was ready to give up as the first taint of blue attacked the fungi. He sensed it first, then saw it. With a desperate effort his only hope of personal survival, he fought on.

... 0.9 ... 0.8 ... 0.7 ...

Had anyone looked out they would have seen the missile's tail — as it hurtled through the clouds, dropping, approaching, shrieking ever closer. No-one looked out, though. They were struggling to close the laboratory door against the intruding fungus. Gunndner and Faber had snatched up solid objects and were smashing Karsten to a pulp, trying to dodge the spurts of burning, greenish blood which erupted from each new wound.

'I haven't betrayed you,' Erzebet was screaming, her hold upon Ylena long relinquished. 'I'm still working. Still fighting for your freedom. You must believe me. You *have* to believe me!'

The skyfire landed on the deck forward of the bridge. The *familiares* spilled out of it, knowing what they had to do.

... 0.6 ... 0.5 ... 0.4 ...

Very slowly, as if manifesting his reluctance, asserting his stature by a last act of defiance, Anhuk appeared.

If duClausky was working for Erzebet, Ferrow reasoned, then he's also working for those *beyond* Erzebet. That makes it *their* machine ...

The timer flashed remorselessly on. Three seconds left.

Ptythonius von Meersburg bowed to the First Keeper. Slowly, he sensed, Anhuk was beginning to understand.

The *familiares* swept onto the bridge, past the cowering Speed. The old man's nerve had broken. They ignored him, rushing down towards the fungus. They bit. They tore. They ravaged. They destroyed the fruit-bodies and stamped down the spores before they could mature.

As the seventh skyfire suffused the vessel, Harding was puzzling over his computer screen. Somehow the trace had hiccoughed, delaying the missile strike by a fraction of a second.

... and if it's their machine it isn't going to alterject us to the Keeper ...

... 0.2 ...

The blue light tore through Karsten, separating his body into thousands of tiny silhouetted fragments. Instinctively Ferrow leaped towards Ylena, pulling her to the floor and protecting her with his body.

'Now!' Erzebet screamed. 'Now!'

The laser flashed, building up a cone around *Harfanger II*. The R B O 6–E streaked towards it like a comet in the night. Only faster.

Johannes, badly burned, sensed the world exploding around him. Nils Gunndner was backed into a corner of the laboratory, his eyes rolling wildly. Faber lay on the floor where he had been thrown when Karsten's body disintegrated. His eyes were frightened but his body, propped up on its elbows, faced the skyfire squarely.

Erzebet and duClausky stood together. She was laughing hysterically. The professor's outline was wavering as the surviving fragments of the fungus retreated back into him. Borne on by the light the *familiares*, Artisson and Toadflax at their head, were leaping nearer.

The missile struck. Too late.

*Harfanger II* and all aboard had entered the Kingdom of the Keeper.

The moments which followed were amongst the strangest of Robert Ferrow's existence. As he struggled to his feet, his senses whirling, he looked around at the laboratory. Everything had that same appearance which he'd noticed for those few moments of alterjection in the bunker. Objects had weirdly prismatic edges, wavering bands of pure colour. The few sounds he heard held an odd quality, as if he were hearing them through ears other than his own.

Somehow he knew that behind himself, in another reality, he'd ceased to exist, that there would be no return from the world he now found himself in. It didn't register that he'd never known about the missile in that past life, that there was no logical way in which he could look back and know his fate. He simply knew.

The strangeness began to fade, giving way before a different but over-riding normality. Ferrow bent down and helped Ylena to her feet. A little way away Faber was struggling to rise, rubbing his eyes in an effort to dispel the strangeness which had permeated his surroundings.

'Is . . . it over?' he inquired, his voice foreign in his ears.

Ferrow shook his head. 'Not until we find the Keeper,' he replied. 'Only then will it actually be over, one way or the other.'

He left Ylena to care for the shaken Nils Gunndner and knelt down beside Johannes. The *glebula* snuffled appreciatively and licked his hand. An interesting moment or two just then, Magister, it told him.

Ferrow could have sworn it was smiling. Are you badly hurt? he inquired.

Not in this reality. A few burns and bruises. Nothing more.

The *glebula* was silent mentally for a moment. Then it said: You know that we can never go back, Magister, don't you? Now we've entered the Kingdom of the Keeper we shall spend the rest of our lives here.

I know, Johannes. I don't think this is the time to tell the others, though. If you can walk we ought to check the bridge.

It struggled to its feet and padded along beside him, falteringly at first. Here and there a decaying patch of fungus remained, staining the walls or floor of the companionway, but its hue had darkened and the firmness of the fruit-bodies had turned to slime. That too was all that remained of the unfortunate Karsten. Occasionally they passed the smothered corpse of a *familiaris*, but there was no trace of Toadflax or any of the other survivors aboard *Harfanger II*.

Ferrow and Johannes found Commander Speed slumped across the floor of the bridge. His eyes were wide and staring and even a cursory glance showed that he was both dead and unmarked. Ferrow frowned, trying to reason out the cause of death, but Johannes supplied him with the answer.

His heart gave out during the transition, Magister. As he died whilst in the act of alterjection he remained alive in neither reality.

'But . . . what made his heart fail?'

Johannes offered a mental shrug. The skyfire? Or the *familiares*? Or even the approach of the missile? Whatever it was, from his expression he was badly frightened. I suspect that would have been enough.

'So, what the hell are we supposed to do now?'

Around them dawn was breaking, several hours too early, Ferrow estimated. As he stared out from the bridge a sudden clicking made him look down at the controls. Without anyone having touched them they had cut in by themselves, setting a course and starting *Harfanger II*'s engines. The storm was over and the vessel surged forward, gathering speed. In the distance, above the bows on the horizon, the Icelandic coast was now clearly visible.

You reckon this thing knows where it's going, Johannes?

Someone knows where it's going, Magister. And I suspect that someone is the Keeper. It would not be unlikely to presume that he's known our ultimate destination all along.

They left the bridge and made their way back below decks. In the laboratory Nils Gunndner was sitting up at a bench, drinking coffee. So was Faber, though the spook was scowling into his mug. Ylena, her face drawn with strain, was pouring cups for Ferrow and herself.

'The commander's dead, isn't he?' she asked.

'Yeah. He's dead. Just like Martin Fallenberg's dead. What I want to know, though, is where are Erzebet and that thing we called duClausky?'

I HAVE DONE ENOUGH. IT IS TIME FOR ME TO GO, the skyfire told them.

Erzebet laughed gently. 'More than enough, little skyfire. But how will you explain your actions to the Keeper, when he asks you?'

It hovered before her, reduced in size to about the diameter of a grapefruit. It pulsed for a moment, then sped away without answering.

They stood outside the ruins of Caillchen's hut, duClausky holding the bag which contained the Irish monk's skull and the tiny monkey figurine. The professor was grinning broadly, permitting greenish tendrils to escape from the sides of his mouth. They had already begun to burst through the scarred side of his face, giving the appearance of a fungoid beard.

'I should have known you sooner,' Erzebet told him. 'The negatives have never let me work alone. What *are* you, duClausky?'

'The relationship is difficult to explain,' the creature began, its voice thick and distorted and no longer accented. 'I am Edvard duClausky, or, at least, the husk which remains of him. And as you suspect I am also something else. If you like, if it makes it easier for you to understand, I am the being which was summoned when the Keeper translated the scroll stolen from him by Caillchen Mac Eamon.'

'You were summoned by the Keeper?' Erzebet gasped in amazement.

The thing offered a species of shrug. 'Think of me as the voice in the skull . . . personified,' it answered. As for my summoning, it was more an escape than it was the work of Tuvianus.'

'Tuvianus? Is that your name?'

The being seemed amused by this. 'My name is not important, Erzebet, No, I am not Tuvianus. That is the name of the Keeper of those days, the one followed by Ilona Yuvicz, who was followed by Deguir de Meaux. And Deguir was the Keeper who intervened at Karlstadt and was replaced by your beloved Ptythonius von Meersburg. The Keeper may lay his plan through decades, but we are older by far than any single Keeper. We lay our plans through *centuries*.'

'And now your own has come to fruition. Are you going to kill me?'

DuClausky chuckled grotesquely. He appeared to be rotting where he stood, fresh growths of fungus breaking through his flesh and clothing. 'I still need you, Erzebet,' he told her. 'I cannot survive the third reality in my present form. Nor may I come to full power without your help. You may yet redeem yourself and become the vice-regent for the negatives upon this planet. Take these things,' he ordered, a decaying hand thrusting the bag towards her. 'Go into the hut.'

Her eyes bright, her features flushed with the promise of ultimate success, Erzebet obeyed. Caillchen's skull-less skeleton crouched before her, one bony hand outstretched.

'Set the figurine in the hand and the skull upon the shoulders,' the creature commanded.

This was her moment. After this there could be no turning back. It was time to lay aside all the wavering and uncertainty, to act, finally, for the achievement of whatever her ambitions really were. If she delayed now the creature would have lost its chance for ever and she would have saved Ptythonius. Only moments remained to make her choice.

'Do it,' duClausky bubbled. 'Do it now!'

'I'm sorry, Ptythonius,' she whispered. 'I've served them for too long to abandon that service now. Forgive me, if you ever can.'

She obeyed.

Slowly the bony fingers closed about the figurine. A foul ichor, basically green but also iridescent with other hues, flowed into the hut from outside, where duClausky had been standing. As it touched the skeleton it seemed to seep through the bones, strengthening them, altering their colour, binding them with an unearthly semblance of bone and muscle. With a slushy, squelching sound to the movement of its joints the reanimated remains of Caillchen Mac Eamon stood up and stretched, breaking the sharded remains of the roof apart as it grew and expanded. Eyes of green fire burned down upon Erzebet from the skeletal face.

'And now for the Keeper,' it announced.

'But the skyfires . . .'

'With one of their number subverted,' the creature declared, 'they will not intervene. Ptythonius von Meersburg will be no match for me alone. And, once he is terminated, without a successor the office of Keeper will lapse. Our battle will be over, for ever.

'And this time it is our side which will have won.'

*Harfanger* II negotiated the barrier island at the mouth of Hornafjörd at a speed which Ferrow would previously have found frightening. All that counted now, though, was the rendezvous with the Keeper. Besides, the vessel was unlikely to respond to the controls, even if he knew how to work them.

With Speed and Karsten gone, and with Faber's background military intelligence rather than seagoing, no-one aboard could have piloted the patrol boat anyway, so all that remained was trust in their arrival at whatever destination had been selected for them.

The town of Höfn, on a spit of land just inside the fjord, appeared deserted. Vessels were active in the harbour and one sailed quite close, permitting a view of its deserted deck and wheelhouse. Ferrow recalled the way that the bunker had appeared deserted when he'd entered the third reality before, and reasoned that the only living things he'd be able to see would also be on an alterjective level. He found the experience disturbing, and began to wonder if there was any connection between alterjective reality and so-called ghost and poltergeist phenomena.

Not that it mattered any more, he thought ruefully. Not if I'm never going back to ordinary objectivity.

To either side of the fjord were green fields which merged into broad stretches of sandy gravel. In the distance, towering mistily above them, was the source of the water in the fjord, the icy fastness of the Vatnajökull glacier.

In the laboratory Faber was scowling, trying to puzzle out in his mind just who had set the bearing at which the alterjective experiment had been undertaken. He'd always believed that he'd decided upon it for himself, but his experience with the fungus and the way in which their course was now being worked out by unseen hands led him to doubt this.

He checked the fridge and found Erzebet's blood sample still safe. He didn't know about the missile which had doomed them all to the third reality for as long as their lives might last.

Nils Gunndner was still badly shaken, as much by his last glimpse of the man he had worked with on the machine, Edvard duClausky, as by the experiences of the skyfire and the *familiares*. Nothing was ever going to be the same for him again, he decided.

Ylena joined Ferrow and Johannes on the bridge. The waters of the fjord were growing shallow, even for a vessel with as small a draught as *Harfanger II*. Quite soon it would be unnavigable.

'And then?' she asked Ferrow.

He smiled and put an arm around her, drawing what comfort he could from her presence. 'That's up to the Keeper,' he told her. 'If there's one thing I've learned about Ptythonius it's that anything's possible where he's concerned.'

In the distance, growing in size as they approached, Ferrow saw the lights in the pale Icelandic sky. 'Johannes?' he queried. 'Take a look at these.'

The *glebula* stretched up on its hind legs and laid its forepaws on the control panel, staring out from the bridge.

Skyfires, Magister, it informed him. Four . . . five . . . six of them. Coming this way.

Ylena gasped. 'They're back,' she cried. 'They've come back to finish us!'

Ferrow shook his head. 'I doubt that,' he responded. 'I've seen those things before today . . . last night. They're the Keeper's creatures. Whatever happens, try not to be afraid. They shouldn't mean us any harm.'

Unless something's happened to the Keeper, Johannes cautioned him.

The lights circled the vessel, then began to close upon it. For a moment all six hovered on the bridge, then three darted down the companionway towards the laboratory below. Faber cried out as they passed through the closed door and began to hover, pulsing and expanding. One reached out for him and another enfolded Nils Gunndner. The third closed about duClausky's machine.

Ferrow looked from the first to the second to the third of the ones around him. The skyfire at Wegrimham hadn't harmed him and he had no reason to suppose that these would.

'I think it's time we had an explanation,' he said grimly.

THE KEEPER WILL EXPLAIN, ROBERT FERROW, the nearest told him. WE ARE HERE TO TAKE YOU TO HIM.

It shot into his chest like a bullet, then rapidly expanded. He gasped with sudden shock as he felt it surround him, then relaxed. Briefly he glimpsed the others obscuring Ylena and Johannes. Then the world began to spin.

Erzebet and the creature beside her approached the entrance to the ice-cavern. Above them, watching, a single skyfire surveyed their progress. The thing which had been duClausky and Caillchen Mac Eamon beckoned.

The skyfire descended.

The Thulean grinned evilly. 'Now for your friend Ptythonius,' it sneered to Erzebet.

'Did you think I had deserted you, friend Robert?' the Keeper inquired.

As the skyfires withdrew, depositing their human and mechanical burdens on the floor of the ice-cavern, Ferrow's eyes swept his surroundings. Around and above him the ice rose like the walls and vaulting of a Gothic cathedral, shimmering with glistening, prismatic hues. Not since the moment of alterjection had he seen anything quite so brilliant or unearthly.

Beside and slightly behind him, Ylena and the others gazed with equal wonder. The sixth skyfire, the one which had taken up the machine, still hovered between Ferrow and Ptythonius.

Ferrow grinned, 'Not exactly,' he replied. 'But you certainly took your time, Ptythonius.'

'Where . . . are we?' Nils Gunndner inquired. 'What is this place?'

'This is my home,' the Keeper smiled. 'You are my guests, and you are welcome.' Then, his voice harder, he ordered the skyfire: 'Destroy the machine.'

Faber leaped forward, an oath upon his lips. Before he could reach it the skyfire violently contracted, then expanded again, scattering a small quantity of what appeared to be ash on the floor beneath it. Faber checked his stride, his eyes wide with panic.

'We . . . we'll never get back,' he whispered.

'Did you ever believe you would?' Ptythonius asked him.

'Then . . .' His voice faltered. For the first time he noticed the figures, many dressed in bizarre and outlandish costumes, all of them wearing clothes from previous periods of history, several even dressed in skins, which surrounded the base of the walls.

'I think it's time you told me the truth,' Ferrow began. 'There's hardly any of it I can understand so far.'

Ptythonius von Meersburg smiled with a confidence he was far from feeling. 'I have called you here,' he began, 'all of you, to witness my act of faith.' He stretched out his arms as if to embrace every figure in the cavern. 'This is both my consummation and my ending, friend Robert. After this there is only the future, whatever that may be.'

Johannes snuffled and looked from Ferrow to the Keeper. The air, to his senses, was almost violent with the promise of coming conflict.

'I have laid my plans, as those before me laid their plans and handed them down,' the Keeper said. 'I have prepared for the moment which is to come in a way that is beyond the knowing of mortal men. Only my peers,' and he gestured to the figures which ringed the cavern, 'may understand at this time. But you will know, Robert. And those with you will know, albeit more briefly. The time is . . . now.'

At the entrance to the cavern two figures appeared, the seventh skyfire gleaming between them. Ferrow and his companions turned, recognising Erzebet and something which might have been duClausky.

Ptythonius held out his hand. 'Will you come to me, my love?' he asked Erzebet von Bamberg.

The Thulean beside her growled and stepped forward, leaving Erzebet and the skyfire behind. Nils Gunndner watched it closely for a few moments, then ran howling towards it, arms outstretched, fingers hooked.

It *was* duClausky. Certainly it was enough of duClausky, the foul thing he'd been tricked into working with, for him to want to take his revenge upon it. All his fears fled in the savagery of that moment. All his life, in whatever reality, fled in the savagery of the moment which followed it.

The creature met him squarely. And ripped him apart.

Ylena cried out and buried her head in Ferrow's shoulder. Faber shuddered at the violence of Nils Gunndner's death, and at the way the thing picked through his bones and began to split them for the marrow.

'Will you come to me, Erzebet?' the Keeeper asked her again.

She stared at him, her eyes pleading. Then she began to advance.

'You have chosen your side,' the creature growled through its feasting. 'He is nothing to you. Will you incur my wrath even as I destroy him?'

Ptythonius von Meersburg smiled sympathetically. 'These understand,' he said gently, gesturing to the figures of his predecessors. 'Even though you may not, they know what has to be. Come closer, Erzebet.'

She drew level with the Thulean. It reached out for her, bony fingers grasping. The seventh skyfire shot forward and seared them off. A foul green ichor dripped from the injured hand.

The creature howled, its eyes rolling in disbelief.

'Did you truly believe the skyfire would betray me?' Ptythonius asked, pityingly. 'More to the point, did you think they would betray their charge?'

Erzebet drew closer, her eyes suddenly wide and unafraid. The Keeper smiled at her.

Faber shook his head. '*This* is it?' he demanded. 'This is your act of faith? Why, that thing has more guts than you have. And more right to live. You're a fraud. You've brought us here to die. That's it. You've brought us here to die!'

'Faber,' Ferrow hissed. 'For fuck's sake shut up! He knows what he's doing. He's always known what he was doing.'

'Has he?' Faber sneered. 'Like you have, Ferrow? You're all mad. All of you!'

The Thulean drooled. It was his last card, and he was playing it well. In all the time Faber and duClausky had been working together the influence had been worming its way inside Faber's skull, preparing him for the possibility of this moment. That was why Erzebet had pretended they'd been working together. She'd felt the influence of Thule without understanding its origin. It was the only explanation she had and she'd been surprised by Faber's original denials.

But now she knew. Her steps began to falter.

Anhuk stared at her. 'Go to the Keeper, Erzebet,' he instructed.

Faber's hand reached for the gravity knife in his pocket. It clicked discreetly open as he held it by his side. As Erzebet drew level he plunged it into her, releasing his grip.

She wavered, then continued, the weapon projecting from her body. Faber cried out as Ferrow's fist smacked into his stomach, doubling him over. A knee came up beneath his chin, knocking him onto his back. Ferrow raised his foot for a skull-crushing kick.

'No,' the Keeper called. 'He has to be alive to watch. Both sides must witness this.'

Ferrow subsided, leaving the whimpering Faber on the floor of the cavern beside him.

'Kill him, Erzebet,' the Thulean howled. 'Destroy the Keeper!'

She reached the Keeper's side. Ignoring the knife, he held her to him. Her eyes were beginning to mist as she reached up and touched his cheek. 'Ptythonius?' she asked, her voice faltering. 'Are we together ... at last?'

'We are,' he sighed, smiling, 'as we always knew we would be. *You* are my act of faith, Erzebet. Your resistance to the negatives, albeit in these final moments, was all I needed. You see, they will never be able to trust their followers again, now that you have betrayed them for our love.'

Gently he raised her face to his. They kissed.

When they parted her blood was salt upon his lips. Her body hung limply in his grasp. Tenderly, with the care of a lover whose beloved is only sleeping, he lowered Erzebet von Bamberg to his feet and set her down. Then he looked across at Ferrow and Ylena, his eyes glazed with fresh tears.

'It had to be like this,' he told them. 'It was the only way that it could ever have been possible. Now we are together, friend Robert, as you and Ylena, in your way, shall be together.

'You see,' he continued, 'it had to be a union of opposites, drawing from the two extremes which are both Thule. That is how the balance is maintained. More than that, it *is* the balance.'

The creature which had been duClausky howled. Faber glanced at it, sensing one last chance.

'We have worked well together, Robert,' the Keeper said. 'I shall never be far away from you now. None of us shall be far away from you, so I shall not say good-bye.'

The Thulean rushed towards Ptythonius. Faber scrambled to his feet and tried to follow, but before he had travelled two yards Johannes had overtaken him and torn the tendons in his right leg to tatters. As Faber rolled over, the *glebula* was at his throat, shredding and rending.

He died screaming.

As the Thulean reached the Keeper, the white fur cloak suddenly emptied. Ferrow glimpsed another figure, a familiar figure, join the others which stood about the walls of the ice-cavern, summoned to witness Ptythonius von Meersburg's act of faith.

Thwarted, duClausky snarled as he surveyed the beings which

ringed him round. Then the skyfires closed upon him.

All seven of them.

The thing shrieked and gibbered as they expanded, obscuring its body from view. Flecks of fungus, dark against the brilliant blueness, hurtled uselessly out to rot upon the cavern floor. Then the lights diminished again and hovered, waiting and watching for what they knew was still to come.

Ferrow stepped forward but was checked by Ylena's arms. His eyes sought out the figure of Ptythonius. It nodded.

I think you should kiss her, Magister, said Johannes.

Ferrow looked at the *glebula*, then at Ylena. 'Sounds like the only thing to do,' he said softly, drawing the white fur cloak close about them both.

# EPILOGUE

Late one evening Ferrow looked in on his former colleagues at Corby. They didn't seem to know him any more.

There was, after all, no reason why they should, he thought. Truth be told he didn't even look the same. Not any longer. Ylena's features had softened his own, giving him a younger appearance than he'd had before. Even Johannes had snuffled uncertainly when he'd seen them for the first time, two scents mingled, two beings in one body.

Two Thules perfectly balanced.

The *glebula* still called him Magister. It would continue to call him Magister throughout whatever lay ahead. For whilst they had seen the end they had yet to discover what their own ending was to be. Perhaps, Ferrow thought, they never would.

Don't be silly, the Ylena part told him. Everything has to end eventually. We both know that.

Perhaps.

They smiled at the desk sergeant and turned away. Outside, Johannes and Toadflax were waiting for them. So, pulsing minutely, were the seven skyfires.

The new Keeper sighed. 'Time for a quick run through the records,' he told them.

'Then maybe we'll find out what the hell is *really* going on.'

The awesome spirits of chaos approach
their appointed hour . . .

——— THE ———

# Time Raiders

## BERNARD KING

**The second in a trilogy of masterful invention**

27 July AD 869. There was something unnatural, ungodly
about the rag-draped skeleton. The weathered white frame
appeared intact, if fallen in, but the skull was missing . . .

30 April last year. His face was like parchment stretched
across a skull which was no longer his own. His eyes, blue
and too young for his wrinkled, gaunt visage, smiled down
at those scrambling away in their panic before him . . .

The immortal forces of Thule insinuate their warring
passions through time, feeding the flame of mankind's
destiny. And as the shadows lengthen, the powers of
darkness thrill to the fulfilment of their deadly quest. But
their ritual is incomplete and they must steal the ancient
talisman from those who uphold the flickering light –
wherever and who ever they may be . . .

0 7221 4868 2   FANTASY   £3.50

*Also by Bernard King in Sphere Books:*
*THE DESTROYING ANGEL*

From the bestselling authors of FOOTFALL

# THE LEGACY OF HEOROT

## LARRY NIVEN, JERRY POURNELLE AND STEVEN BARNES

Civilisation on Earth was rich, comfortable – and overcrowded. Millions applied for the voyage but only the best were chosen to settle on Tau Ceti Four. The Colony was a success. The silver rivers and golden fields of Camelot overflowed with food and sport nurtured by the colonists' eco-sensitive hands. It was an idyll, the stuff of dreams.

Just one man, Cadmann Weyland, insisted on perimeter defences: electric fence, minefield, barbed wire. Against what? Surely humans are the most destructive creatures in the universe? Surely the planet is friendly? Surely it's safe to walk in the fields after dark?

And beyond the perimeter the nightmare began to chatter . . .

'A version of ALIENS by writers who know the difference between Hollywood science fiction and the Real Stuff'
**TIME OUT**

Also by Niven and Pournelle:
FOOTFALL

By Larry Niven:
RINGWORLD
INCONSTANT MOON

0 7221 6407 6    SCIENCE FICTION    £3.50